Joe Poyer was born in Michigan, USA, in 1939. He graduated from the Michigan State University with a B.A. in Communication Arts, and is at present the Manager of Project Operations for a pharmaceutical company in California, where he lives with his wife and two sons.

He is the author of *North Cape* and *The Balkan Assignment*, both of which were tremendously successful. *The Chinese Agenda* is his third novel.

*Also by Joe Poyer and available
from Sphere Books*

NORTH CAPE
THE BALKAN ASSIGNMENT

The Chinese Agenda

JOE POYER

SPHERE BOOKS LIMITED
30/32 Gray's Inn Road, London WC1X 8JL

First published in Great Britain
by Victor Gollancz Ltd 1973
Copyright © Joe Poyer 1972
Published by Sphere Books 1974

TRADE
MARK

Set in Linotype Baskerville

Printed in Great Britain by
Hazell Watson & Viney Ltd
Aylesbury, Bucks

ISBN 0 7221 6986 8

For Olin Witthoft for his unfailing
confidence and encouragement

And, for that rarest of all commodities,
honest criticism, my thanks to Bill Fairbairn

Something hidden, Go and find it.
Go and look behind the Ranges—
Something lost behind the Ranges.[1]

Kipling

[1] Kipling, R., "The Explorer," *The Five Nations: The Writings in Prose & Verse of Rudyard Kipling*, Charles Scribner's Sons, New York, N.Y., 1921, Vol. 21.

AFRICA

CHAPTER ONE

The three men waited on the dock as the boat crept sluggishly up the river, engines pounding against the heavy current. The late afternoon sun filtered down through the overhanging jungle canopy to ripple along the boat's length in a patchwork of color. One of the men on the dock, a small, painfully thin figure, sighed once, partly in relief, partly in despair, and the other two exchanged apprehensive glances.

The racket from the engines increased for a moment as the helmsman eased the throttle forward and turned the bow into the dock. She was now side-on to the three watchers and they could see that the boat had been badly battered. A line of splintered holes ran from the bow to the waterline amidships and the port forward edge of the deckhouse was badly shot up. The bow wave swept under the rickety pilings and the boat edged alongside. A black sailor jumped down onto the dock and looped a snubbing line around a piling, then trotted back along the length of the boat to catch a second line tossed to him from the stern. The ear-splitting racket increased as the man at the helm threw the wheel over, then died abruptly as the stern bumped against the dock. General – courtesy of the Gambian Government-in-exile – Emile Jacques gave a distinctly Gallic shrug of apology to his two companions. The sailor climbing back onto the boat caught the gesture and grinned at Gillon.

Gillon stared at the two men on either side of Jacques. Both were well-dressed but distinctly out of place in the jungle setting in their business suits and ties. And, both had that hard indefinable air about them of men who are at their best in any situation simply because they fully believe in their own competence. Anyone who found his way into the camp was of the deepest concern and though Jacques must have satisfied himself that their business was both urgent and legitimate, Gillon found himself growing angrier by the minute. He was well aware that it was impossible for anyone, and especially anyone as distinctive as an Oriental and a Caucasian to travel together in Africa without it being known from Cape Town to Cairo in a matter of hours.

The two men watching the battered boat saw a man of middle height, with broad, rangy shoulders and a shock of immensely red hair glaring down at them through red-rimmed eyes. His face was smeared with a mixture of engine oil and cordite and his gaze, travelling over each in turn, was contemptuous. A dark smear of dried blood lined one cheek and a once-white shirt was streaked with oil.

Beyond the dock, stretching back into the gloom of the rain forest and resembling an abandoned lumber camp more than a military base, were a series of prefab buildings surrounded by brush and grass huts and a few tents, all huddled together in mutual support under the jungle canopy into a small, cleared area edged with concertina wire. Soldiers could be seen moving slowly in and out of the buildings and along the few paths, while scattered here and there were the reclining bodies of a few uniformed troopers, most of them asleep. Gillon snorted in disgust and waved a hand at Jacques.

'Hullo, Emile.'

Jacques waved back and turned to speak with the other two men for a moment. Then he grasped the railing and pulled himself up and onto the deck. The other two followed as he started slowly aft to the deckhouse, examining the damage as he went. He stepped down into the cockpit and squeezed Gillon's shoulder.

'You have had a rough trip, it would appear.'

'Goddamn it, yes, we had a rough trip,' Gillon snorted, and instantly Jacques assumed his well-practiced air of hurt patience that Gillon had learned to recognize during their two-year association. Jacques leaned back against the coaming with the resigned air of one willing to wait out a storm in good cause and Gillon gritted his teeth and swore to himself.

'Yes, we had a hard time.' His carefully conserved control deserted him in a rush of shouted words. 'We put shells into the oil barges then shot up the tug. Before we could sink her in the channel off Point Loma their damned air force showed and I lost my best gunner. Two twenties through the chest. There's hardly enough of him left to bury. Now they'll get that damned tug off and we'll have to go out and do it all over again.'

Gillon stopped abruptly, too weary to continue. To hell with Jacques, he thought, and leaned against the deckhouse and shut his eyes, wishing he could shut his ears and his senses to the stolid African evening. Under the canopy of the rain forest there would be no surcease from the oppressive humidity that filled the air. Even off the coast the humidity never left them. Jacques' nasal voice, telling the two men that indeed the ship had fought hard and valiantly, that indeed there was no one that knew small patrol ships – as many times as Gillon had corrected him, Jacques still referred to the riverine boats as ships – as well as Gillon, added to the misery created by the humidity and Gillon opened his eyes and stepped away to the lee side of the boat, where he could at least feel the stirrings of the water-laden air on the back of his neck. But even that did no good and he finally swung around and snapped:

'Emile, for God's sake, shut up, will you. What the hell do they want anyway?'

The two men exchanged glances, glances that questioned Jacques' judgment without words more than anything they might have said. Nor did Jacques miss the implication.

'He is overwrought for the moment, gentlemen,' he replied hurriedly. 'Overwrought and overworked. You can see for yourself that he . . .'

'Emile, for Christ's sake . . .'

Jacques capitulated and drew himself up. 'Permit me, gentlemen, to present Colonel Robert Gillon of the Gambian Independence Forces, Captain of the . . . the . . . this, uh, ship, since it does not at present have a name. Colonel Gillon was formerly Major Gillon in your Armed Forces, Mr. Jones; the Army I believe.'

'Jones!' Gillon snorted. 'Sure, why not? Everywhere you turn in Africa these days you fall over a spook.'

'Colonel Gillon,' Jacques persisted, his voice taking on a warning note, 'permit me to present Phan Duc Phnom, Deputy Minister of Internal Affairs, Royal Kingdom of

Laos, and Mr. Jones, attached to the American Embassy in Laos.' In spite of everything, including forty years' absence from Europe, Jacques would remain a *continental* to his dying day.

Gillon nodded and ignored Jones's outstretched hand. 'How's the embassy business . . . uh, Jones? Sorry, I'm not very good at names. And you, what do I call you, Your Excellency?'

Phan Duc Phnom looked at Jacques dubiously. 'Mister will do, Colonel Gillon.'

Gillon sighed and rubbed his forehead.

'Look, I'm tired, you must be tired – or at least you are if you have any sense. Let's quit playing around. Jones or whatever. You are from the CIA, NSA, DIA, ABC or God knows what. If you have anything to do with Laos, you have my deepest sympathies, Mr. Phnom. Now, once more, what the hell do you want?'

Jacques started to interrupt but Gillon cut him off. 'Stop it, Emile. We all know what the score is . . .'

Jacques persisted, however, glaring at Gillon. 'These gentlemen have traveled a long, dangerous way to talk with you, Robert. At least, you can show them the common courtesy of hearing what they have to say.'

'I suggest,' Phnom interrupted, 'that since Colonel Gillon is tired and we are tired as well, perhaps it would be better to wait until morning to begin our discussion. Then, we would all be at our best.'

'Very nice of you I'm sure, gentlemen,' Gillon said sarcastically. 'Now, I would appreciate it if you would all get the hell off my boat so we can finish up and get some sleep.'

The three men exchanged glances once more, then started down the gangway without another word. In the embarrassed silence, Gillon grabbed Jacques by the arm and held him back.

'Emile,' he said softly, tightening his grip and glaring down at him, 'how many times have you told me that no outsiders come into this camp at anytime?'

The older man saw his own frustration and fear mirrored in the angry face. Half smiling, half pitying, he stood his ground against Gillon's anger.

'Is that all you can do?' Gillon snarled at him. 'Stand

there and grin like a fool? If you hunted all over Africa you wouldn't have done any better. A diplomat and a spook, for God's sake. The only two professions in the world where a flapping mouth is a basic requirement. Why the devil didn't you go and get M'bouti and bring him here with a division?'

Jacques stepped closer and laid a hand on Gillon's shoulder. 'Go and get some sleep, Robert. You are tired and you are not seeing things clearly. I understand your concern and fully appreciate it. And you know that I, of all people, would do nothing to endanger this camp. I do what I must, even though I wish I did not have to.'

Jacques said this last with such a sad smile that Gillon relented, although he knew that Jacques was a consummate actor. He was too tired to argue any further and let go of his arm.

'All right, Emile. I'll get some sleep and we'll talk in the morning. But, I want you to put a guard on those two tonight. Somebody you can trust to stay awake. And I don't want them to know they are being watched either.'

The Belgian nodded. 'I have already done so, even though I know who they are and why they are here.' He waved once and trotted down the gangplank to join the two men who waited for him on the bank.

Gillon watched him go with mixed feelings of anger, respect and affection for the old man. Forty years he had spent in Central Africa, through more wars than he could remember. Belgium was a faded memory and even the *War* was thirty years in the past, as were the last traces of Jacques' optimism, liberalism and faith in man. There were only innumerable petty squabbles to be fought now, all masquerading as National Wars of Liberation, civil wars, revolutionary wars, struggles of the proletariat and so on. All the modern terms applied to senseless killing by the Western and Eastern worlds in their struggle for hegemony. One hundred years ago they would have been called imperial wars and two hundred years ago tribal wars. But now they were immensely more deadly than the cattle and women raids of the tribal days; fought with the latest obsolete military

13

equipment short of nuclear weaponry, the dead were measured in the thousands and sometimes millions.

As Gillon watched the old man walk up the path, his back still as ramrod stiff as the day he left the Ecole Militaire, he knew that if he wasn't careful, thirty years from now he might very well be walking up a similar path. Why he stayed he really was not certain. The high pay certainly did nothing to offset the boredom, and what adventure was there in dying in ninety-degree heat and ninety-eight per cent humidity with your chest torn open by an AK-47 bullet? But he knew, as with any job, if one was not careful, one fell easily into a rut in which the effort required to extract oneself grew in proportion to each passing year. As had happened to Jacques. In the beginning, in the 1930's, it had been his sense of duty that had kept him in Central Africa. And then had come the War and its aftermath. Through the fifties, the beginnings of inertia mixed with a fading professional conscience had by the 1960's led him easily into the new wars in old colonies with new nationalistic names. Trained military officers were in short supply and he never lacked for employment, hence the rut had grown deeper and deeper. Jacques would die here. Not by an enemy bullet since he was a staff officer and not by a firing squad if captured or surrendered. The other side was always in need of trained officers, especially staff officers, and as long as you were flexible enough . . . no, Gillon thought to himself, Jacques stood an excellent chance of dying of old age, providing chronic alcoholism or some obscure tropical disease didn't single him out first.

Gillon flicked his cigarette into the oily water and turned away to shamble across the cockpit and swing himself down onto the dock.

CHAPTER TWO

Gillon lay on the hard cot for a long time, chain-smoking and staring at the lighter patch of sky visible in the gloom through the screened window. The interior of the hut was rank with the moldy smell of heat and humidity and the thin mattress beneath him was soaked with his sweat. In spite of his exhaustion, the tenseness and anger that he still felt, combined with the heat to keep him awake. His mind raced like an engine gone wild and, try as he might, he could not turn it off.

He twisted on the soggy mattress and pushed the thin pillow higher under his head to lift his neck away from the dampness. He had spent two long years, monotonous years, in Gambia, during which times the rebel forces had lost ground steadily in spite of the vast quantities of material that had been poured in to support them. Even the British advisers in the South and the new air force so thoughtfully supplied by the Israelis as they replaced the last of their obsolescent equipment were clearly not enough to stem the growing demoralization and fast approaching final defeat.

With seemingly unlimited Soviet bloc support, the incumbent government was growing stronger by the day, extending its hold ever farther into the countryside in spite of the brutal ineptness of its army, until finally, the rebel forces held only the Northeast, inland from the coast, and the eastern border areas which formed a narrow corridor to the forces in the South.

The night sounds of the rain forest were in full swing, a threnodic counterpoint to his musings. Through the folds of mosquito netting, the heavy jungle growth completely obscured the sky, trapping all the heat and moisture of the day and releasing it slowly throughout the night. Every so often, the quiet would be broken by a raucous laugh from the barracks or the muttered oath of a sentry as he tripped over something in the path of his beat.

It was just after midnight that Gillon was shocked out of a light doze by the sharp explosions of bangalore torpedoes on the perimeter wire. A sudden rattle of small-arms fire was drowned in the first carumping shock of incoming mortar rounds. Still half asleep, Gillon swung off the cot reflexively, kicked out the screen and dropped through the window, pistol in hand, before the second wave of mortar shells struck. Scattered throughout the din was a ragged blend of hysterical screams and shouts from attackers and attacked alike.

Awake now, he paused for his bearings and, crouching, ran lightly to the corner of the hut, where he sprawled on his stomach to peer around the edge of the foundation. A slit trench, the only safe refuge from the .82 mm mortars, was eight feet away across cleared ground. From where he lay, he could see the flicker of machine-gun fire sweeping the compound area from beyond the fence.

Gillon faded back into the brush near the hut and made for the eastern side of the compound. This sector was quiet, indicating that the raid was on from the west and as he glanced back over his shoulder, he saw flashes of fire starting on the northern edge. He moved quickly along the fence, checking to see that the nervous sentries were all in place and ready. Satisfied, he raced toward the river. As he ran, he could hear the cough of a mortar going off and seconds later the roar as the shell struck. The explosions were spaced far enough apart to indicate no more than two mortars were in use and that suggested that the attack had been hastily mounted and he cursed Jacques and the two visitors all over again. Ahead, he could make out the barbed strands and flopped to a halt. Once on the ground, he wriggled around until he had a clear view of the wire in both directions. At the point nearest the upstream edge of the wire, he saw the dull gleam of a metal helmet and that told him that the machine-gun crew was holding its position. Faintly surprised that they were in place rather than run off to join the fire fight or, worse yet, ducking for cover in the jungle, he turned and at a half crouch, half run, made for the boat.

Breathing heavily, he crouched behind a dock piling. Flashes of fire from the forest two hundred yards behind showed him that the attackers were hurrying to extend a flank down to the upstream edge of the compound. They were probably after the boat, he thought, and the two guards who were supposed to be on the dock were nowhere to be seen.

As Gillon started to climb up onto the dock, a figure materialized at the foot of the walkway and sprinted towards him. Gillon was taken by surprise and the figure slammed into him, sending the pistol spinning from his hands. Gillon went down and a heavy body straddled his, knocking the wind from his lungs. Thick, muscular fingers went around his neck and a vise clamped down on his windpipe. He gagged and gasped simultaneously.

Just as suddenly as it happened, the hands relaxed and the pressure on his chest lifted. Through the red haze filling his exploding head, Gillon felt himself being lifted to his feet and pushed in the direction of the boat and dimly he heard the cheerful voice of his second-in-command, Nbtobi, apologizing for not recognizing him sooner.

Nbtobi practically lifted him over the taffrail and pushed him down on the deck and he gagged and went into a coughing spell that threatened to split his already tortured throat. Gillon rubbed his neck and glanced up at the dark face, now split in a wide grin.

'Goddamn you, you idiot,' he choked.

Nbtobi chuckled and handed him the pistol. 'Some karate expert!'

Gillon's throat felt as if it were about to come apart into two raw halves. Nerve endings from skull to chest were screaming and his eyes refused to focus properly. Nbtobi disappeared for a moment and returned with a canteen, which he pushed at Gillon.

'Here, drink some water . . . but carefully.'

Gillon took the canteen and let a dribble slide down his raw throat. The first swallow burned like fire into his gullet.

Without a word, Nbtobi hurried out of the cockpit and a moment later Gillon started as the boat's remaining machine gun exploded into action and began hosing the wire along the upstream flank.

Gillon stumbled to his feet and went forward to the deck cannon. Nbtobi had the only operable machine gun but he could make more than his contribution with the Bofors. More than once the combination of machine gun/Bofors had gotten them out of tight spots and it was likely it would do so again.

Gillon knelt down and threw open the deck plate covering the ammunition hatch, pulled up the drum

17

and settled it onto the gun's breech, swung into the saddle and pedaled around until he was sighting it on the line of tracers laid down by Nbtobi's weapon.

He flicked the selector switch to semi-automatic and pulled the trigger. The gun bucked solidly against his shoulders and he traversed the wire, laying down a ceiling of exploding steel well over the heads of the defenders, but into the area held by the attacking forces. Nbtobi dropped the fire angle on the gun to concentrate directly on the wire to pick off any attackers that might have gotten through.

Gillon reached the far corner of the compound and released the trigger. Between the Bofors and the machine gun the fire from the far side of the wire had practically died away. Mortar rounds, however, continued to drop in on the compound and he raised the muzzle elevation and lobbed a few shells into the jungle at points he thought most likely. A few minutes later, the mortars ceased firing and the area around the compound was still.

Gillon leaned his head back from the gunsight and hunched his shoulders. When he rubbed his hands on his thighs, he found that he was wearing nothing at all. His reaction to the first explosion had been automatic enough to send him through the window, pausing only long enough to grab up his pistol.

'Think they're gone?' Nbtobi asked softly.

'More likely . . .' Gillon stopped. He found that he couldn't speak above a whisper. During the firing, he had forgotten about his bruised throat.

'Hey . . . Gillon, you all right?'

'Yeah, my . . .' Gillon tried again, gave up and climbed stiffly down and pattered across the deck to the machine-gun mount.

'I'm okay,' he croaked. 'My throat . . . can't talk.'

'Sure am sorry about that,' Nbtobi chuckled. 'Thought you were a friendly native come to toss a grenade or something.'

Gillon cleared his throat experimentally. 'Damn that Emile . . .' he muttered. 'He ought to have more . . . sense than . . . to bring strangers . . . into the area . . .'

Both men were silent, listening for sounds that might

indicate a renewed assault, but the night remained quiet and empty for a few moments more as the stunned defenders recovered. Then, suddenly a voice was heard shouting, marshaling order into the stunned camp, and single pistol shots rang out along the wire. Gillon and Nbtobi looked at each other and then both shrugged. Killing was an old story in this war and so was savagery. Prisoners were only taken for the information that could be tortured from them.

'Come on, let's go up and see what's happened,' Gillon muttered, and swung a leg over the lee board. Nbtobi laid a hand on his shoulder in warning.

'Listen,' he whispered.

A sheet of flame flared in the compound and the breaking matchstick sound of a collapsing hut followed. Then Gillon heard it, a faint splash of water.

'The stern,' Nbtobi murmured, and drew his pistol from his waistband. He backed away in a deep crouch until the deckhouse was between himself and the stern. Gillon edged over the side of the boat down onto the dock, then pattered silently back to the stern, where he lay down at full length and leaned his head around the transom to examine the dark river. One minute, two minutes, three passed and he was no longer sure of what he was seeing. The river's slow movement along the boat was making him dizzy. A dark arm broke water for just an instant. A moment later, a head emerged and moved toward the boat. Gillon got slowly to his knees, and then suddenly stood up full, leaned around the stern and fired twice. The arms thrashed water for a moment and a cry of pain cut off almost before it started and the head disappeared. Four feet away, Nbtobi leaned over the stern and fired down into the water. Something flew through the air and landed with a clunk in the cockpit. Gillon heard Nbtobi scream and he dove off the dock onto the muddy riverbank as the grenade went off. Its sharp crack was followed immediately by a louder, more solid explosion and flame billowed high over the stern. The concussion pounded Gillon's ears and flung stinking mud into his face.

A raging sheet of flame spread swiftly from the petrol tanks in the stern. Nbtobi must have been killed by the exploding grenade; Gillon was almost certain of that and helpless to do anything more than swear savagely. He could only watch the boat burn. Voices came from behind him and the sound of feet running down the path to the dock. Several soldiers pushed past and fanned out along the bank. A few shots were fired into the river, more for his benefit than anything else.

'Robert?' A hand took his arm and gently turned him away from the burning boat and led him back up the path.

'Robert,' Jacques repeated as they walked on toward the camp. 'We are finished here. I have given orders to move at daybreak. We will never withstand another assault. Therefore, you must talk with the two men who came to the camp tonight, and you must do it now.'

Gillon swore and shook his arm out of Jacques' grasp. 'I told you that it was a fool thing to do, to bring those damned spooks here.'

'Do not lecture me, Robert. I know as well as you, perhaps more than you, what risk I was taking.' Jacques paused and swung Gillon around to face him, suddenly angry with the younger man.

'I have been a soldier for nearly forty years. There is little or nothing that you can teach me about military matters. So, you will shut your mouth and listen to what I have to say. These two have come a very long way on an important assignment and I know for certain that they were not the ones who led the Army to this camp . . . our location has been known to them for several days now. It was always a matter of time. I have told you that we are finished. We will move the camp at dawn, but that is merely a delaying tactic. The Lisbon negotiations will collapse in a few weeks because the government will have won. To save their own necks, the National Front will capitulate soon, throwing us to the wolves. I have seen it happen before and am well acquainted with the signs.'

Gillon began to interrupt, but Jacques shook his head and continued on.

'I will not stand by and see these people executed as traitors after the real traitors in Lisbon are finished with them. Nor do I wish to face a firing squad myself.

We will stay in the jungle for one more week and then I will negotiate my own terms with the M'bouti . . . terms that will be favourable to everyone concerned. By that time, I want to see you well away from here. It will not be so easy for an American after the war is over, no matter what promises will be made. The Russians will have the upper hand.'

Gillon shook his arm free and angrily started up the path, shocked at what he had just been told. He swung around, his voice barely under control.

'You mean to tell me that you are going to sell out what we've spent nearly two years building up here . . .'

'Merde,' Jacques exclaimed. 'After all these years and you still have pretensions of loyalty to a government, and one that by no stretch of the imagination can even be called your own?'

'No, of course . . .'

'Then do not accuse me of such nonsense either,' Jacques shot back. 'They would and will do the same to me if given the slightest opportunity. I intend to see that they are not given that chance. I will protect as best I am able those who have worked and fought with me. What I can no longer protect I warn them of the coming danger. They may then run to the next country who requires their services, or they can stay with me.'

Gillon listened, knowing that what Jacques was saying was true, thrusting down the ugly suspicion that perhaps Jacques had already contacted the M'bouti and that tonight's raid was the result of those preliminary discussions.

'All right,' he said wearily. 'Let me at least get some clothes on first.'

CHAPTER THREE

A single Coleman gasoline lantern hissed angrily from the ceiling, filling the stifling room with white light and heavy, sharp-edged shadows. Both Jones and Phan were seated at the deal table, which had been cleared of its usual accoutrements of maps and dirty dishes.

21

The smell of cordite and oil smoke was heavy in the room, trapped by the blackout curtains on the windows and door. Outside, Gillon could hear shouted orders and the sound of shovels and padding feet as the troops worked to clear away the debris of the attack. Gillon and Jacques sat down at the opposite side of the table and Jones could see that Gillon was angry, that he blamed them for the night's attack. But there was nothing he could do about that now and he shrugged it off to be settled later.

They were a contrast he decided, the big American and the diminutive Belgian. That both were professional soldiers was obvious to anyone who was at all familiar with the breed and if there was one thing that he was, it was familiar with the military – from the outside looking in, thank God.

To find someone like Gillon here, and a mercenary at that, was certainly a contradiction. Gillon's military record had been excellent. A major at thirty, young even for the Special Forces in the early days of Vietnam, he had clearly been a man on the way up until suddenly, he had resigned and disappeared. The resignation would not ordinarily have been noteworthy except for its suddenness. The manner in which it was carried out had suggested irresponsibility to some and perhaps they were right after all, Jones thought. In some respects, Africa with its growing-pain wars could be considered a secession from the 'real world.' Here there was no real responsibility because loyalty was not required beyond certain bounds and, because there was no responsibility, there were no pressures beyond those one imposed on oneself in order to remain alive. Seen in this light then, he did not have much hope for what he had to do. But then, he had no other choice than to try. They had made that clear enough to him in Paris.

He cleared his throat and stared hard at Jacques, who finished pouring the brandy. The Belgian picked up the glass and drank it down quickly, then with a half-smile, nodded knowingly.

'I have much work to do, as we leave shortly. *Bon soir, monsieur*. I know that you will excuse me?'

Phan inclined his head to Jacques' half-bow, but remained silent, and Jacques turned away and pushed out through the curtain.

Gillon sank wearily back into the chair and picked up a cigarette package from the table. He lit one and tossed the pack down in front of Jones. Jones eyed him, but said nothing.

'All right, now that you have put me properly in my place, can we get down to business?'

Gillon snorted without looking up.

'There is a group of Chinese Nationalist agents in western Sinkiang Province, very near the Soviet border. . . .' Jones began.

Gillon looked up in disbelief. 'For God's sake, what is this? Sinkiang?'

Jones leaned across the table and smashed his fist down hard, making the half-full glasses of brandy jump.

'Shut your damned mouth and listen to what I have to say, then you can make all the wise-ass remarks you want, but by God, you hear me out!'

Gillon put the cigarette back into his mouth and sat back, not at all impressed with Jones's outburst.

'All right,' he said in a controlled voice. 'Go ahead, but keep it to the point.'

Jones nodded and sank back down into the chair. At least Gillon would listen to what he had to say, he thought. He had gained that much.

'There is a team of Chinese Nationalist agents in Sinkiang,' he said again. 'There has been at least one such team in Sinkiang since the Communist take-over in 1949. They are parachuted into the area in twenty-man teams, stay for two years, then head south and make their way out through Afghanistan . . . those of the teams that are left. Every so often, Taiwan manages to arrange an airdrop of supplies, but other than that, they can do little more.

'These teams are in there in the hopes . . . or so Taiwan says . . . that if the counter-revolution ever comes, they can provide the nucleus of a trained striking force in the West, where the Chinese are the most vulnerable to guerrilla operations. Since the Peking Government has become solidly entrenched and Taiwan has lost hope, active support for the strike teams has been failing. So, in the last few years, it seems that the teams have been more inclined to banditry than espionage.

'The team in there now apparently takes their job very seriously. It seems they have come onto something very big and now they are yelling for help to get it out.'

'What?' Gillon asked carefully.

'We'll talk about the *what* later,' Jones replied, his voice brusque. 'Right now, we have other problems. They asked for help through their radio contact, which happens to be Mr. Phan's department in Laos. He relayed their message on to Taiwan as usual but this time, there was great deal of messaging back and forth. Just about the time we decoded the messages, the Nationalist Chinese took us into their confidence.'

'Nice of them,' Gillon interjected acidly.

'Yes, it was, and no, it wasn't. They really had no other choice. They had to give their strike team some kind of help and they had neither the resources nor the methods of doing so. The strike team wanted their find out of China, but they could not take a chance on trying to bring it out the usual way. This stuff had to get out fast and it had to get out with a high assurance of success.'

Jones paused and mopped his brow. The humidity, excessive at any time, was almost unbearable in the closed-in room.

'So the Nationalists asked the good old U.S. of A. for help, knowing that you were probably stupid enough to give it?'

'Something like that,' Jones acknowledged. 'As soon as we found out what they had, we were more than willing to help . . . but we couldn't pull it off by ourselves either.'

Gillon pulled another cigarette from the pack and lit it, grinning all the while. He exhaled the first deep puff and chuckled at Jones. 'That's not in the code of the West, *podner*. There's no such word as *can't*.'

Jones ignored the sarcasm this time and continued. 'The data they had to bring out were of concern to more than us alone . . . the U.S.S.R. was equally involved.'

At that Gillon broke into laughter. 'How about that?' he chortled. 'The U.S. and the U.S.S.R. both needing help from each other. That's never happened before. No . . . no . . .' Gillon pushed himself upright in the chair and waved his cigarette at the two men. 'I take that back. They have needed each other before. Without the one, the other couldn't have kept these stupid little wars going, so that they would have someplace to dump their obsolete weapons and recoup some of the money they've wasted in the past twenty-five years.'

'And no one to employ your unique talents, Colonel Gillon.' Phan eyed Gillon across the table, his lips pursed.

'Right you are, Mr. Phan, or whatever your name is; no one to keep my paychecks coming in. This war, I forget which side is picking up my bill . . .'

'All right, Gillon,' Jones said, his voice tired. 'Knock it off. I'm not going to debate political philosophy with you. If you'll keep your mouth shut for a little while longer and let me finish, we can all get some sleep.'

Gillon nodded, grinning. 'Pray, continue.'

Jones took a deep breath and plunged ahead, even though he was certain it was hopeless by now. He was more than ever convinced that Gillon was a total washout. There wasn't enough of anything left in him to appeal to . . . except his cynicism and, try as he might, he could see no way to use that to his advantage.

'The Nationalists were totally opposed to Russian intervention in the beginning.' He went on quickly to forestall the expected comment from Gillon. 'But they had no other choice. There is no other way into Sinkiang than through Siberian Russia and that clinched it. The problem was presented to the Russians in Moscow the day before yesterday and they agreed to a joint venture. They would supply two team members, transportation and the jump-off zone; we would supply the equipment, four team members and the key.'

'Key?'

'The strike team lives on the ragged edge as long as they are in Sinkiang, or they don't live at all. They trust no one including their own government. They insist on calling the shots and since they could just as easily turn what they have back to the Red Chinese to buy immunity, we are being very careful to do exactly as they ask.'

'All right,' Gillon said, and leaned forward to clasp his hands on the table. 'You've done enough talking in riddles. Let's have it with no more nonsense. It's been a big night and a bigger tomorrow.'

Jones and Phan exchanged looks and Phan nodded.

'The data they have,' Jones said without preamble, 'contain photographs and microfilmed documents describing the results of the latest series of the Chinese ICBM nuclear warhead tests completed last month. As best we can tell, the data are authentic.'

Gillon nodded. He was not greatly impressed, but acknowledged the possible importance of this information to Jones.

'The strike team has no way to get this information out quickly. They can't transmit by radio for any length of time or, no matter how much they move around, the Chicoms would be able to pin-point their location. So they want someone to come in and pick it up. Taiwan, in turn, has asked if we are interested enough to go and get it. As you can guess, the data would be of marginal value to the Nationalists for anything other than trading purposes. Since they can't get to it, they figure that they have more to gain by playing the good guy and giving us a crack. I suppose they also feel if we are stupid enough to involve the Russians, then that's our lookout. And since we too have no other choice, the Russians are involved.'

'Okay, the United States has to go in and get the data. So what's holding you back? Your people have had plenty of experience with this sort of thing.'

'The *key*, Gillon, the key. That's what's stopping us and that's why we are sitting in the middle of this lousy jungle, getting shot at. The key, Gillon,' he repeated, having lost his temper completely. 'You, damn it, are the *key* to the whole stupid situation. You've got to come along with me to find this ridiculous team out in the boon-docks and we'll probably get our heads shot off while we're at it.'

'Me . . .' Gillon stuttered in surprise. 'Me . . . like hell, buddy. I'm not going . . .'

26

'The pay is good,' Jones said wearily. 'One hundred stinking thousand tax-free dollars for a week's work ... think about that before you say no, and think about this too,' he added as Gillon got to his feet, still shaking his head. 'An old friend of yours, Jack Liu, is the leader of that strike team. He told us in no uncertain terms that there is only one person in the whole damned world that he would trust in the situation he is in now. No one, absolutely no one else, and that's why you, buddy boy, are the *key*.'

'Jack . . .'Gillon sat back down, clearly stunned. He stared at the table for a long minute before he murmured, half to himself, 'So that's where he disappeared to.'

Jones watched him carefully, knowing that he had struck the right nerve, but wondering if it would prove tender enough to provoke the right response.

'Yeah, and when he heard that the Russians have to be in on it as well, we almost lost him. You are the only one he trusts and that's that.'

'And so they sent you out here to get me to go along on your hike into Sinkiang . . . complete with a hundred grand in bribe money . . . you poor bastard,' Gillon finished softly.

'That may very well be,' Jones replied. 'But I'm trying anyway. I'm not going to give you the patriotic pitch, and I'm not going to tell you how vital that information is to preserving peace. You know all that nonsense as well as I do. I'm saying that I need your help, that the pay will be damned good and that your friend Jack Liu asked for you, specifically. Right now, the Red Chinese know that he has this information, they know that he has made radio contact with someone outside China. The bets in Washington, Taiwan and Moscow are that he can't stay far enough ahead of the Chicom hunting parties to actually deliver. But he knew that when he sent out the first message. Unless we can get in there, get that data and get him out at the same time, he's dead and for nothing. Now, I don't know what there is between you two, but I do know that he said that he would hand the data over to you and only you . . . otherwise we wouldn't be trying to convince a two-bit broken-down mercenary that we need his help.'

Jones finished this last savagely, but Gillon wasn't listening any longer.

Jones may not have known what was between him and Jack Liu, but Gillon certainly did and he cursed Liu for calling the debt in this way. Even in the intensely humid room, seven thousand miles from Laos, the taste of dirt, the hammer-like sun grinding down on his back, the rotten jungle-smell of decaying vegetation and the pain in his chest where the grenade fragments had lodged and the rifle butt that rose and fell with monotonous regularity on the backs of his legs were as sharp and intense as that day, three years ago, when it had happened.

'Well . . .' Jones broke into his reverie. Gillon brought himself back into the hot room with an effort and stared at the two men across the table. 'Where exactly is he?' he asked, his voice hoarse and dry as if suddenly full of that red, powdery dust once more.

Jones smiled in puzzled delight, not quite believing that he had heard correctly.

'All right, all right, that's more like it!' he chortled. Still grinning, he snatched a thin brief case from the floor and extracted a map and spread it open on the table. Gillon glanced at Phan but found him watching Jones's movements with the same bland expression that he had worn since Gillon had entered the room. But, tired as he was, Gillon thought he detected the least bit of relaxation in his posture, as if this were as close as he would ever come to an expression of any kind.

Gillon saw that the map that Jones had opened was a composite assembled from carefully matched aerial photographs. Contour lines had been superimposed and details accentuated. After a moment's study, he identified Lake Alma Ata and, once oriented, traced the Kazakhstan/Sinkiang border. Jones pointed to a mark some sixty miles west of the border and south of the Dzungarian Plain, roughly two hundred square miles in area.

'Liu is somewhere in this area,' Jones said.

CHAPTER FOUR

The flight from Conakry had been uneventful after the helicopter flight from the interior at dawn. They flew due north at thirty thousand feet, straight over the African bulge. The terrain below turned gradually from the deep-green rain forest to the lighter green of savanna grasslands and then to the grayish-brown of rocky, scrub-covered uplands. By the time they had been in the air three hours, the land had faded into the sere brown, barren wastes of the Sahara.

Jones spent most of the flight forward in the cockpit while Phan slept. Gillon, although dead tired, had been too tense to manage more than catnaps during the long flight. It wasn't until the azure Mediterranean was visible as a thin line along the horizon that Jones came back to tell him that the next stop was Rome. He apologized for having left him alone for so long, but he felt that sleep would be much more beneficial than company. He then led Gillon aft to a small lavatory, pointed out clean clothes and shaving necessities and left him to luxuriate in a long, hot shower and shave.

The Jetstar swept in over the clean, blue and white vista of Rome at 1100 hours, local time, banked steeply north of the city and followed the traffic into Campagnano International Airport. As they turned off the taxi strip, Jones noted with obvious relief that a NATO staff car was streaking toward them as the 'follow-me' jeep led them to a remote part of the field. He got out of his seat and walked back down the aisle to where Gillon, freshly shaved and in clean clothes, looked as if he felt 100 per cent better. Gillon glanced up at him then and pointed with his thumb at the NATO staff car now pacing them.

'Is that our welcoming committee?'

Jones dropped down into the seat. 'Yeah, the first of the grind, I'm afraid. We get a mission briefing here before going on. They'll bring us up to date on the political situation and tell us what our jump-off point inside the Soviet Union will be.'

'Also,' Gillon asked quietly, 'whether or not they have heard anything more from Liu?'

Jones looked at him hard, wondering just what it was between these two men that had caused Gillon to change his mind so quickly. They had told him in Paris that Liu's specific request would be the only thing that would convince him and he had a vague feeling that even though Gillon was strictly supercargo, his involvement with Liu might really be the key to the success of this whole mission after all. He resolved to find out before they went much further.

'It could be,' Gillon continued, 'that the Chicoms have already gotten Jack. What then? If he isn't answering radio transmissions except when he decides to, how are we going to know? Do we go, unless we hear definitely that he has been caught, or what?'

'No, the drill is that Liu will make a radio contact tonight. We were to tell him only yes or no.'

'Yes, meaning I've agreed to come?' Gillon asked.

Jones nodded but was prevented from saying anything more as the cockpit door opened and the radio operator hurried down the aisle.

'Ready for guests, Colonel?' He grinned at Jones. 'There's a whole pack of them piling up out there and another car on its way.'

He continued on up the aisle to the hatchway and as the aircraft swung around and came to a stop, he pulled the latch bar down and shoved open the door. Instantly, Gillon felt the mild air of the Roman spring course through the stale air of the cabin.

'Colonel?' Gillon asked.

'Yep. For the moment, I'm a colonel in the U.S. Air Force, Intelligence.'

Gillon turned in the seat to face Jones. 'For the moment, heh. Just what is your name, anyway?'

Jones grinned at him and without answering went to meet the first of the brass coming aboard.

After two continuous years in the African bush, Gillon felt overwhelmed by the press of people that flooded aboard. There were uniforms of the various branches of the United States military, as well as what appeared to be the Soviet Army, and several business-suited individuals, all were introduced to Gillon and he promptly forgot every name. A colonel hurried past to the front of the cabin to put up a screen while an enlisted man threaded a movie projector in the back. Curtains were pulled over the windows but not before Gillon saw a squad of Italian soldiers scurrying to take positions around the aircraft.

Jones was pressed back against the bulkhead by the crowd of people and Gillon could see his expression changing from surprise to intense anger. Jones elbowed free of the press of people, none too gently, and rushed up the aisle to confront a tall, spare individual wearing a major general's uniform. So, Gillon thought, this shindig was worth the time of a major general. He looked for the Soviet officer and from the stars and ribbons on his shoulder he was, as well as Gillon could recall, a lieutenant general. He took a second look at all of the uniforms, both American and Soviet, with their abundance of medals and ribbons and shoulder braid, and decided that if the Sulkinhov effect – the theory that held that an army's effectiveness was inversely proportional to the flashiness of its uniforms – held true, both armies were in big trouble.

The colonel finished with the screen and called for attention and there was a shuffling of feet and shifting of bodies in the suddenly cramped interior of the aircraft, but the noise did not diminish one bit. A moment later the lights went out and the movie projector's beam lit up the screen, stopping the roar of conversation as effectively as a command. For a moment, Gillon had trouble identifying the scene. The colonel, having extracted his collapsible pointer, tapped the screen.

'This, gentlemen,' he boomed in a professional narrator's voice, 'is the Tien Shan mountain range of western Sinkiang Province, People's Republic of China. These photographs were made available to us for this briefing, courtesy of the Soviet Air Force.'

So, Gillon thought absently, it was an air force uniform, not army.

'These photographs show, in some detail, the area

31

where we expect to find our contact. As you may know, the Tien Shan is one of the remotest and, consequently, least explored mountain regions in the world. Today, it effectively separates the Union of Soviet Socialist Republics and the People's Republic of China. It is some eight hundred miles long and one hundred fifty miles wide with an average height of sixteen thousand feet. Its major peaks, Pobeda and Tengri Khan, are 24,409 and 22,940 feet high respectively and are the highest in the Tien Shan range.'

Our contact. Gillon wondered if he was intending to go along and snorted loudly. The colonel glanced down the row of seats, searching for the source of the interruption, and Gillon waved to him.

'Right now,' he continued, ignoring Gillon, 'we are looking at a pass some twelve thousand feet high, known as the Dzungarian Gate. This gate, or pass, if you will, allows access to the interior of the Tien Shan. The latest maps we have, with the exception of those made up from aerial and satellite photos, are based on those of a German/Russian expedition in 1905 that traveled into the area for the express purpose of mapping and mountain climbing.'

The terrain unreeled slowly as the aircraft flew southward, as shown by a small compass set into an instrument panel superimposed onto the lower left-hand corner of the picture. After a few moments of high elevation shots, the zoom lens went to work and narrowed the field of view at a dizzying rate. The crumpled terrain took on the look characteristic of mountain ranges. Steep passes and high-walled mountain flanks, all of them covered with snow, Gillon noted, passed in review. The colonel was silent a moment as the harsh terrain, more suited to the moon than to earth, appeared on the screen. Gillon studied the picture intently as the aircraft flew deeper into the mountains. Tall stands of pine became visible, sometimes as individual trees along the top of a ridge, but more often as dense forests to about ten thousand feet in the deeper valleys. The rest of the terrain, beneath the snow and ice of winter, he knew would be alpine meadow and scrub bush.

Jones dropped into the seat beside Gillon. 'Now you

know why we were so anxious to have you along,' he whispered. 'And not just because Liu asked for you. I can use whatever experienced mountain help I can get.'

'You must be crazy,' Gillon chuckled. 'I haven't been in that kind of mountain for nearly ten years. And that country calls for snowshoes and skis.'

'It'll come back to you,' Jones replied comfortably. At least, he thought, some of that damned hostility of his is dying down.

'We can offer you gentlemen no more than this quick look at the terrain,' the briefing officer continued. 'It is all we have. With the help of the Soviet Air Force Mapping and Photographic Service, we have been able to prepare what we feel are adequate maps to guide you to the rendezvous with *your* contact. Two members of the Soviet intelligence service will accompany you to act as guides. All the equipment which you will need is being put aboard now and you will have time to examine it during your flight.'

The projector went dark and the lights were snapped on.

'The agenda for this mission into China is, of necessity, somewhat lacking in fine detail. Unfortunately, there has not been time to do much more than select a team, provide the equipment and hope that you will be able to work out the details of the operation yourselves. We are relying on your resourcefulness to offset the lack of support.' The colonel paused for a moment and rubbed his nose.

'Because of the sensitive nature of our relations with China at the moment,' he continued in a hesitant manner, 'it is of course essential to the security and interests of the United States and the Soviet Union that you do not allow yourselves to be captured or . . . well, captured.'

He nodded abruptly and hurried down the aisle while a distinguished-looking man in a dark business suit took his place at the front of the cabin and, with an air of controlled patience, waited for the colonel to collect his belongings and leave. The guard at the hatch saluted and swung the hatch shut again.

'What the hell did he say?'

Jones nudged him and nodded to the front of the aircraft.

'Gentlemen, I am here to brief you on the present political situation. As you can see, our military colleagues are unable to supply you with any significant information concerning conditions on the ground. But I think that you will see that in the political realm, it will be somewhat different.'

'Son-of-a-bitch,' Jones stage-whispered loudly enough for his voice to carry. He smiled serenely in reply to the dirty looks from the State Department people and the appreciative laughter of the military.

'The situation, briefly, is this. You will be violating the borders of a sovereign nation; one, further, which is extremely sensitive to any infringement of its sovereignty. After twenty-some years, diplomatic relations have just been re-established. In spite of this, we are told, the information which you will collect is of sufficient importance to risk jeopardizing all our work. But, that being the case, I must emphasize what the previous speaker stated and that is that you are to take special precautions against being captured or in any other way, being discovered . . . as must the government.' He paused for effect.

'The government of the United States will take no actions of any kind to protect you should you be captured.'

Jones growled and started to rise, then thought better of it and sank back into his seat.

'If you or any member of your team is captured or killed, the government will disavow any knowledge, etc. . . .' he quoted loudly from a popular television program.

The diplomat stared at him frostily. 'I am sorry, sir, but that is how it is.' His voice was hard. 'If you are captured, there is nothing that we can or will do for you . . . and conversely it is important that you do absolutely nothing to . . .'

Jones shot to his feet at this point and shouted angrily, 'General Masue, who the hell let this bastard on board?'

Masue pushed his way forward from the tiny lounge, where he had been talking with another officer. 'I beg your pardon . . .'

'I said,' Jones repeated furiously, pushing his face directly into the general's and forcing him to back up until he collided with an aide, who stumbled and plopped down into the seat occupied by the Soviet general. During the ensuing squawks, which he ignored, Jones poked General Masue in the chest, 'who let this bastard in here? This damned mission is supposed to be so top secret that even your mistress doesn't know about it. Who in hell brought all these people in here. . . ? Get them out now and unless you have anything else of importance, real importance, get your own ass the hell out of here as well.'

'Just a minute, sir . . .'

Gillon suddenly revised his opinion of Jones. Anybody who talked to brass that way couldn't be all bad. He got to his feet just in time to intercept the diplomat, who had come hurrying forward. Gillon caught his outstretched arm and jerked. The diplomat swung off balance and before he knew it, his arm was twisted up behind his back and the other caught at his side in a hard grip. Gillon rushed him down the aisle to the hatch and kicked it hard. The guard swung it open in time to receive the diplomat, business suit and all, and they both collapsed in a heap on the runway.

Gillon swung back to the shocked aircraft. An air policeman was reaching for a pistol but one of the men who had come aboard, heavyset and with a weather-beaten face, shot out a hand and pinioned the guard's arm against the wall.

'Don't, or I'll break it off and feed it to you,' he told the guard softly.

'Now, the rest of you who don't belong or have anything constructive to contribute . . . out,' Jones roared, and jerked a thumb at the hatch. Another State Department official started to protest, but stopped promptly as Gillon started up the aisle toward him.

'You heard . . . out!'

A few moments later the aircraft was empty of everyone but Gillon, Jones, the flight crew and two new men; one of whom had stopped the air policeman from drawing his weapon. Gillon eyed them expectantly but Jones shook his head.

'Fellow members of the suicide squad . . . Michael Leycock and Charles Stowe.'

Gillon nodded and shook hands briefly.

'What the devil was that all about?' the one introduced as Charles Stowe demanded. 'I thought you were keeping this thing dead quiet.'

'I thought we were too,' Jones said ruefully. 'It seems, however, that we were overruled.' He stepped across the aisle and stooped to peer through a window. The guards were still in place but the staff cars were beginning to pull away. As he straightened up, the pilot stuck his head through the cockpit door.

'What now, Colonel?'

Jones jerked a thumb at the ceiling. 'Out of here, just as fast as you can. Did they give you the flight plan?'

The pilot nodded. 'Direct flight to Volgograd for refueling. About five hours. All the equipment is aboard as well.'

'All right,' Jones nodded. 'Let's go.'

The pilot nodded once and closed the cabin door. A moment later the seat belt sign winked on.

THE SOVIET UNION

CHAPTER FIVE

Gillon watched as the aircraft gained altitude over the spiny ridge of mountains that ran the length of the Italian boot. The others had settled down to sleep, all of them showing the same signs of exhaustion as he; but, too keyed up to sleep, Gillon slumped in the wide seat and smoked cigarette after cigarette until the light blue Adriatic appeared and he finally fell asleep.

Hour after hour the Jetstar flew on, crossing the Adriatic, passing over the Dinaric Alps lining the Yugoslavian coast, deeper and deeper into Central Europe until first the Black Sea and then the broad strip of the fertile Caucasus was obscured by dense storm clouds.

Jones dropped down into the seat across the aisle several hours later, waking him to offer a cup of coffee.

'Feeling better now that you've had some real sleep?'

Gillon started to shrug and realized that he did feel better.

'Yeah . . . yes, I do. Thanks.' He sipped at the coffee for a moment, waiting for the caffeine to clear away the last of the cobwebs.

'We'll reach the jump-off point just after dawn,' Jones volunteered. 'If it will do us any good.'

Gillon looked up in surprise at the sudden bitterness in his voice. 'Why do you say that?'

Jones twisted in the seat. 'Because I just got a radio message a little while ago. Peter Lin was found dead in his apartment this morning.'

He noticed Gillon's blank stare. 'Pete was Phan Duc Phnom. He and I have been together for nearly three years.'

'Three years,' Gillon repeated. 'I thought he was a Laotian government official.'

Jones nodded. 'He was . . . but we also worked together.'

'I see,' he said, not sure what it was that he did see. 'How did it happen?'

'Somebody from the embassy went to his apartment to

pick up some papers. No one answered the door and they got the landlord to let them in. The place was torn apart and Pete knifed to death. It was made up to look like a robbery but that's nonsense. Pete held a third-degree black belt in Kenpo Karate. No one, not even two or three people with knives, could have gotten close to him.'

The cobwebs were gone now and Gillon had to lean closer to hear Jones as he had deliberately pitched his voice low so that the other two would not hear.

'There are too damned many people who know about this shindig . . . in Rome, Washington, Moscow, wherever. You can't maintain secrecy with that many people involved.' And he smacked the seat rest in anger.

Gillon nodded and suddenly he felt the cold, fey touch of death, and shivered involuntarily. Both men knew that Lin must have talked. A dose of carefully administered hypnotic, and his killers would have found out all he knew . . . providing, Gillon thought, that the killer knew generally what kind of questions to ask. Which meant that if he had been at all successful, he would have to be familiar with the broad outlines of the mission, and that meant that he must have been aboard the aircraft in Rome.

Gillon sat for a moment, mulling this chilling fact over in his mind. Finally, he had to ask the question.

'How much did he know?'

Jones looked at him, face noncommittal.

'Only the barest facts. He knew about the strike team in Sinkiang, about the data they were supposed to have . . . no specifics, just what you know, that a combined American/Soviet team was being put together.'

'Did he know where or when . . . anything at all in any detail?'

Jones thought for a minute. 'No,' he said slowly. 'No, no way. I didn't know myself until I read through the operations plan about two hours ago. I doubt if there are more than five or six people anywhere who know the full details.'

'Who?' Gillon prompted.

'How the hell . . . ?' Jones started to snap, then

thought better of it. Gillon waited patiently while Jones thought it through.

'Probably the Director of Planning at headquarters, maybe his staff aide, the Soviet intelligence chief and possibly one or two of his people . . . that should be all. These plans aren't even typed up by one person. Pages are spread at random through several typing pools.'

'No one else. How about somebody in Rome? That idiot general, maybe?'

'No, I doubt it. No one is ever trusted with full details of any plan unless they absolutely need to know.'

Gillon was silent for a moment, staring out the window. There was something missing here, some question that hadn't been answered, but for some reason it completely escaped him for the moment. He shrugged irritably and told Jones what had occurred to him, that the killer may have been in the group that boarded in Rome.

'So,' he finished, 'it could be that after we threw them off, they decided that shaking your friend down to learn anything more was worth the gamble.'

'Could be,' Jones responded dubiously. 'If that's the case, then they are damned desperate and might go after somebody else, figuring that if they can put enough pieces together they can puzzle out the plan. That would mean, then,' he finished slowly, 'that they have a pretty good idea of what's going on. And now they are looking to fill in the pieces.'

He was silent a long time, then reached over and slapped Gillon on the knee. 'Maybe you aren't out of the jungle yet, buddy.'

'I never figured I was,' Gillon replied soberly.

Jones leaned even closer. 'Don't say anything to the other two yet. No sense in having everyone upset.'

Gillon nodded, he could see the sense in that. 'Which brings up a question. How much do you know about these other two birds?' Against his will, he was beginning to take more of an interest in the mission. Then the stupidity of that position dawned on him. Win, lose or draw, they would all need to depend on one another. It was imperative that he know as much about the other two as possible, their strengths and weaknesses particularly.

'Leycock by reputation and Stowe by both reputation and experience. Both of them are extremely capable men. You rarely get the chance to pick the people whom you will work with on an assignment . . . they pretty much do that through some magical psychological testing and computer matching and, as usual, they fouled this one up. Leycock, I might have picked based on what I know of him; but not Stowe, not ever.'

Gillon raised his eyebrows in an elaborate questioning pose and Jones shrugged.

'You're going to find out anyway, so I might as well tell you now. Stowe doesn't work for the Agency. He's a National Security Council boy. Supposedly . . . there are only ten of them . . . they are the elite and they report directly to the President when they are on assignment. Stowe is one of those damnable know-it-alls who thinks that he's the only person capable of doing anything right. There is no love lost between the Agency and the NSC operatives, because we are senior, but they are completely independent of Agency control . . . except when on a combined effort assignment.'

Jones glanced over his shoulder but Stowe was asleep in his seat. 'This mission was approved on the highest levels and, as usual, the President assigned operational responsibility to the Agency.'

Oh hell, Gillon thought to himself. This whole damned thing isn't weird enough, but that we have to have interdepartmental politics involved as well.

'Anyway,' Jones went on, 'Stowe has the reputation for being an overbearing ass, even though he is apparently capable enough. I expect to have some discipline trouble from him before the mission is out, but nothing more than that. Otherwise, I've always found that he knows what he is doing and since he spent some time in Tibet a few years ago he should be able to handle himself in the mountains.'

'You say you worked with him before?'

Jones glanced out the window. 'Yes,' he replied in a tone that indicated this was forbidden territory.

42

'What about Leycock?' Gillon asked, deciding that he might get further if he played the game.

'Another one of us mountain men. He's been with the Agency since he left the Army ten years ago. His last assignment, according to his record, was leading a counter-reaction team in Bolivia.'

'And just what is a counter-reaction team?'

'A fancy way of saying anti-guerrilla unit. It's the latest fad in counter-insurgency warfare. Supposedly, it's designed to work in areas where the insurgency is still in Phase One . . . a backwoods operation, in other words, with hit-and-run tactics and no pitched battles. The counter-reaction teams are recruited from the local countryside and usually include a policeman, some farmers, a few businessmen from the city, a doctor and a lawyer . . . they try and get a cross section of the local society, in short. Then they train these people and send them into the bush after the guerrillas to meet them on their own ground. Each group consists of about twenty men and they are supported and supplied by helicopter. The idea is based on the old British local forces idea that worked in Malaya. The U.S. uses it quite a bit in Laos these days.'

'I see,' Gillon nodded. 'Then Leycock led one of these outfits in Bolivia . . . after Guevara, I would imagine.'

'Well, some of his units, yes, and quite successfully too. They worked pretty high in the Andes, so he knows his way around in the mountains . . . or so his record tells me.'

Gillon shook his head. 'I sure hope it's right. The Tien Shan is going to be one devil of a place to find out that some clerk mixed files.'

Jones nodded agreement. 'Before that, he was in Cambodia and then southern Laos with the Special Forces, a Montagnard unit, I believe. They are supposed to have made some raids into North Vietnam. You might ask him about them since you both worked the same neighbourhood.'

Jones stretched and shook his head. 'God, I'm exhausted. Want some more coffee?'

Gillon shook his head and Jones stood up. 'Then I

think I'll go up front and get another cup and see if anything else has come in from Rome.'

Gillon nodded and went back to staring out the window at the clouds. He had never considered that his army days in Indo-china had qualified him as an expert in covert-style warfare. But for all he knew, they were counting guerrilla experience as college credit these days. He was happy to discover that at least one of the qualifications for membership in this select group of idiots was mountain experience . . . actual on-the-ground experience and not classroom textbook experience. He well knew what they could expect from the terrain, altitude and weather once they got into the Tien Shan – assuming they made it that far. May was not the most ideal month to hike into ten- to fifteen-thousand-foot passes.

Gillon had not been in the mountains in nearly ten years . . . real mountains, mountains over ten thousand feet and covered with snow and glacial ice all year around as distinguished from mountains with rain forest and grasslands. He knew well that they would need both skis and snowshoes to pack in the supplies they would need for a week. There would be no time to teach an amateur what he needed to know to survive a howling blizzard and below-zero temperatures. Ten years and he hoped that he was neither out of condition nor had forgotten how to survive, himself.

He continued to stare out the window for a while, watching the extremely few lights that were scattered across the vast, silent steppe some thirty thousand feet below. They had outflown the storm while he slept and the skies were clear. Above them, by shading the double plastic window from the cabin lights, he could see bright, ice-sharp stars and far to the north, on the very horizon, the faint ghost dance of the northern lights. Proof enough that they were moving north. Ala Kul, Jones had told him earlier, was to be the jump-off zone. Try as he might, he could not place Ala Kul even though Jones had explained that it was a large salt lake near the Sinkiang border. He got up and went to the back of the cabin, where Jones was poring over the mission plan and borrowed a map showing the Central Siberian area and the western Sinkiang region. Returning to his

44

seat, he adjusted the overhead light and began to examine the map. After a moment, he found the tiny blue speck labeled Ala Kul, some sixty miles due west of the border. On the southern edge of the lake, he spotted a small Soviet air base, presumably used for border patrol. The airfield lay far enough away to be beyond the range of Chinese radar, but close enough to allow them to fly into the mountains quickly. Foothills overflowed the border at this point and their northern slopes were portrayed as quite steep, leading up to an almost sheer massif where they joined the main line of the range, the Tien Shan mountains. An aircraft taking off from Ala Kul could, if it hugged the ground to the border, use the radar shadow of this massif to penetrate the range, drop a load and be gone before the Chinese could spot it by radar. There were one or two advanced radar stations marked along the highest ridges, but the Soviets were apparently not worried about these, as they could not monitor the wide, steep, but very high passes through which a carefully piloted aircraft could slip.

A hand fell on his shoulder an indeterminate time later and he awoke with a jolt.

'Join us,' Jones shook him again.

Gillon sat up in the seat shaking his head, surprised to find that he had dozed off.

The cabin was brightly lit and strewn with sleeping bags, Primus stoves, cold-weather clothes, carbines, skis, snowshoes and a hundred and one other items.

'We decided that it would be a good idea to see what the bright boys back in Virginia packed for us. Once we leave the hospitable Soviet Union, it'll be too late to holler for matches.'

Leycock was busily making up four individual packs and Stowe stood up, rubbing the backs of his legs. He turned to Gillon and looked him over slowly.

'Do you know how to use any of this?'

For a moment, Gillon could not decide whether the question was meant as a joke or an insult. Stowe's manner provided no clue and he decided that, this early in the game, the benefit of the doubt was in order.

He nodded. 'Yeah, I do. I understand that both of

you know your way around in the mountains.' He noticed that Leycock had stopped work and was watching Stowe.

'You do, huh?' Stowe grinned. 'My kid brother does a lot of hiking in the Cascades. But I sure as hell don't count that as knowing how to use this equipment.'

And now he knew. Gillon stepped quickly across the aisle. 'Look, friend. We're going to be together for quite some time. We need to reach an understanding. So, you give me any more smart talk and I'll tear your head off.'

Gillon's move was so quick and unexpected that Stowe stepped back involuntarily. Leycock sat back on his heels and laughed. 'Chuck, I do think that you've met someone who's not going to take any nonsense. I'd leave him alone, if I were you.'

Stowe considered Gillon for a minute, as if deciding which tack to take. Gillon waited patiently, watching his face for any sign of a quick move. Finally, Stowe grinned.

'All right. I apologize. If you say you know, then you know.'

'Darned right, Stowe,' Jones said quickly. 'Gillon cut his teeth on the Swiss Alps when he was a kid. Not only that, but he took the cross-country silver medal in the 1964 Winter Olympics.'

Stowe shrugged. 'All right, then I apologize. I've had to work so long with stumblebums like these that I've come to consider anyone that runs with them a stumblebum . . .'

'I don't run with anyone,' Gillon said flatly.

'Yeah . . . I can see now that you don't. Anyway, I do apologize.' Stowe stuck out a large hand. 'It is certainly nice to have an expert *who is an expert* along for a change.'

With some misgivings Gillon shook hands. Stowe was a large, rangy individual, and the strength of his grip was certainly no childish attempt to impress him. He would be a mean customer in a fight, he decided, and it was better to have him on the same side.

Both Jones and Leycock were grinning openly. In the closed intelligence community, reputation counted for all. No matter what a man's abilities, good, bad or indifferent, it was his reputation, which often had no bearing on his demonstrated abilities, that counted.

Gillon nodded and smiled thinly at Stowe. Stowe seemed to take that as an acceptance of his off-hand apology and Gillon, ignoring him for the moment, bent down to examine the equipment that had been laid out on the desk. Because he was expecting it – a test of a sort – he sensed rather than saw Stowe's leg coming at him as Stowe threw himself almost horizontal with the effort he put behind the side thrust kick to Gillon's thigh. Stowe was to his right, so Gillon shuffled forward with his right foot to take himself out of the line of the kick. So fast was his movement that Stowe was caught by surprise and, in trying to correct his aim, lost his balance for an instant.

That was all Gillon needed and his right hand smashed into a downward block that knocked Stowe's extended leg away. Spun off balance, his left foot acting as a pivot, Stowe stumbled and Gillon stepped forward, snapped his right foot out and caught Stowe behind his left knee and sent him crashing to the deck. Instantly, Gillon was on him, his own knee crushing down on Stowe's exposed thigh. One hand pressed his left arm down and the other, the left, touched a thin-bladed throwing knife to the inside of Stowe's ear.

'The next time you try that,' he said softly, pressing down on the point until it drew blood, 'I'll carve your brain out. Do you understand?'

Stowe grunted an acknowledgment and Gillon stood up quickly and backed away, dipping the knife back into his boot. The incident had happened so quickly that Leycock and Jones were immobilized by surprise. Stowe climbed slowly to his feet, staring at the blood on his fingers where he had pressed them to his ear.

'By God, you cut me . . .' he said, astonished.

Jones whistled slowly. 'He sure as hell did!'

'You, buddy boy, are damned lucky to be alive,' Leycock murmured. 'I sure am glad I didn't try that.'

Stowe stared at Gillon, his face ugly, then back at the blood on his fingers and stared, 'Next time friend, I'll make damned sure that you get no warning of any kind.'

And Gillon knew that he wouldn't either, but at the moment, he did not care. He was still shaking inwardly. If he had not been expecting the kick, the incident could have become very nasty.

After a moment more, Stowe turned away, intense anger evident on his face, and went aft to the lavatory. Leycock and Jones wandered forward to the galley, just aft of the cockpit, and Gillon, left alone for the moment, returned to an examination of the equipment laid out on the deck. He was breathing heavily and the adrenaline shock was beginning to drain away. He noticed that his hands were shaking slightly and he was glad the others were gone so they would not notice.

Forcing himself to relax he first checked over the mountaineering gear, tents and sleeping bags. The first were excellent quality Swiss mountain tents of very lightweight, close-woven parachute nylon. Each would accommodate one man and his gear. A single T-brace of aluminum tubing supported the triangular tent and the entire affair could not have weighed more than two pounds. The sleeping bags were five-pound goose-down mummy bags of the type supplied by the U.S. Army to the Ski Corps. Each was capable of keeping a man warm and alive in temperatures to twenty below. Lightweight wool liners added an additional five-degree safety margin. With the sleeping bags and tents, they should be able to survive a blizzard in the Antarctic.

Each pack was also supplied with an alcohol compass, tiny Primus stove, sufficient dehydrated food in individually wrapped meals for five days, two changes of nylon mesh underwear, socks and gloves, and a personal pack containing first-aid supplies, toilet articles and liquid soap with a label stating that it would not harden in below-freezing temperatures. Gillon snorted at that. Satisfied that the packs had been made up by experts in mountain survival and that everything that he would have chosen was included, he turned his attention to the outer clothing and the weapons.

Each of them was supplied with a one-piece white coverall designed to be worn over the mesh underwear. Each suit was fitted with a hood that could be drawn tightly around the face by means of a cord. Gloves, lightweight silk affairs without padding, were supplied and at the cuff of each coverall, thickly padded mittens with trigger slits were attached with plastic zippers that allowed them to be removed if required. Lined face masks were contained in roomy pockets inside the jackets. The boots, vacuum-insulated, were one piece with each suit and over these, ski boots could be drawn. The entire suit was made of the same closely woven nylon as the tents and lined with a two-inch layer of goose down, the best insulator so far discovered for cold-weather use. Each pack was mounted on a sturdy Hima-laya frame, constructed of duraluminium, and bore stickers showing that they had been purchased from Frost-line Equipment in Seattle . . . no better supplier of mountain gear in the world.

Gillon had been accustomed to the M-16 carbine for several years, considering it one of the best all-round weapons for counter-insurgency warfare yet developed. But when he picked up one of the carbines stacked against the cabin wall, he knew that he might have to change his mind. He had heard about the AR-18 but had never seen one before. A slightly smaller version of the M-16, it was a substantially lighter and, at first glance, simpler weapon. It used the same .222 caliber ammunition and if it weighed five pounds when fully loaded, Gillon would have been surprised. He stripped it down and found that it came apart much like the M-16, but went back together again much more easily.

He sat back on his heels and surveyed the neat piles of equipment before him. At least from the standpoint of supplies, he decided, this idiot-mission had been well organized. He looked up warily as Stowe came back into the cabin. A wad of tissue stuck out of his left ear and his face was not exactly what Gillon would have described as friendly.

Stowe hesitated a moment as if undecided and then shrugged.

'Oh hell.' He grinned at Gillon. 'I guess I had that coming. I should have guessed from the way what's-his-name, Jones, kept quiet about you that he was setting me up. The Agency boys don't think much of me or my outfit because we don't do things by the book.'

So that was it. Gillon thought to himself. A setup to teach Stowe who was boss and at the same time to find out if he was as good as his record indicated. Very neat, very neat indeed. His respect for Jones rose another notch.

'Forget it,' he said carefully. 'We were both set up.'

Stowe nodded and went on forward. Gillon sank down in his seat and stared at the cabin lights reflecting in the window, considering, wondering what other surprises they might have in line for him.

They were not unique, he thought, Jones, or whatever his real name was, Leycock and Stowe. He was the unique one, unique in the sense that he was part of a dying breed – the professional soldier. When you came right down to it, he mused, it really was not such a bad life. Most of your decisions were made for you and your responsibility was only to carry them out – within narrow limitations. But either the world had grown too small and the weapons too terrible or else civilization was at long last passing from intemperate adolescence to maturity. It seemed to him that warfare had been taking on two or three new aspects since the end of World War II, new aspects that were rapidly consigning overt warfare to extinction. The so-called Wars of National Liberation – Malaya, the Philippines, Korea, etc. – had pretty much died out in the mid-1960's, as the Communists changed their tack from indirect or direct aggression to internal subversive movements such as had taken place in Indochina. That one had been a mistake all the way around, resulting from considerable misunderstanding on the part of North Vietnam and the United States as to the intentions and commitments of the other and so it had blown up into a full-scale land war. It would be, he knew, a long time before that ever happened again.

The little wars, Gambia, Bolivia, Nigeria/Biafra, Colombia, etc., were really internal affairs, civil wars of a kind, but complicated by big-power interference. But even these were dying out as the emerging nations gained maturity and learned to handle their problems in other, less deadly ways. Africa could never be compared to the two-hundred-year reign of terror that had wreck-

50

ed Central Europe – and in particular the Balkans. All considered, Africa, with little in the way of human resources, had moved quite peacefully from direct imperialistic control to a series of independent nations in less than twenty years. The few wars that had broken out, with only one or two exceptions, had been confined to within national borders rather than to aggressive attacks on other nations.

Warfare had become a push-button affair – as had long been expected – in which highly trained technicians monitored surveillance consoles, fingers poised over triple-locked buttons that could unleash forces capable of destroying civilization. Except for skirmishes here and there and chronic problem areas – war, active, overt war was fast disappearing. But disappearing by becoming submerged in the third aspect, the silent wars. The wars of international surveillance or espionage involved the same old power blocs, but considerably fewer people and with much less dangerous effect. And Jones, Leycock and Stowe represented the new soldier. To him their work was a game, a silly, almost useless game involving 99 per cent newspaper clipping and only 1 per cent direct action. But to them, it was a deadly life-or-death struggle, as overt war was to the professional soldier.

Cro-Magnon and Neanderthal, the new driving out the old. And that's what he was, the old species watching himself give way to a younger, more clever breed. He would hold his own while the new breed slowly gained ascendancy, but slowly, surely, his would die out.

CHAPTER SIX

Sometime after dawn, Gillon woke again to find that he felt rested for the first time in months. He stretched, then wandered forward to find some coffee. Jones, Stowe and Leycock were still asleep in their seats and in the cockpit, Gillon found the radio operator stretched out on a small fold-down bunk. The pilot was dozing at the controls and the co-pilot staring moodily through

51

the cockpit windscreen. The sun was just clearing the horizon and the land below them was in darkness. From one horizon to the other, Gillon noted with interest, the skies were perfectly free of cloud. During the long night, they had obviously outflown the storm cell.

Gillon drew two cups of coffee in the galley and handed one to the co-pilot. In silence, they watched the sun inch higher and higher until with a sudden burst of radiance, a flood of golden light sped swiftly toward them as they raced to meet the sun. The co-pilot polished a pair of sunglasses on his shirt and put them on. Gillon contented himself with shielding his eyes against the glare of the moment. Within minutes, the countryside was flooded in the clear, soft light of dawn, revealing a carpet of gold-polished white wool.

Gillon went back to his seat and gathered up his shaving kit. Twenty minutes in the tiny shower facility on the aircraft and he literally felt like a new man.

Sometime later, Gillon finished the large breakfast put together by Jones and Leycock and was enjoying the first cigarette of the day. He had just spread a copy of the map describing their route into the Tien Shan on his lap when a flicker of light caught his attention. He turned to the window in time to see the sleek shape of a Mig 21 sliding into place off their port wing. Its pilot glanced over at the Jetstar and waved. Gillon felt the Jetstar rock abruptly as their pilot waggled his wings in answer. Through a window across the aisle, he could just see a second Mig arriving to lead them in.

'Company,' he announced, and pointed toward the Mig on the starboard side. The other three hurried to the windows.

'Sure is,' Leycock muttered. 'I hope to hell they're expecting us.'

'If they weren't, you wouldn't be standing here making dumb remarks,' Stowe muttered.

'Christ almighty,' Leycock exploded, 'doesn't anything ever help your disposition?'

Jones gave Stowe a disgusted look, shook his head and wandered back to his breakfast, leaving Stowe staring after Leycock with a faint grin on his face.

Ahead of them, Gillon spotted a peculiarly flat, somewhat bowl-shaped area and a quick map check showed it to be Ala Kul. Moments later, the Jetstar bore around to the north, the Migs following smoothly, and a small airfield on the southern edge of the lake slid into view. As the turn was completed, the Migs accelerated ahead to lead them in.

Jones walked back from the galley, leaning heavily against the centrifugal pull of the aircraft as the pilot completed the turn, and dropped into the seat beside Gillon. He pointed to a line of distant mountains and there was an undercurrent of anticipation and excitement in his voice.

'Those are the Tien Shan! The Chinese border is just about in line with that farthest peak.'

Even from a distance of nearly seventy miles, the Tien Shan looked bleak and forbidding, Gillon thought. And damned dangerous as well. Snow lay thick down to the foothills and in the higher elevations deep winter raged. And, he thought, most of their time would be spent at elevations above nine thousand feet. Interminably, the mountains stretched from horizon to horizon, northeast to southwest. In the early morning light, they were a steel-blue barrier, the jagged peaks wreathed with heavy clouds. The sight of these almost unknown mountains – although unknown only to the West, inhabited as they had been for thousands of years by Siberian, Mongolian and Chinese tribesmen – did nothing to increase Gillon's enthusiasm.

This view of the mountain range from ten thousand feet and a vantage point of seventy miles made it clear why the Soviets had insisted that the mission start from Ala Kul. It would be a straight flight due south to the massive escarpment that marked the beginning of the Tien Shan. In some ways the escarpment reminded him of the eastern flank of the Sierra Nevada range in California. At midrange, the northeastern wall of the Sierras was a single, three-hundred-mile-long massif rearing above the Owens Valley. The Sierras had been caused, he knew, by some eons-old series of cataclysms that had literally snapped free the crust of the mantle and tilted it upward like a broken paving block. He wondered if a similar event might not be responsible for the Tien Shan.

Gillon turned back to the airfield in time to see the Migs touching down. Moments later, the edge of the runway flashed past beneath and the Jetstar was down and taxiing after the Migs as they made for a hangar on the far side of the field. The airfield had a curiously deserted air about it, in spite of the bustle around an Aeroflot TU-144 airliner loading passengers at a small terminal. Heads turned in curiosity as the Jetstar taxied past and Gillon wondered if the national markings were still in place. They had been when he boarded the plane in Conakry, but they could easily have been changed in Rome without him having noticed.

The Jetstar eased to a halt in front of an old worn-out hangar. Staring through the window at the weather-beaten building, Gillon reckoned that it must have been built at least thirty years before, probably before World War II to protect the Russian southern flank as the Japanese had moved westward. Now it merely served as a forward base from which this 'safe' area of the Chinese border could be watched. There was, Gillon realized, only the remotest possibility that the Chinese would dream of mounting a land attack through the barrier imposed by the Tien Shan. Border actions might certainly be fought in the high passes and meadows, but hardly anything more serious. Only someone with the courage and stubbornness of a Hannibal would even dream of trying, and technology had long ago replaced elephants with less efficient means of locomotion. And further, since this territory was never in dispute with the Chinese, there was little likelihood that they would press for border adjustments as they had done further north along the Sinkiang border, or in the Far East along the Ussuri River.

Gillon studied the building opposite them some three hundred feet. To judge by the multitude of signs nailed to its front the hangar did double duty as an administrative center. Weather-beaten and paint peeling, it nevertheless did not induce that empty feeling that most such World War II-vintage military buildings all over the world did, whether still in use or not.

Jones got up and reached into the rack for his parka. Gillon did the same, and, shrugging it on, he joined the others in the aisle, stretched and waited for the next development. Shortly, the co-pilot stuck his head into the cabin.

'Captain says you may as well go on and get out. The control tower doesn't speak English and now they won't even answer us. Nobody else seems to be around.'

A worried frown appeared on Jones's face for a moment, but he motioned toward the back of the cabin. 'Let's go see what the holdup is all about.'

Leycock nodded and with a glance at the carbines in the overhead racks, walked to the hatch, unlatched and shoved it open and pushed the button to extend the ramp.

The sun had been up for less than two hours, but already the sky was an intense cobalt blue with scattered, blindingly white clouds. The terrain, incredibly flat, stretched unbroken, west to the horizon. To the east, it butted sharply against the distant Tien Shan escarpment. From the level of the airfield, the mountains were completely covered with snow; the slopes icy gray and blue with long lines of shadow lacing sharp white ridges. The intervening distance was ethereal, mirage-like in quality, so that it seemed no more than a walk of a mile or two to the rearing barrier of snow and ice.

Gillon turned to the north; again a similar vista. Flat steppe covered with snow stretching away to the horizon, the monotony of the terrain somewhat relieved by the demanding line of peaks curving away to the northeast. Gillon was struck by the majesty and serenity of these vast mountains.

He shook his head and glanced around to see if the others were as affected as he was by the quiet immensity of Central Asia. After a subdued moment, Leycock coughed in the cold air and the spell was broken.

'God almighty,' Stowe muttered, stamping his feet. 'This place is about as deserted as those mountains.'

'Don't let it fool you,' Jones said tightly. 'Neither is. This place is full of Russians and they are probably wondering who the hell we are because some damn fool clerk in Moscow forgot to process the paperwork. And,

55

over there,' he said, pointing toward the mountains, 'are more Chinese soldiers than you ever thought existed, all waiting for us to come bumbling across their border.'

His words were strangely prophetic and Gillon was to think back on them bitterly in the coming days.

Stowe snorted. 'You're probably right . . .'

'Over there,' Leycock interrupted, pointing across the field. A bright red snowplow, almost black in the distance, was plodding comfortably down the far runway. A crystal plume of blown snow towered thirty feet above the cab, spraying a fine mist of flashing rainbows as it drifted slowly in the bright sunlight.

'Hey, you guys, wake up.' The co-pilot was standing above them in the hatch with a pack in either hand. He tossed both down and reached back inside for two duffle bags, which he passed down to Gillon.

'What are we supposed to do with these now?' Stowe yelled up at the co-pilot.

'For God's sake, if you don't know by now, then you better get back . . .' He stopped abruptly and stared at the hangar.

'Who the devil?' Jones began, and took a few paces forward.

The sound of booted feet trotting in rhythm floated around the side of the hangar and Gillon moved up next to Jones just as a squad of Russian soldiers trotted into sight. There were ten soldiers, five abreast and all carrying rifles at port arms while a sergeant trotted beside them calling cadence. Gillon and Jones stared at each other in surprise and both stared back to the Jetstar just as two jeeplike vehicles roared up behind, one jamming to a stop in front of the aircraft's nosewheel, effectively blocking any movement, and the other skidding to a halt beside them. A young officer vaulted out as the soldiers reached them, rifles levelled.

'What in hell is going on here . . . ?'

The officer pushed Jones back and pointed. Instantly, four soldiers sprang forward to grasp each of them by the arms. Four more stepped in front of Jones and looked him up and down.

'*Amerikanets?*'

Jones glanced around at the other three and nodded vigorously.

'Yeah, yeah . . . *Amerikanets* . . . *Amerikanets* . . .'

The officer nodded. '*Da, Amerikanets . . . Amerikanets. Shpion.*'

'Like hell,' Jones shouted, and fumbled through his long-forgotten college Russian. '*Nyet, nyet Amerikanets shpion, drug K Rossii.*'

The Russian officer merely snorted at that and motioned to the soldiers, who closed in tightly and began herding them toward the hangar. Gillon managed a glance over his shoulder in time to see the pilot stop, halfway down the ramp, beside the co-pilot, mouth open in surprise. A rifle barrel jammed painfully into Gillon's back was as good as a command in English to face forward and he did so, promptly. The officer, who had jumped back into his jeep to follow, climbed out again as they reached the building and pushed ahead to shove open the door. They were shoved inside and, with gestures, the officer made them understand that they were to sit down along the wall.

Stowe jerked his arm away and shook his head. 'Like hell I will!' he shouted.

His guard reversed his carbine and swung it hard to his midsection, but Stowe stepped to one side, parried the swinging weapon and kicked the soldier neatly in the back of the left knee. He went down in a heap and several soldiers rushed Stowe. The soldier he had knocked down, a short, thickset Tartar by his deep complexion and slanted eyes, got slowly to his feet and started toward Stowe, who stood waiting, shoulders hunched against the pressure of the arms that held him immobile. Gillon took a deep breath, forced himself to relax and eyed his guard warily, estimating his chances of jumping him; from the corner of his eye he saw Jones and Leycock tensing.

The officer snapped a command and the soldier hesitated. The officer spoke again, his voice cold and flat, and the Tartar stepped back, hitching his carbine sling and glaring at Stowe, suggesting plainly that the incident was by no means forgotten.

The officer, hands behind his back, stepped forward. 'Very much . . . regrettable . . .' he stuttered in heavily accented English. 'No permission . . . here . . . war base.' He waved at the floor again.

'Sit . . . please.'

When they still hesitated, the officer lost his patience and they were shoved down against the wall by the soldiers. Three remained, rifles ready, while the others withdrew to the far side of the room. At a brief word from the officer, they relaxed, dug cigarettes out of their parkas and lit up. One of the soldiers, a corporal from the markings on his hat, stepped forward and tossed a pack across the room to Leycock.

Leycock looked at Jones, who shrugged. Leycock dug one out and handed the pack to Gillon, who took one and motioned to his pocket for a match. The soldier shook his head in warning and produced a small box of wooden matches, which he tossed across the room. Gillon caught it and lit the thin, flattened tube and inhaled the heavy, greasy smoke, thinking that the cancer potential must be fantastic.

Stowe, still angry, hurled the cigarettes back across the room.

'Damn it, this is ridiculous. There's got to be somebody in the place who speaks English . . . or something besides Russian. This is nothing more than a lousy Communist stall . . .'

'Shut up, Stowe, before you get your head blown off. These people aren't fooling.' Jones sat back against the wall and stretched his legs out comfortably. But Gillon noticed that the hands he shoved into the parka's pockets were shaking slightly.

'You might as well make the best of it, because until someone comes to bail us out . . .'

'Maybe you think so . . .' Stowe started to get to his feet. The racketing blast of a carbine smashed through the room and splinters burst from the wall above Stowe's head. He sat down abruptly. The Tartar soldier that he had knocked down lowered the muzzle until it was pointing directly at Stowe's head, smiling in expectation.

Gillon relaxed slowly and settled back against the wall, being very careful that he made no sudden moves. Jones, too, half on his knees, hands pressed against the floor to spring, subsided as the machine gun waved in his direction. Stowe leaned forward slowly, then turned back to stare at the line of splintered bullet holes just above his head. For once, he was completely speechless. The Soviet officer had been halfway across the room when the firing started; now he turned slowly, as if afraid of what he might see. His gaze raced over the four Americans and he exhaled in relief as he realized that the shots had been fired in warning. Before he could react further, the door on the far side of the narrow room was flung open and a second Russian officer strode in. He took in the room in one quick glance and without breaking stride, walked across to the young officer. His voice was quiet enough as he spoke in Russian, but it was too carefully controlled, his anger too obviously suppressed. The soldiers, surprised by the sudden shots and the even more sudden entry of the officer, were galvanized into action. The one with the carbine snapped to attention and the others retreated as fast as they could to the far side of the room. The first officer came quickly to attention, his face burning as he tried to explain.

Apparently, he was successful, as far as Gillon could tell, because the newcomer nodded and snapped a single word. Both the soldier and the young officer were visibly relieved as he turned and strode across the room to stare down at the Americans.

'You are Americans?' he asked abruptly.

Jones nodded. 'Yes, we are Americans.'

'And what are you doing in the Soviet Union?'

Gillon could detect no trace of accent in his well-modulated voice. He could have grown up in any one of the northern mid-western states; the only fault Gillon could detect was the too exact pronunciation.

'What the devil do you mean, what are we doing in the Soviet Union? We are on a top-priority joint mission and our orders require us to report to a Colonel Andre Dmietriev.'

'There is no such person here,' the officer stated firmly. 'You are American military personnel? You arrived in an aircraft belonging to the United States Air Force?'

Jones shook his head. 'No, we do not belong to the military, the aircraft was , , ,'

'Not military,' the Soviet officer interrupted smoothly. 'If not military, then what?'

'Look, this is ridiculous,' Jones stammered. 'If we didn't belong here, why did you let us land? Our pilot had clearances for this airfield, clearances that were issued in Moscow. We received permission to land from your own control tower!'

'And what would you do if a strange aircraft appeared on your radar screen? We sent fighter aircraft in pursuit but before they could make contact, you had asked for permission to land. Since you did not take evasive action when my aircraft appeared, we decided to let you land and then find out why.'

'Nonsense,' Jones snorted. 'If you had any doubts at all, you would have shot first and asked questions later. You are too damned close to the Chinese border for any other action to be considered.'

'We are friendly with the People's Republic of China and would have no cause to show alarm if one of their aircraft accidentally strayed across the border.'

Gillon laughed at that and turned to Jones. 'Brother, this guy is worse than a divorce lawyer. It looks to me like your people have fouled up this mission from the word go.'

Jones turned on him, an angry retort ready, but Gillon ignored him and studied the Russian.

'All right, buster, there's one way that you can find out what's going on here. Either your people don't think you can be trusted' – he paused to see if the Russian would take the bait – 'or they forgot to send you the message . . . that is, of course, assuming that it ever left Washington.'

'It did,' Stowe answered abruptly. 'My people are in charge of liaison. I sent it out myself and got a forwarding acknowledgment before I left for Rome.'

Jones, completely baffled, stared hard at Stowe, then sat back and began whistling tunelessly.

'All right then, something happened.' Gillon felt his

patience ebbing fast. 'Get on the radio or telephone or drums or whatever the hell it is you people use to talk to one another and find out what the devil is going on.'

'And who would you suggest I ask?' The question was logical but the tone of voice was quite sarcastic.

'Start with the GRU,' Gillon replied coldly.

The officer straightened in surprise. 'The GRU . . . why should I contact them?'

'Because,' Gillon snarled, his patience exhausted, 'we are supposed to be co-operating with them, or with one or another of your silly intelligence units. If it isn't them, they can tell you which other agency. If your people spend as much time checking up on each other as ours do, they'll know.'

The officer studied him for a long moment, as if not quite sure that Gillon was serious. Angrily, Gillon stared right back.

The Russian took a deep breath and rubbed his forehead and eyes in weariness. 'Your suggestion will be taken into consideration,' he replied slowly. 'For the moment, you will remain under arrest since you have crossed the borders of the Union of Soviet Socialist Republics illegally, landed a foreign military aircraft in a restricted area, resisted arrest and imported weapons in violation of Soviet laws. You will be placed under guard. I must warn you that any attempt to escape will be dealt with swiftly and harshly. I have given my men orders to shoot to kill. You must realize that you are very lucky that you were not shot down and killed during your landing attempt.'

With that, he stepped back and motioned the soldiers forward. Jones's face reflected his shock and anger, but appreciating the uselessness of further argument, he remained silent.

The two officers conferred in Russian for a moment and then the colonel turned and left abruptly and the lieutenant sauntered over and stared down at them in scorn.

'Look your fill, sonny boy,' Leycock growled. 'As soon as your boss gets his signals right, I'm going to wipe your feet with your silly face.'

The lieutenant pursed his lips at Leycock. He may not

have understood the English, but the meaning was clear enough. He nodded and four soldiers came forward and, at gunpoint, they were herded back out into the icy cold of the Siberian morning and then marched toward a ramshackle building standing well back from the apron. What little paint had once coated the wood had long since peeled away under the onslaught of winter cold and summer sun. The walls were almost the same gray as the bare concrete apron. They were marched up to the door and the lieutenant hurried up the steps to push it open. It resisted, and, suddenly angry at being made to look foolish, he bent and slammed it open with his shoulder. The door thudded back against the wall and the guards motioned for them to enter. One by one they climbed the rickety steps.

The interior of the building was almost as cold as the exterior. A guard hurried to the stove, a battered old potbellied affair almost completely red with rust, standing in the center of the room, and shoved in several sticks of wood, crumpled some sheets of newspaper and doused it all with kerosene. He stepped back and tossed a match into the stove and the fire lit with a loud, soft pop.

The two-story building was constructed in the clapboard style that Gillon had seen used on World War II-vintage military bases the world over. Interior walls were screened off by thin panels of fiberboard ending several inches short of the ceiling. The floor was tiled with crumbling rubber squares whose edges had curled through years of winter cold and summer heat. Gillon stumbled on one and received another jab with a rifle for his clumsiness. They reached the stairs at the far end of the barracks and were motioned up to the second floor. Puzzled, Gillon followed the others up the steps. As far as he could see, the building was completely unoccupied and had been so for years. There was no reason to take them up to the second floor, until he remembered the pipes radiating from the stove. Two went to the ceiling and since hot air rises, presumably the second floor would warm faster. Very strange, he thought to himself. Why should they care whether we are cold or not?

At the top of the stairs, one of the guards pulled open the door of the first room in line and motioned Leycock inside. He hesitated a moment, then shrugged and grinned.

'I guess we really don't have much choice, do we?' He stepped inside and the door was closed and they watched as the guard attacked a padlock and snapped it shut.

The guards shoved them on down the corridor to the next room, where Stowe was detached and the process repeated. Jones was next and the last room, at the end of the corridor, was for Gillon. As he stepped inside, he saw a soldier dragging a chair to the head of the stairs. Obviously, they were going to be watched very carefully.

The door was pushed shut behind him. It stuck in the jamb and Gillon heard a muffled curse and a heavy boot kicked it shut. A padlock snapped into the hasp and footsteps walked down the corridor. The soldier paused at the head of the stairs and spoke with the guard, then clattered down to the first floor and a door slammed. In the sudden silence that followed Gillon shoved his hands into his pockets and glanced about the room. It looked like it was going to be a long day.

Shivering, he walked over and pressed his hand to the register set into the wall at floor level. He felt only the barest stirrings of hot air and stooped down to examine it more closely. The register was almost closed and when he poked at it with a finger, it resisted and he concluded that it was rusted shut. Extracting the thin-bladed throwing knife from his boot top, he considered it thoughtfully, the Russian guard, the layout of the airfield and his chances of reaching the aircraft after dark. He concluded that they were pretty good, but that the chances of flying the Jetstar out of the Soviet Union were next to nil. With over four hundred miles to go to reach the Afghan border, the nearest . . . if China was excepted . . . they would be after him in minutes. And the Jetstar, fast as it was, did not have the turn of speed necessary to outrace a Mach 2 fighter-interceptor. He shrugged and used the point of the knife to push open the register, then slipped it back into the boot top and stood up.

It was strange, he thought, that the Russians had not bothered to search them. Gillon did not believe for one minute that the Russian officer did not know why they were in the Soviet Union. Soviet Air Force lieutenant generals were not sent to NATO briefings in Rome for curiosity's sake. And then to allow things to be screwed up at some backwater military base was more than he could believe possible.

Gillon wandered over to the lone, dirty window. He shook a cigarette out of the half-empty pack and lit it, staring thoughtfully at the airfield below. There were very many things about their treatment that puzzled him besides the fact that they had not been searched. For instance, the Jetstar. Right now he could see the Russian lieutenant strolling across the apron. The pilot saw him too and a moment later appeared in the hatch, hesitated, then climbed down and walked to meet him, hands waving in expressive gestures. The two met, and started back to the aircraft, deep in conversation. Gillon grunted; either the pilot spoke Russian or the lieutenant spoke better English than he had acknowledged. How interesting.

At the foot of the ladder, they were joined by the co-pilot and radio operator. The pilot waved at the barracks, the lieutenant shrugged. The pilot ticked off points on his fingers, the lieutenant shrugged. The co-pilot yelled, the lieutenant shrugged. The lieutenant spoke for some minutes, shrugged again and started back to the administration building. The co-pilot gestured obscenely while the pilot glanced towards the barracks, then shrugged himself. Empathetically, Gillon shrugged with him and grinned at his own reaction. All very strange. Apparently the Russians were making no move to lock up the flight crew.

A few minutes later, a ground support truck drove up and the co-pilot superintended the coupling of the nose gear to the trailer hitch. The truck then drove away, towing the aircraft with it and Gillon watched as it was pulled around to the far side of the hangar and parked. The truck uncoupled and disappeared and the flight crew apparently remained inside the aircraft. After a few minutes in which nothing else happened, Gillon lost interest.

The TU-144 had completed loading by now, had left the terminal and was now waiting at the far end of the runway. A green light winked in the distant control tower and snow boiled off the runway behind the tail as the roar of the engines, running up for takeoff, reached him. The aircraft rolled ahead, gathered speed down the runway, lifted smoothly and disappeared into the morning sky in a northwesterly direction. The slow rumble of the aircraft's engines faded. The snowplow had finished its task and disappeared. Nothing else moved on the field. The winter stillness of bright sun and burnished cold closed down.

Gillon turned away from the window to survey the drab, bare room with distaste. A steel-frame bed covered with a thin blanket and thinner mattress stood against one wall. Other than the bed, there was not another stick of furniture in the room. It was, though, he noted with some gratitude, beginning to warm up as the fire in the stove on the floor below gained ground on the entire winter's cold.

He walked to the door and knocked loudly, then listened, hearing nothing but the noise of the guard shifting in his chair at the far end of the hall. He knocked again. First a groan, then footsteps started down the hall, pausing at each door. Gillon knocked again and the footsteps hurried to his door and stopped outside. The padlock clicked, then a rifle's safety catch. The door was pulled, stuck, and pulled again, harder. It swung open and the guard stood framed outside, carbine pointing into the room.

Gillon smiled at him in what he hoped was a friendly fashion.

'How about something to read?' he asked, not really expecting the guard to understand and pantomiming the flipping of magazine pages. It took a moment or two but finally he made the soldier understand and as a final touch, pantomimed smoking a cigarette. The soldier understood that right away and he pushed the door shut and hurried off down the hall.

Now, how about that, Gillon thought to himself, and

pushed the door wide open. The little devil forgot to lock it. A careless guard . . . not likely. These people did not impress him as being careless, or forgetful. Perhaps they wanted him to try and walk away from the room? Then they could shoot him and claim that he tried to escape. Again not likely; otherwise why go to all the trouble to lock them up in the first place; why not just march them outside and shoot them down?

Gillon scratched his head, pushed the door shut and wandered back to the window to stand thinking until the guard returned and pushed the door open. He stepped into the room, a wide grin on his face and arms full of magazines. On top of the pile rested two packs of cigarettes. Gillon grinned back and relieved him of the load, noting that his rifle was carelessly slung over his shoulder, where it would be out of the way . . . and out of reach as well.

'*Spasebo.*' Gillon grinned back and the guard touched his cap and pushed the door closed. Gillon carried the magazines over and dumped them on the bed . . . and swore loudly. All of them were printed in bright colors on relatively good quality paper, and of recent vintage. But they were all in Russian. Ah well, he decided, lit a cigarette and slumped down on the bed, bunching his parka behind his head for a pillow, and picked up the top magazine. There was nothing else to do and long hours ahead to kill and since no explanation of the quirky things that were happening was forthcoming . . . at least the magazines were full of pictures.

The day ground on to its conclusion in a burst of color over the western edge of the airfield. The weather had faded during the long afternoon from its wintry beauty of sunshine, blue shadow and ice as a heavy cloud cover edged across the sky. The change in weather brought a drastic drop in temperature and, by evening, the single window overlooking the runway was completely frosted over. Gillon used his knife to scrape away the frost and stared out into the darkness. Feeble lights marked the limits of the airfield; red along the runways and blue for the apron and taxiways. Thin splashes of color circled the snow beneath each light, but as there were no halos visible in the air Gillon knew that the temperature was well below freezing and the air intensely dry.

Behind him on the bed, the remains of an excellent hot meal shared space with the unreadable magazines.

As he gazed through the frost-rimmed patch of cleared window, a snowflake drifted by. A moment later another and another until the sky was full of soft, gliding flakes fluttering down in the still air. At least the snow, he knew, would keep the temperature from dropping much below zero – not that it would be of much concern to him in his present predicament. Whatever game the Russians were playing, they were not about to let them into China. He had concluded that the Russians, in spite of the potential importance of the documents, had contracted a case of diplomatic cold feet. A clerical error, or whatever, could easily become a face-saving device. Rather than admit that they were afraid of the Chinese, the Kremlin could easily justify their withdrawal from the mission by claiming an administrative error had delayed the start of the mission until it was too late. Then they could apologize and send the Americans packing.

He heard footsteps below and the sound of someone kicking his heels against the risers of the steps to dislodge caked snow. A moment later, footsteps came up the stairs and marched down the hall. Doors were unlocked and a voice called in bad English for them to come out.

His own door was thrown open and a heavyset non-commisioned officer glanced at him with indifference and motioned him out.

Gillon picked up his parka and stepped through the door to find Stowe, Jones and Leycock and three armed soldiers gathered in a little knot in the middle of the hall waiting for him.

'We were just comparing notes,' Leycock said as he joined them. 'Apparently we've all come to the conclusion that the Russians have gotten scared and are stalling until it's too late. Then they'll send us to Moscow and see us out of the country. What do you say?'

Gillon, somewhat surprised that all four of them had reached the same conclusion independently, nodded in agreement.

'I don't know if anybody else could see the Jetstar,' he added, 'but they towed it around to the back of a hangar and left it there. That's all, just left it there. As far as I know, the crew is still inside.'

'I saw that too,' Jones murmured. 'This whole setup really stinks . . . the guards are just too damned careless . . .'

The non-com came up at that point and shooed them toward the stairs. They went down the steps, along the hall and out into the cold night; a cold so sudden in its intensity that it caught them all by surprise, whisked their breath away and left them coughing.

'You know . . .' Stowe managed to choke out finally. 'Somehow or other . . . I'm damned glad they . . . fouled up.' He caught his breath and pulled the sleeve of his jacket across his mouth and chin. 'Can you imagine spending twenty-four hours a day for two or three days out in this stuff?'

'Just hope to God,' Jones said, 'that they don't intend to send us to a labor camp. Otherwise, you'll see a hell of a lot more of this kind of weather.' The grimness in his voice drove away the touch of euphoria that had begun to affect them all.

They were lined up in single file, two soldiers to a man, and trotted through the falling snow under a blaze of arc lights to the same administration building in which they had been questioned that morning, each expecting to be told that everything had been straightened out but that it was too late and therefore the mission had been canceled. Gillon found himself hoping that he was wrong, a reversal of his previous attitude, he realized with surprise. But he suddenly understood that if the Russians were going to renege, then Jack Liu would be left holding the bag. And if that happened, there was nothing, absolutely nothing that Gillon could do for him. The interior of China was a hell of a long way in space and time and condition from the Laotian border area.

They were brought to a halt outside the door and while the non-com slipped inside and slammed the door shut, they all, guards included, stamped their feet and huddled against the icy wind. The non-com came back out a moment later and motioned them inside. Gillon gasped in the sudden change of temperature and the combination of heat and bright overhead fluorescent tubes filled his eyes with tears, blinding him for a moment. He rubbed his fingers across his eyes to rid them of the tears and finally could make out a group of men standing in front of him. From their bearing and uniforms, they were officers, and Gillon realized with a shock that two of the men were Orientals, wearing the khaki uniforms and green collar tabs of the Army of the People's Republic of China.

THE TIEN SHAN

CHAPTER SEVEN

Four officers, two of them Russian, two of them Chinese, faced the four Americans. The Soviet officer, a colonel, whom they had met earlier waved his hand to indicate that they were to line up against the wall. Collectively stunned by the unexpected turn of events, they shuffled into position and only then did Gillon hear Stowe begin to curse non-stop under his breath as the shock of the Chinese uniforms began to wear off. Afterward, Gillon could not recall when he had ever been as surprised, surprised to the point of being unable even to formulate words of protest. Both sides stared at one another for a long moment and the silence in the overheated room was devastating.

'What the hell . . . ?' Jones began.

'Be silent,' the Russian officer snapped, and that broke the moment of time in which they had all been suspended. The colonel bent over to converse with one of the Chinese officers, then straightened at his nod. The two Chinese officers continued to stare impassively at the Americans. In spite of their controlled features Gillon could sense that they were angry, intensely angry, but at the same time also pleased, as if they had been vindicated. The colonel murmured once more and the Chinese nodded carefully.

'We have checked your story, as you suggested,' the colonel began, and nodded toward Gillon. 'As we suspected, it is a lie from beginning to end. There is no officer named Andre Dmietriev at this base or anywhere within the Soviet armed forces and your tale of orders to report to this fictitious gentleman at this installation is worse than foolish. I can only surmise that you were planning some type of intrusion into the People's Republic of China when your aircraft was forced down here.'

He paused and looked at them carefully, as if to gauge the effect of his words. Stowe was now standing rigidly against the wall, staring at him. Leycock had lounged back and was gazing around the room as if bored. Only Jones appeared to be angry, a slow, red flush suffusing his face, but he held himself in check.

The colonel drew himself up straight and clasped his hands behind his back.

'You are accused by the People's Republic of China of attempting to gain illegal entrance into China to rendezvous with bandits and then to carry out sabotage, murder and espionage. Your attempt to involve this nation in your scheme is reprehensible, to say the least.'

A feeling of complete unreality swept over Gillon. Something had gone wrong, terribly wrong. The colonel sounded to Gillon as if he were reading a prepared script. Gillon shook his head and the Russian caught the slight movement.

'Ah, you seek to deny it, do you? Well, this information and my instructions come to me from the highest levels in Moscow.'

He paused to lend weighted emphasis to his words. 'You will be placed into the custody of General Lin Chuo' – he nodded to his left – 'and flown to Peking, where you will be put on trial for crimes against the People's Republic of China.'

When he finished, the four Americans stared at him in stunned silence. Even Leycock had lost his air of boredom and his mouth was open in total surprise. Jones started forward, only to be shoved back by a guard. He shook himself free, shouting, 'You can't do that. We have not violated Chinese territory. We are still in the Soviet Union and therefore the Chinese Government has no legal jurisdiction.'

'Ah, but there you are wrong, my dear sir,' the Chinese general broke in, his English soft and accentless. 'In China, it is held that the thought is partner to the deed. You have contemplated a crime, planned it carefully and attempted to carry it out. Therefore, legally, you have committed that violation, even though you were prevented from doing so. To have allowed you to commit the crime would have been foolish in the extreme.'

Jones spat out a curse. 'That, sir, is in China, This is the Soviet Union . . .'

74

'It will do you no good to argue,' the other Soviet officer, who had so far remained silent, interrupted. 'The decision has already been made. You will be flown tonight to Peking and there stand trial for your crimes.'

Gillon looked at the officer who had just spoken. Tall, broad and bullnecked. He wore the uniform of the Soviet Army but his lapel was adorned with the insignia of the GRU, the Chief Intelligence Directorate of the Soviet General Staff. So, they really had checked as Gillon had facetiously suggested. A shock of graying blond hair surmounted a seamed and weathered face. This man spent a good deal of time outdoors, he thought.

General Lin laughed at Jones. 'We have conclusive evidence that you were to meet a group of Nationalist Chinese gangsters and together engage in sabotage to the nuclear testing installations at Lop Nor. Understandably enough, in this time of strained relations, the Soviet Union resents your attempts to involve them, to use their national territory as your starting point. And, I might add, the Soviet Government has been very cooperative.'

If that was the story the Chinese had been told, Gillon thought, it helped bring into perspective everything that had happened so far. The Red Chinese could very well have learned the broad details of the mission in Taiwan . . . they probably had as many spies in the Nationalist government as the Nationalists had in the Communist government. They would have known that the Americans had been asked to help. From Phan Duc Phnom, they would have learned that the Russians were involved before he died. A little pressure applied to the Kremlin could easily have forced them to reconsider their commitment to assist the Americans. Now that the Vietnam War was over, the U.S. was relatively free of foreign encumbrances while the Russians were heavily committed in the Middle East and more and more so in Northeast Africa. The wisdom of engaging in a border clash with China, that and the effect on Sino-American rapprochement that the capture of the Americans would have, must certainly have seemed attractive. And so they were being tossed to the lions. From the sick look on Jones's face, Gillon knew that he had reached the same conclusion. So much for their optimistic conclusion less than ten minutes ago that the Soviets were sending them to Moscow. They were going on a trip all right, but in the opposite direction . . . to Peking. Stowe had remained impassive following his initial outburst and Leycock was now staring at the floor, as if disinterested in the proceedings.

'Just how did . . . ?' Gillon started to ask, but the GRU officer cut him off sharply and snapped an order in Russian. Before he could demand that his question be answered, they were pushed into position by soldiers and forced out into the freezing night. They were marched at a trot to an aircraft waiting on the apron, where its brightly lit interior spilled out in yellow patches onto the snow- and ice-covered concrete.

As they reached the foot of the ladder, Stowe unexpectedly sidestepped away from his guard and before the soldier could react, had lashed out, hitting him in the face. Instantly, Stowe was smothered by soldiers. One swung his carbine, hitting him a glancing blow across the shoulders that nevertheless was sufficient to stun him. Stowe went down without a sound. Gillon started forward but a bayoneted rifle thrust toward his stomach brought him up short. The GRU officer materialized at his side and Gillon roared at him.

'Tell this bastard to back off or I'll take that rifle away from him and shove it down his throat!'

The intelligence officer threw a surprise glance at him and, grinning, ordered the guard to back off before pointing to the guards lifting Stowe off the snow.

'If you do not wish to receive similar treatment, then you will all behave yourselves.' Jones cursed him roundly but he turned away, still smiling.

The area surrounding the aircraft had been lit by a series of portable floodlights and, though the light was dimmed by the heavy snowfall, Gillon saw that the aircraft was an old Russian turboprop transport with Chinese markings. Two Chinese guards waited at the head of the steps and two more below. The Russian guards had backed away, leaving Gillon, Leycock and Jones standing at the foot of the ladder with the two Russian officers and the Chinese General Lin. Gillon surmised that the second Chinese officer, who had remained inside, was to go on to Moscow. A moment later four Russian soldiers pushed past, loaded down with the duffle bags and packs, and disappeared up the ladder and into the aircraft.

General Lin lit a cigarette and standing to one side watched the three Americans with an air of expectancy. The soldiers trotted back down the gangway, and Stowe was carried up and into the cabin.

Gillon, watching them haul Stowe's unconscious form up the steps, had turned to say something to Jones when his guard jolted him with the rifle. Gillon started to swing round on him but the two Chinese guards at the bottom of the steps pushed him away. The Russian jabbed him again with the rifle butt, eyes glistening with anticipation. Gillon forced himself to swallow his rage and followed Jones up the stairway, his anger barely contained. They ducked and stepped into the brightly lit interior, blinking against the lights. Stowe had been shoved down into a seat at the back of the cabin. As they walked past, he groaned and pushed himself carefully into a sitting position, rubbing the back of his neck. Jones, Leycock and Gillon were led up the aisle and motioned into seats well away from one another. The Chinese guards followed them down the aisle, stopping at each seat to handcuff each by one wrist to a steel bar let into the bulkhead beside the seat.

Two of the Chinese soldiers took up positions at the front of the cabin, their backs against the bulkhead separating the cabin from the cockpit. A moment later, a Russian sergeant pushed down the aisle, bringing with him a curious assortment of odors, alcohol, heavy, biting Balkan tobacco and the freshness of cold air and snow, as well as a large duffle bag, which he slung into a seat across from Gillon. He paused to stare down at Gillon for a moment, his face expressionless, then turned back and slid into the seat directly in front of him. Gillon noticed that the sergeant was wearing the same GRU insignia and, puzzled, Gillon glanced over his shoulder in time to see General Lin come aboard, followed by the Soviet GRU officer. Both were laughing at some joke and they settled themselves companionably into seats in the back of the aircraft. One more Chinese soldier hurried aboard, trotted up the aisle and disappeared into the cockpit. Almost immediately, the starboard engine began to turn, its high-pitched turbine whine rising until the engine exploded into a cloud of smoke that was whipped to tatters as the propeller bit into the cold air.

Very curious, Gillon thought. Two Soviet military intelligence operatives aboard the same aircraft taking them into China, Perhaps they had been sent along as witnesses, although that hardly seemed necessary. Very curious indeed. Again that same sense of bewilderment swept over him. Very little of what was happening made sense. There was something missing, something definitely missing, but he could not put his finger on it. The information that Jack Liu was holding for them was important, in fact downright more important to the Soviets than to the Americans. As the State Department clown had pointed out, the United States was taking a big chance with this mission whereas the Soviets, with a three-thousand-mile contiguous border and their already strained relations with China, were not. And surely the situation, the data at stake, were not important enough to risk threatening the Soviet Union with war. Since the Communist take-over in 1949, the Chinese had always been militarily conservative, fighting beyond their borders only when forced into it. They did not enter the Korean War until American troops were standing on the Yalu River border; did not attack India until the Indians had repeatedly sent troops into China; never did send combat troops to Vietnam. And their previous set-tos with the Soviets had been limited to a lot of name-calling and border skirmishes only in areas historically belonging to China. It just did not make sense and . . . if the Soviets had gotten cold feet, why turn them over to the Chinese? Why not just send them packing and be done with it? Then if the Chinese protested, they could say with a clear conscience and nothing to hide that they had in fact been approached by the United States for help, but had turned them down. That would avoid any possible conflict with China as well as set back the Sino-American rapprochement . . . a situation patently dangerous to Russia if allowed to progress very far.

The way he saw it, turning them over to the Chinese was tantamount to admitting involvement, no matter what was said officially. Gillon shook his head, nothing seemed to make sense, yet he knew that none of the three governments involved ever took a step without a plan. The plan itself might often be utterly foolish, but every action had a logic of its own. Both engines were running to power now and Gillon felt the plane move forward, edging slowly away from the hangar area. When they reached the end of the taxiway and began turning slowly into position, Gillon spotted another aircraft ahead of them just gathering speed down the runway. Gillon watched it reach flight speed and leave the runway. For a moment, the aircraft was silhouetted against the white snowfield and he was positive that it was the Jetstar. The aircraft banked sharply around to the north and disappeared from his field of view.

North, he thought. If they were going north it probably meant Moscow. At least the Russians were not giving up the Jetstar to the Chinese. Gillon hoped that the flight crew was still aboard and that they would prove resourceful enough to find a way of notifying Washington of what had happened. Since they had been warned that the State Department would not intercede if they were caught, their chances of getting out of this situation were not good. Gillon shifted uncomfortably in the seat. The sharp metal ring of the handcuff bit painfully into his wrist. There would be a trial in Peking, he knew, one in which trumped-up evidence would play a big part. And if the Chinese were really going to use them as evidence that the United States was hypocritical in its dealings, the trial would receive wide international publicity and the sentences would be severe. Probably not death, but at least twenty years in prison. Somehow, death might be preferable.

The transport had turned onto the runway; the engines ran up and, as the brakes were released, it leaped forward, rushing down the icy runway. Gillon felt the tail section begin to sway back and forth but a moment later, the wheels broke free and they were airborne. The runway dropped beneath and Gillon's field of vision expanded, then steadied as the ground fell away, encompassing first the apron, then the hangar area and finally the entire airfield before it disappeared astern. Then there was nothing but the wide, empty steppe with here and there an occasional light to mark a lonely building and to the east, the pale towers of the Tien Shan.

The flight into China was silent. For a long time, the transport had circled, climbing for altitude to clear the twenty-thousand-foot peaks of the Tien Shan. Gradually, the distant features of the steppe had faded below, leaving nothing but a faint glimmer of starlight on snow. The flanks of the Tien Shan had merged into black silhouettes of grinding teeth, blocking the stars with their bulk.

The murmur of conversation from the back of the cabin, where the two officers sat together, had died away following takeoff. Gillon sat back in the worn seat and tried to relax. He had calculated that with the probable range of the aircraft they would make two refueling stops; the first at Urumchi in Sinkiang, the second somewhere in Kansu and then the final landing at Peking. Six thousand miles almost and at an average speed of 300 miles an hour, they would reach the capital in twenty to twenty-four hours.

Gillon looked around the cabin again but the high seat backs obscured his view and the handcuff kept him in place. From the sound of his deep breathing, Jones was asleep, and Leycock and Stowe were both out of his line of vision and hearing. The two Chinese soldiers remained stolidly near the front bulkhead, swaying gently with the easy motion of the aircraft, and Gillon wondered if they were going to remain there during the entire flight. The Russian sergeant was slumped well down in the seat, his feet propped on the armrest of the seat across the aisle, asleep to all appearances.

An hour after takeoff, Gillon heard laughter from the back and the rustle of what sounded like a map being unfolded. A few minutes later he looked around to see General Lin standing in the aisle beside his seat, facing Jones.

'We are now in the People's Republic of China,' he said, smiling down in a friendly fashion at Jones.

'Shove it,' Jones murmured.

'Come now, that is no way to talk. We all play a game. Unfortunately, you have selected the losing side.'

'No,' Jones said mildly, 'not the losing side . . . just a real loser for a teammate.'

'How is that?' Lin inquired politely.

'The Russians,' Jones snarled. 'It's too bad that during the kangaroo trial coming up we won't be allowed to tell the full story.'

Lin bent over to beam at him. 'That really will not be necessary, really not necessary at all.' Gillon had to strain to hear this murmured response.

'However, no matter how well-intentioned your motives, it will do you no good. Your government has trifled with mine long enough. Many of us have warned that the perfidious American warmongers were only disguising themselves . . .'

Lin continued in this vein and Gillon grimaced. One of the hawks, he thought. There was no hope for them at all if these people were in, or near to being in, control . . . no matter how much he was forced to admit that there might now be some justification to Lin's charge.

'Shove it,' Jones repeated, and Lin chuckled, then suddenly cuffed him on the ear.

'You bloody . . .' Jones half rose from his seat. Gillon saw it coming but there was nothing he could do to prevent it. Lin drew his pistol, reversed it in his hand and used the butt to hit Jones viciously across the temple. Jones groaned once and slumped back, blood welling out of a deep cut above his temple. Gillon found himself on his feet, swearing violently, his right arm caught against the bulkhead by the handcuff. Lin smiled thinly and turned, raising the pistol to strike again. A shot blasted through the cabin and Lin jolted forward, caught his balance and turned to the rear of the cabin. Gillon saw his look of utter astonishment as he faced the Soviet GRU colonel, now standing in the aisle. The colonel took slow aim and fired the pistol once more, striking Lin squarely in the chest. Lin's own pistol dropped from his nerveless fingers and he crumpled forward.

Behind Gillon, the sergeant was moving like a dancer, twisting out of his seat and drawing his own revolver at the same time. The colonel fired once more, shifted his aim, slightly, pistol hand lying across his left forearm. Gillon stared for an eternity down the muzzle before it fired for the third time . . . past his shoulder and struck the Chinese soldier on the left side of the cabin. At the same time the sergeant shot twice, dropping the soldier standing to the right of the door. The cockpit door was thrust open and a rifle poked out. The sergeant jumped to the left and fired twice inside as the colonel raced up the aisle. The cockpit guard crumpled to his knees and the sergeant fired once more, into the back of the neck, and he slumped face forward onto the floor in a welter of blood. The Russian officer hurdled the body and slammed into the cockpit. Three shots were fired in quick succession and the aircraft banked abruptly to the left and fell off the port wing, throwing Gillon forward and wrenching the skin from his wrist, where the handcuff dragged at the flesh. The transport tipped into the slow twist that preceded a spin, then, just as abruptly as it had begun, righted itself and, a moment later, the engines were running up to full rated power, dragging the nose up, and she began to come level once more.

Gillon untangled himself from the seat and got shakily to his feet. The three Chinese soldiers were dead. One body had rolled across the cabin in the violence of the spin and lay on its back, sightless eyes staring at the ceiling. Lin was on his back, astonishment still evident in his staring eyes, a thin trickle of blood running idly down his cheek.

The sergeant had been thrown hard to the deck by the sudden movement of the aircraft. He got to his feet, shaking his head, swayed in the aisle a moment and grabbed a seat back to steady himself. Then he walked carefully to Lin, stooped down and went through his pockets until he found the key to the handcuffs. Without a word, he reached back and handed the key to Gillon, then bent over Jones's unconscious figure.

Gillon found the key that fit his cuffs, unlocked them,

82

and tossed the set to Leycock, who released both his and Stowe's. Leycock tensed and Gillon heard the hiss of his indrawn breath. He turned to see the GRU colonel standing in the cockpit doorway, pistol still in his hand but grinning from ear to ear. The colonel laughed and snapped the magazine out to show that it was empty. As if nothing had happened, he slipped a fresh magazine into the pistol, snapped the slide back to load a cartridge into the chamber, put the safety on and shoved it back into his holster. Still wary, Leycock came up the aisle and knelt down beside Jones. The sergeant backed out of the way while Leycock undid the handcuffs and examined his bleeding head.

The sergeant walked down the aisle to the colonel and spoke to him in Russian, gesturing at Jones. Gillon caught a trace of concern on his face and hastily leaned over the seat. Stowe came up and together the three of them got Jones lifted out of the seat and onto the carpeted floor.

His breathing was shallow, his skin almost gray and covered with a thin film of sweat. Leycock rubbed his wrists and chest and Stowe hurried back down the aisle to where the packs were piled in one of the rear seats and came back with a first-aid kit. He found an ammonia ampul, broke it and waved it under Jones's nose. Jones coughed and feebly pushed the ampul away. Leycock pressed him back to the floor and his color and breathing began to return to normal. After a minute or so, Leycock held up three fingers.

'How many?'

'Seven, dammit, let me up . . .'

'Okay, but take it easy . . .'

Leycock helped him into the seat and stepped back while Stowe went to work with swab and antiseptic to clean the gash that the pistol butt had left above his temple.

'Ye gods, take it easy,' Jones whispered between clenched teeth.

Stowe grunted and finished up, dabbed an antibiotic ointment on a sterile pad and taped it in place. Then he shook two tablets out of a bottle and offered them to

Jones. Leycock handed him a canteen and they both insisted that he swallow the tablets.

'They're just aspirin. And you are going to have one hell of a headache in a few moments.'

Jones nodded and swallowed the tablets, then leaned his head back against the seat. Stowe adjusted it until it was almost horizontal.

'All right, Colonel, fun and game times are over,' Gillon said tightly, turning to the two Russians talking together at the front of the cabin. 'What the hell is this all about?'

The colonel smiled easily and came down the aisle to them. 'I would not really blame you if you were angry. It is a very dirty trick to play. But we had no other choice. My name is Andre Dmietriev and this is my friend and associate Sergeant Anton Rodek. We are the two other members of this apparently ill-fated venture.'

Gillon was surprised by the announcement. But then, he thought, nothing had made sense so far. Why should it start now?

Stowe moved up the aisle as if to back him up and Leycock got slowly to his feet, his hands relaxed at his sides. Gillon glanced at Stowe, noting that his face, although still pale with the after-effects of his beating, was set into hard lines of anger.

'Ill-fated is the word, Colonel. Perhaps you will explain what all this nonsense is about and who these people are . . . were,' he corrected himself.

'Certainly, but first . . .' He said something to Rodek in Russian, Rodek nodded and stepped into the cockpit. Dmietriev waited a moment, a look of concentration on his face, and Gillon felt the roar of the engines deepen and the deck under his feet tilted upward slightly.

'Sergeant Rodek is an excellent pilot. He feels that perhaps a bit more altitude is necessary. In view of the height of these mountains,' he finished, half-apologetically.

Gillon had almost forgotten that they were well into the Tien Shan by now and he stooped to peer through the window.

'No,' Dmietriev smiled, 'I am afraid it is too dark to see anything. The moon will not rise for several hours

84

yet. Now come,' he invited, 'let's be seated and I will tell you what has happened.' He gestured to the seats and, rubbing his aching wrist, Gillon sat down on the armrest. Stowe took the seat across the aisle from Jones while Leycock remained standing.

'I am afraid this deception, hard on you as it was, was completely necessary. As you probably know, one of your operatives was murdered in Rome.'

Behind him, Gillon heard the sudden intake of breath as Jones reacted to this news. Gillon felt the same way. How the hell had the Russians found out so quickly?

Dmietriev laughed at their response. 'But you forget, we are supposed to be partners in this operation. We knew of course as soon as your people did that your operative had been killed . . . knew from two sources, I might add. Your people and our own channels of communication.'

Dmietriev paused and looked at them. Gillon could feel the hostility that was being directed toward the Russian by the other three. It seemed foolish to him, but then he thought, perhaps if he was as involved in intelligence work as they were, he might feel the same way. It all seemed like pure nonsense to him, serving only to aggravate the differences between nations.

'So,' Dmietriev continued, 'we are now quite certain that he was killed by the Chinese. I say this because within hours of your man's death, the Ambassador of the People's Republic of China handed our Foreign Minister a note of diplomatic protest couched in the strongest terms. This mission is as important to us as it is to your country, perhaps more so since we share common borders with China. As far as my country is concerned, that data must be retrieved at all costs . . . and this was stressed to me by no less than the Minister of Defense himself. So we devised this little drama to convince the Chinese that we had nothing to do with you, that everything was the exclusive idea of the United States. I must say that there are certain elements in my government, as there are in the Chinese Government, that have reacted with strong approval to the idea of destroying whatever progress had been achieved to date in the American-Chinese talks.'

Dmietriev glanced at his watch as he continued. 'So you were put under arrest as soon as you landed at Ala Kul . . . I trust it did not prove onerous?'

He was met by a stony silence and chuckled. 'We knew that the Chinese would be arriving within hours of your aircraft . . . we could only hope that it would be after and not before. Both of your arrivals coincided so closely in fact that we did not have time to explain to you what was happening . . . which from my standpoint was just as well, as your reactions were certainly convincing.'

'You are saying then,' Stowe broke in, 'that this whole business was just a sham to convince the Chinese that the Russians had nothing to do with this mission . . . ? You really didn't expect them to believe that, did you?'

Dmietriev laughed. 'If you were a bit more familiar with the art of diplomacy, my friend, you would see that as having no bearing on the matter at all. Of course they did not believe us . . . but that is not what they were asking. The Chinese Government warned my government that there would be serious repercussions if we allowed the mission to take place. So we agreed that the mission would be halted by simply arresting you and your friends and turning you over to the Chinese Government.

'Now that we have done so, we are no longer responsible for what happens. You see, a Chinese officer stayed behind to report to Peking as well as to the Chinese Embassy in Moscow. He saw you put aboard this transport, saw his fellow officer and the three soldiers go aboard, but did not see either Sergeant Rodek or myself follow. After he boarded the aircraft in which you arrived, a message came for General Lin informing him that two Soviet military personnel would accompany him to Peking . . . Sergeant Rodek and myself . . . to assist in the trial. Of course the message was unimpeachable as it was in the latest Chinese military codes.'

Gillon raised his eyebrows at this news and Stowe, Jones and Leycock exchanged glances.

'Of course, the message was completely false,' Dmietriev continued modestly. 'So far as the Soviet Union is concerned we have complied with the Chinese request. If the escort should prove incapable of controlling their prisoners, that, of course, is their problem.

'So it will appear that you left Ala Kul earlier tonight after General Lin sent a wireless message informing Peking of the time of departure . . . and after being seen aboard by one of their own people. In addition, a second message was sent from this aircraft confirming that we had crossed the border. Our flight records will show that this aircraft left on schedule and radar logs on both sides will show that this same aircraft crossed the border still on schedule. In fact, the pilot was to report his position every half-hour. It has now been fifteen minutes since he last did so and we are wasting valuable time talking. This aircraft will crash in twenty minutes and we do not want to be aboard when it does so. It will appear,' he finished triumphantly, 'that once having overpowered your captors, you were unable to fly the aircraft and it crashed in a remote area of the Tien Shan. Very neat, hey?'

'Very neat is right,' Jones murmured. 'You say twenty minutes? Where will that put us?'

'Right in the middle of the scheduled drop zone. Unknown to them and fortunately for us, they were flying very close to the route we would have taken if we had not been discovered. It is the only sensible way to cross the Tien Shan to Urumchi, where normally an aircraft would refuel.'

'So we haven't really lost anything then,' Leycock put in, more a statement of fact than question.

'Nothing but time,' Jones answered. He glanced at his watch. 'We are now about four hours behind schedule. That means that we must camp on the north side of the pass and wait to cross tomorrow . . . tonight really. So we lose more than fifteen hours total.'

'You are right, but I am afraid that can not be helped. And, if we waste any more time, we will lose more than that.' Dmietriev stood up.

'I suggest, Mr. Jones,' he said formally, all trace of his bantering tone disappearing, 'that you have your people change into their cold-weather gear and check their equipment and weapons.'

Jones nodded and struggled up out of the seat. Leycock tried to make him sit still, but Jones insisted that he was all right. Gillon watched as he got to his feet, still protesting. Jones was moving carefully, holding his head erect, as if even the slightest movement hurt him. Great, he thought, they hadn't even started yet and already one of the group was injured, and injured worse than he was willing to admit. Gillon had a premonition, sitting on the armrest of the seat in the warm, well-lit cabin of the aircraft, that there were drastic days ahead for Jones as well as for the rest of them. Shaking his head, he followed Jones and Leycock to the rear of the cabin to sort out gear. Stowe busied himself with checking and loading weapons. Dmietriev disappeared into the cockpit and after a moment, Rodek came hurrying back through the cabin to his duffle bag. He placed it on a seat, opened it and began to pull out cold-weather clothes and weapons similar to their own. Two AK-47 machine guns were included and two large-caliber pistols that Gillon could not identify. Two long paper-wrapped parcels were produced from the galley, where they had been hidden behind an oven unit, containing skis and snowshoes for both Russians. The other bag contained hiking packs, sleeping bags and wax-paper-wrapped blocks of gelignite explosive. Whistling soundlessly, Rodek went to work and Gillon stopped for a moment to watch him. Rodek inserted an igniter into each block of explosive and lined them up on the seat one after another. When he had finished, six two-pound blocks of gelignite stood in a row, enough to blow the entire aircraft to kingdom come and then some.

CHAPTER EIGHT

While Rodek went about his own tasks, the four Americans completed a final distribution of supplies to the packs. Then each of them stripped down and struggled into the insulated underclothing and one-piece snowsuits. Gillon found that his suit fitted as if it had been tailored for him. Jones watched, grinning, and admitted that his uniform sizes had been obtained from the Army.

'We made allowances for any weight you might have gained since.'

Gillon snorted. 'I weigh less now than I did the day I resigned.' They finished just as Rodek completed dressing and pushed past and into the cockpit. A moment later, Dmietriev came hurrying out.

'Five minutes,' he snapped. 'You will find a cargo parachute in one of those bags. I suggest that you lash everything together and the first one out the door will have to be responsible for watching it go down.'

He threw off his own clothing and began to dress quickly. 'There are also six parachutes in the galley. I supervised their packing myself this afternoon; you can be quite certain they will open.'

This was one phase of the exercise that Gillon was not looking forward to at all. His entire jumping experience consisted of the U.S. Army airborne course at Fort Benning, nearly twelve years before, and he had not jumped since.

Leycock and Stowe fetched the chutes from the rear of the cabin and dumped them down on the floor. Stowe held one up, a standard backpack type which Gillon recognized as a sport parachute that provided a great deal more steerability than the standard military chute.

'Just a backpack . . . where are the safety chutes?'

'Sorry.' Dmietriev grinned. 'No way to get them aboard. You will just have to take your chances and rely on the Soviet Air Force.'

The news apparently did nothing to cheer Stowe, from the scowl he gave Dmietriev, but he slipped his chute on anyway and buckled it up.

Dmietriev unfolded a map and spread it out on his knees. He studied it for a moment, then called Jones over to him. As Jones got up from the seat and made his way back to the Russian Gillon couldn't be sure but he thought he noticed a slight stagger in his walk. The two of them bent over the map for several minutes, then, satisfied, Jones nodded, made some notes on his own map and came back up the aisle. Dmietriev folded his map and slipped it into his parka, then glancing at his watch once more, hurried back up the aisle, parachute dangling from his arm.

'All right, you guys,' Jones called out, 'let's get finished up. Three minutes to the jump zone.'

Rodek stepped out of the cockpit and gathered up his pack and parachute. An air of expectancy began to build as Jones chivied them forward to the crew hatch. Dmietriev was standing half in and half out of the cockpit door from where he could keep an eye on the control panel. The aircraft was flying so slowly that they were being buffeted from side to side by the winds. Dmietriev had stopped the air-conditioning system and the air was rapidly growing thin . . . and very cold. Stowe and Rodek dragged the body of one of the Chinese soldiers out of the way and Jones started to undo the hatch. Dmietriev glanced over his shoulder, caught Rodek's eye and nodded. Rodek knelt and fussed with the gelignite charges he had placed in seats on both sides of the fuselage in back of the wings. Dmietriev jammed a long crowbar through the rubber seal and worked it into the crack between the hatch and the coaming. He motioned to Gillon and together they heaved once, twice and on the third time, the hatch slammed open, punched through the two-hundred-mile-an-hour slipstream by the cabin's higher air pressure. Instantly, the cabin was full of whirling debris as the air rushed out and he grabbed a seat back to steady himself against its tug. The temperature plummeted abruptly and Gillon gasped in surprise at its icy clutch.

Leycock stumbled forward with the backpacks and duffle bags lashed into a single large bundle and placed them near the door. He opened the cargo chute pack and extracted the rip cord, which he tied to a seat stanchion. It was difficult to hear over the wail of air rushing past the aircraft and Leycock pointed to himself and then down, indicating to Jones that he would go first. Jones nodded in a distracted way and Gillon started to move toward him, then thought better of it. There was nothing that could be done now in any case. There was no turning back. Unless this aircraft crashed somewhere in the mountains or reappeared on the southern side of the Tien Shan, their carefully constructed diversion would be for nothing and Chinese fighter aircraft would reach them before they could get back across the border.

Through the open hatch, he could make out the dark silhouettes of the surrounding peaks reaching almost level with the aircraft. He glanced into the cockpit and located the altimeter; it read 18,000 feet, hardly higher than some of the peaks around them. Dmietriev stepped out of the cockpit, glancing at his watch again, and motioned them to gather around him.

'We are coming up on the jump zone.' He shouted to make himself heard above the scream of air past the open hatch.

'Jump when I give the signal and all go out as fast as possible. As each man lands, shine your flashlights so that the others can find you. Do you all understand?'

They nodded and he turned to Rodek, who had come up after finishing with the last of the charges. Rodek nodded and shouted in Russian.

'He says,' Dmietriev translated at the top of his voice, 'that the fuses are set to go off in ten minutes. That should give us plenty of time. The aircraft will be fifty miles southeast of us when it crashes.'

Gillon was conscious of his laboring lungs as they fought to draw in sufficient oxygen, as well as an icy feeling that had nothing to do with the cold wind blowing in through the open hatch. He felt giddy and nauseated. The sickly gleam of the lights in the foggy interior of the cabin emphasized the shadows on each face, accentuating the apprehension that each of them felt. The remaining minutes passed slowly and Gillon swallowed hard several times. He was aware that he was sweating heavily and he knew that his tightly clenched hands would be shaking badly if he had not shoved them hard into his parka. Each of the six men stared desperately at the open doorway, each conscious of his own fear, none daring to look at his companion, frightened even more of what he might see in the face of the man next to him than of what dangers lay in wait below.

Dmietriev hurried back into the cabin to check the fuses a final time. A moment later, he returned to the doorway and peered out into the night, then stepped back and tapped Leycock on the shoulder. Without hesitation, Leycock kicked the bundle of packs and duffle bags through the doorway and followed the instant the static line snapped free. Jones was right behind, then Rodek. Stowe made a perfect start, vaulting out to drop feet first. Gillon stepped to the door right behind him, placed both hands on either side of the frame, took a shallow breath of the icy fluid into his lungs and pulled himself out.

He had pulled harder with his right arm than with his left and had twisted so that he was looking back at the aircraft. He was aware of the fuselage sliding past as he began to drop, slowly at first, so that he seemed for an instant suspended next to the airplane looking back at Dmietriev, who had just stepped to the hatch. Then with breathtaking speed, it disappeared and with it his point of reference. Then began the silent flow of cold air past his body and the sensation of falling deserted him until the shock of the opening chute snapped him up like a broken puppet on a string. He glanced up to see the square canopy opening like a black and white flower above his head. Just past the edge of the chute he could see Dmietriev's chute beginning to billow.

Gillon, remembering his first, painful lessons at Fort Benning, caught the harness lines and pulled hard to the left to steady his descent. Quickly, the pendulum motion canceled and the chute came under control. He could see the drifting canopies of the others strung out in a curving line, as if they were all sliding down an invisible cable. The terrain below was all but invisible; the snow-covered mountains were little more than pale blurs in the starlight and only the faint images of jagged peaks could be discerned around him. Above, the Milky Way wheeled across the sky, presenting itself for inspection in a way that only the parachutist ever sees. The crisp, thin, cold air of the high altitude carved each star from crystal and fixed it to the deepest black velvet.

He looked for Dmietriev again and finally spotted him, some thousand feet behind and several hundred feet above, his chute fully opened and the black dot that was the Russian intelligence operative dangling below. Searching back along the way for the aircraft, he found that he could not even find the running lights.

As Gillon turned his attention back to the ground, a bright flash of light caught his eye, imprinting itself upon his retina. He jerked toward the light to see it flash toward the peaks and for an instant he thought it might be a meteorite. Puzzled, and suddenly apprehensive, he swung wide, using the harness straps to turn the chute, but whatever it was, it was gone.

As he forced his attention back to the imminent landing, he knew that the flash could only have been the aircraft exploding prematurely. It had not lasted long enough to be a flare and too long to be a meteorite. And if it was the aircraft, then the wreckage would fall into the relatively accessible area well below the Dzungarian Gate, some twenty miles southwest. It surely would have reappeared on the Chinese radar screen in the interval before it exploded and its sudden disappearance would mean that search parties would be airlifted into the area immediately. That brought the chilling realization that the search parties could be at the wreckage within hours of dawn.

Ruthlessly, he thrust those fears down for another time. If he did not concentrate on his landing, it might not make any difference to him whether the Chinese found the wreckage or not.

Their landing area, just west of the bend in the Agiass River, was relatively flat, although high, and formed a wide, but short plateau south of Musart Pass, through which they would reach the interior of the range. There was, he knew, an ancient lamasery less than two miles from their landing site on the northern edge of the plateau that supposedly had been abandoned for nearly one hundred years. They were to wait there for moonrise.

A blur of white rushed to meet him and he had only enough time to will himself into relaxation before the amazingly hard surface of compacted snow slapped him. He collapsed on impact and rolled onto his side in the classic landing position that he had been taught so many years before, surprised that he still retained the proper reflexes. He sprawled face downward and the wind snatched at the chute and dragged him several yards before he managed to turn over onto his back and release the harness. The chute billowed for a moment in the wind, then, shorn of its balancing weight, collapsed.

Gillon got to his feet, gasping deep breaths in the relatively thick air of the nine-thousand-foot plateau. The air was like liquid nitrogen in its intensity, almost as cold here as it had been at 18,000 feet. After a moment, he caught sight of a tiny point of light several hundred yards north of his position. He stripped off the chute harness and gathered up the canopy, wrapping it into a bundle with the shrouds, and started toward the point of light, his own flashlight glowing. Dmietriev had landed not more than two hundred feet away and Gillon detoured to help him with the chute. In less than ten minutes, the six of them had assembled around the pile of packs and duffle bags that Leycock had dragged into the shelter of a rock outcropping.

'The aircraft exploded before it should have,' Dmietriev said without preamble, speaking in short choppy sentences that betrayed his anger. 'Both Sergeant Rodek and I checked the explosives very carefully. One of the fuses must have been defective. However, that does not alter the fact that the Chinese will be able to find the wreckage now sooner than we had anticipated. I would guess that they will have reached the crash site by midmorning. By midafternoon, it is possible that they will have discovered that the bodies of four Caucasians are missing. By nightfall they will be scouring these mountains for evidence that you parachuted to safety.'

Jones was half sitting, half kneeling on the pile of equipment, and, as he looked up at them and in the meager light from the torches, Gillon was shocked to see how worn and exhausted he appeared to be. Leycock saw it too and knelt down beside Jones.

'How do you feel . . . ?'

Jones waved a hand in irritation. 'I feel perfectly all right. Stop fussing over me.' He looked down at the snow for a moment before speaking again. 'You can bet that when they do come, they won't confine their search

94

just to the air. They'll have ground parties out and in force.'

'Damn those fuses!' Stowe muttered. 'All right, Mr. Agency man, you are the fearless leader. Where do we go from here?'

Jones bit back an angry retort and Gillon turned to stare at Stowe. It was a good thing that he wasn't running the show, he thought, otherwise Stowe would be off to a very bad start . . . with a set of loose teeth.

Jones had apparently decided to ignore the comment, because he looked around in the darkness as if considering. 'We can't go stumbling around trying to climb the pass until moonrise. And we can't stay here without shelter.' As he spoke, the wind stiffened momentarily, as if to remind them of its presence.

'I think that we had better stick to the original plan and head up to the lamasery for a few hours. We could all use the time to adapt to the altitude anyway.'

Stowe started to say something and Leycock, as if guessing that it would be a smart crack, dug an elbow into Stowe's ribs to silence him. Stowe grunted in anger, but remained silent.

Jones waited for objections and, when there was none, heaved himself to his feet and picked up his pack. 'All right, open the duffle bags and pick out your weapons, then bury the chutes and bags.' The six men looked at one another, realizing the hopelessness of their position before they even began, but knowing that there was nothing else to be done.

'Well,' Jones snapped. 'What the hell are you waiting for? Get busy.'

Rodek cut the lashings and dragged the duffle bags out and zipped them open. Silently, he handed out the rifles, keeping the two AK-47s for Dmietriev and himself. Leycock scooped a hole in the glazed snow, broke through the thick ice crust with his knife and in a few moments had dug a pit in which to cram the parachutes and empty bags.

Gillon glanced at his watch, noting that it was still set on Rome time. He mentioned it to Jones, who immediately ordered them all to reset at 2130, local time. They had at least four hours to moonrise and the remaining five to six hours of darkness should be enough to see them over the pass, he calculated. Staring about him at the ghostly pale peaks and the frozen landscape of the plateau, he agreed with Jones; this was no time to go stumbling about in the dark, risking turned or broken ankles.

The surface of the snow had been packed hard enough by the incessant wind that snowshoes were not needed. Since the route lay upslope, they strapped the carrying cases for the skis down the side of the packs and, with each other's aid, lashed the snowshoes on the back. Then, roped together to prevent straying only, since the slope was neither rugged nor steep, they started out, Jones in the lead, Gillon following, then Rodek, Stowe, Dmietriev and Leycock.

Jones had set an easy pace because of the altitude and the fact that there was no need to hurry . . . as yet. Their landing zone was approximately two miles below and to the north of the lamasery, and within forty minutes its forbidding black bulk was in view, silhouetted against the star field. Jones brought the party to a halt in the shelter of a jumble of boulders and untied the safety line from his waist. With a warning to Gillon to remain where they were, he trotted away to the right and disappeared into the darkness. Again, Gillon found himself impressed with the precautions that Jones was willing to take. There was less than one chance in ten thousand that the Chinese could be waiting in ambush for them, but apparently, those odds were too much for Jones. In view of everything that had gone wrong so far, Gillon felt they were much too high for him as well.

The wind was unbelievably cold, blowing nearly thirty miles an hour up the pass and added to the 0°F temperature, the wind chill gave an equivalent temperature of forty below zero. Gillon was beginning to think that his feet had frozen to the snow in spite of the heavily insulated boots and clothing when Jones reappeared.

'All right,' he called, 'let's go in.'

They went up the slope quickly, all of them anxious to get out of the fierce wind. Gillon had forgotten how cold, cold could be. Two years in Africa and four years before that in Indochina were not the best way to train for mountain conditions, and he wondered if there was any truth to the old legend that your blood thins in warm climates.

As they came up under a great stone arch that had once surmounted the main gate, Dmietriev shone his torch along what remained of the old wall. The hewn rock glistened with its coating of frost. Gillon went closer to examine the construction with his flashlight and found that no mortar had been used, that the huge blocks of stone had been carved to fit one exactly onto the other. Frost had crumbled away the edges where the blocks met, but each had been fitted so closely that it would have been impossible to insert the thinnest knife blade between any two stones. Mortar would have been valueness, he realized. With the constant expansion and contraction of the rock caused by summer heat and winter cold, it would have crumbled away in a few years.

Inside the walls, the squat shape of the lamesery itself loomed several hundred feet beyond the entrance. It was hard to discern details in the starlight, but it appeared that the roof had collapsed on one side of the building. The compound itself was empty and flat, the snow having covered all debris. Jones led them directly to the main building and up the long sweep of carved steps to the main doorway, gaping wide like a dead mouth. The doors had long since disappeared and Gillon, estimating the size of the doorway to be nearly twenty feet high by thirty feet wide and surmounted by a massive carved stone lintel, wondered how they had been carted away . . . or for that matter how they had been brought here in the first place.

Inside, the wind was reduced to a few eddies wending through the doorway and scattering the snow about into meager drifts. Jones took them down the ice-coated main hallway to a smaller room, where even the whine of the wind was lost.

'This looks like a good place to wait it out,' Jones said suddenly, startling them all. His voice echoed through the room. The heavy atmosphere failed to lift when Dmietriev lit and fixed a small candle into a metal reflector. The minuscule flame provided just enough light to see by, but at the same time, cast looming shadows on the far walls. Gillon took his flashlight and shone it around at the room walls. They were completely devoid of decoration, in contrast to the usual oriental penchant for intricate and colorful design. Dirt and frost stained the stone walls and piles of debris were scattered here and there across the floor, which was of the same carefully fitted stone construction as the walls.

Finding nothing of interest, he returned to the others. Jones had pulled his sleeping bag from his pack and spread it on top of a foam pad. Gillon studied the pinched faces of the others. Already he could see the beginnings of altitude sickness in their blue lips and hollow cheeks. Rodek was moving slowly about the room, fixing his sleeping bag and arranging his backpack and rifle within easy reach. His every movement suggested the start of stomach cramps and lack of energy. Thoughtfully, Gillon dug the first-aid kit out of his pack and swallowed three aspirin tablets with a mouthful of icy water from his canteen. This was his preventive technique . . . or his superstition . . . he was never sure which, for preventing altitude sickness, the mild hypoxia that resulted from too much exertion at an altitude where the pressure of oxygen in the air was too low to penetrate the arterial walls in the quantities to which the body was accustomed at sea level. It was a common malady in mountain travel and usually passed after a day or so, but its effects, until the body adapted, were a general feeling of languor, nausea, restless sleep and a gasping for breath, all of which combined to make the victim wonder why he had come in the first place and swear by everything he held sacred never to do so again. His theory was that the aspirin dilated the blood vessels, especially those feeding the brain, and the extra blood/oxygen capacity staved off or reduced the hypoxia. The best way to start a hard trip into the mountains was to sleep at altitude, thus allowing the body to begin its process of adjustment under conditions of the least exertion possible.

Satisfied that every precaution possible had been taken, he climbed into his sleeping bag and in spite of the sleep on the trip from Rome and the long day of enforced relaxation at Ala Kul, he quickly fell asleep.

Gillon came awake with a start. Jones drew back and motioned for him to lie quiet. A moment later, someone moved across the room and the tiny candle went out, plunging the room into darkness.

'Get out there and see if he needs any help,' Jones called in a low voice. Gillon heard the soft sounds of booted feet trotting down the narrow hallway.

Almost immediately, Leycock was back. 'All right, they are still a long way off.'

'Good. Get back out there and stay with Rodek then,' Jones answered.

'What's going on?' Gillon demanded.

'Get up and be ready to move. Rodek spotted something or someone coming this way.'

Gillon slid out of the sleeping bag as the candle was relit and slipped his cold boots on. With the ease of long practice, he shook out the sleeping bag, then shoved it into its stuff bag. He zipped his pack closed and lashed the bag to the frame, then picked up his carbine and loaded a cartridge into the chamber and flicked the safety catch on.

'Ho, boy. The soldier is ready and raring for action,' Stowe's voice was sarcastic.

'Shut up. Get your own stuff together and get out into the courtyard.' Jones toured the room quickly, checking to see nothing was left behind that would betray them. 'All right. Let's get out there and see what the hell is going on.'

The almost full moon was just pushing its way past a long ridge to the east, and through the main gate the snow gleamed in the pale flood. The growing moonlight had washed away the shadows that gave substance to the rubble-strewn yard and left a smooth, glistening sheet that stretched to the walls. The three men crossed the courtyard quickly to the base of the wall, where the rubble of years was piled.

Gillon clambered up the broken steps, careful not to

thrust a foot through the thin crust of snow into the rocks beneath. The monastery appeared to have been constructed as much for defense as for prayer. The walls were massive; huge blocks of stone piled fifteen feet or more high and ten feet thick, each carved from the granite of the mountain. They reached the top of the wall and went up slowly to the battlements to where Leycock and Rodek were leaning against an abattoir that jutted abruptly above the level of the wall. Both were staring off to the northeast through binoculars.

Jones called out and, startled, Rodek swung around with his carbine ready, then lowered it and waved a hand as he recognized them. Gillon walked along the wall to where Leycock waited, and accepted the proffered glasses.

At first glance, the pass below was empty of all but wind and snow. The moon, now well clear of the ridge, flooded the snow-covered terrain with a harsh white light that provided better visibility than he had expected.

Leycock nudged his arm and pointed. 'Just over there, below that pinnacle.'

Gillon shifted the glasses until he caught a flicker of movement in the shadows beneath the towering rock spire. A moment later, a line of men and animals emerged into the moonlight.

'My God,' he exclaimed. 'There must be a hundred people in that . . . that . . . what in hell are they?'

'Some kind of caravan, I guess.' Leycock answered. 'I thought caravans had disappeared years ago.'

'Apparently not,' Gillon muttered. 'Are you sure they aren't Chinese soldiers?'

Leycock shrugged. 'As far as I can see, they don't look like soldiers. And if they were, why would they be traveling with camels?'

'But,' Gillon countered with a question of his own, 'if they aren't soldiers, why are they traveling at night?'

'That's what's got me worrying,' Jones said as he came up and took the glasses. Gillon pointed out the location and Jones spent several long minutes studying the distant figures.

'Damn,' he said finally.

Dmietriev questioned Rodek in Russian and Gillon half listened as he used his own glasses now to watch the caravan. Rodek protested and Dmietriev spoke again, more forcefully this time, and still Rodek disagreed. Finally Dmietriev shrugged and borrowed Gillon's glasses. After a moment, he nodded to Rodek.

'What is it?' Stowe demanded.

'Sergeant Rodek thinks that the caravan is composed of nomads, probably from somewhere in the Dzungarian region or perhaps from further east in Inner Mongolia.'

'Nomads,' Stowe snorted. 'You mean like Tartars and Mongols? Nonsense . . .'

'Not Tartars,' Dmietriev interrupted. 'Probably Mongols of some kind. There are a few of the ancient Khanates left that still use the caravan trails. That is the reason for this monastery. Why else do you suppose it was built in the middle of nowhere? It is part of the eastward chain of Persian caravanserai.'

Stowe shrugged. 'How the hell should I know? You're supposed to provide the local color.'

'Are you saying then,' Jones interjected, 'that these people are traveling some kind of caravan route and are not out looking for us?'

'I do not see how they could be searching for us already. Certainly there would have been no time to bring that many men and animals into these mountains. I doubt very much that they have even heard of us. I do not know a great deal about caravans, but it would seem to me to be very early in the season for them to be traveling and very late at night as well. I would guess that they are starting early to be as far ahead of the other caravans as possible. Probably, the authorities do not even know they are on the trail.'

The six of them were silent for a moment. Jones's face was, for a short time, a study in indecision. Then, abruptly, he made up his mind.

'We had better get the hell out of here, no matter who they are. Chuck, you and Andre go down and smooth out the tracks we left in the courtyard as much as you can. Mike, check outside and do the same thing.'

Stowe nodded and Dmietriev and Leycock followed him down the steps. Jones glanced at Rodek and casually stepped around so that his back was to the Russian. Rodek ignored them and went back to the wall to watch the caravan.

'I don't know who this traveling menagerie is, but it seems mighty damned coincidental to me that they show up now. It could be that Dmietriev is right and they are just trying to get the jump on the competition, but I still think it's better that we get out of here and the faster the better.'

'Yeah,' Gillon nodded. 'I don't like the idea that they are still traveling this late at night.'

He went back to the wall and studied the caravan once more. The moonlight was too dim to show more than the grossest details, but that was sufficient to show the strength of the approaching party. The entire scene was right out of *The Arabian Nights*, he decided. Large, swaying camels plodded along under heavy burdens paced by men muffled and swathed in greatcoats against the bitter chill. They came steadily on and without a doubt now, the monastery was their destination.

'Come on, let's go,' Jones muttered, and started for the steps. Rodek followed and Gillon put his glasses away and started after then.

'I just thought of something else, too,' Gillon called after Jones. 'If they are going to stop here, they may be crossing the pass . . . hell, they *will* be crossing the pass. We could have them dogging our trail for the next couple of days.'

Jones nodded and kept on. 'Yeah, you could be right. We'll just have to be extra damned careful, then.'

Gillon followed Rodek down the steps wondering how much of the exchange the Russian had understood. He knew less about him than about any of the others. He had had a chance to observe Jones, Leycock and Stowe on the long flight from Rome . . . although he had to admit that most of what he knew about their backgrounds had come from Jones. About Dmietriev, he knew little more than that he was an excellent shot, fast as a striking snake, and a good actor, all of which he would have expected from a Soviet intelligence field agent, or any nation's field agent for that matter. But Rodek was a blank. The fact that he spoke, or pretended to speak no English led him to think that the Soviets were still playing their own game. Until Rodek decided to break his zombie-like silence, there was little more that he could learn about him.

Dmietriev and Stowe were waiting for them and they trudged through the gateway, where Leycock joined them. They had fashioned drags using their packs and they pulled these along behind to obscure the tracks they left in the snow. Jones led them to the south until the monastery was between them and the approaching caravan. He stopped here and, using his flashlight, unfolded the map and knelt down in the snow while the others gathered around. He traced out the route to the rendezvous. The way that had been marked would take them across the plateau to skirt Isskgal Glacier and then three miles southwest to Musart Pass at 11,480 feet. That meant a climb of nearly four thousand feet in less than three miles. Jones wanted to clear the pass before sunrise if possible and make camp on the far side for the day. They would then trek down through the trees after nightfall to about ten thousand feet, bypass the Jiparleth Glacier and into the heavy forest the second day to be in position for the rendezvous at dawn on the third day.

There was a heated discussion as to the wisdom of following the marked route. Stowe objected on the grounds that as the Chinese had been able to discover the existence of the mission, they could very well be in possession of their route of march. He argued hard for an alternate route that would take them northeast, even farther away from the suspected crash site and down through a low valley in a lengthy circuitous route that would add fifteen miles to the march.

Jones finally cut the discussion off by getting to his feet and picking up his pack and carbine.

'If nothing else, the Chinese won't know the route. I laid it out while the rest of you were sleeping. Also,' he continued, 'these winds will wipe out any tracks in a few hours.' But Stowe was unconvinced and continued to press for the circular route to the northeast, claiming that the safest approach lay from the opposite direction. When Jones refused angrily, pointing out that they lacked the time to make the longer trek, Stowe stamped off to gather up his pack without another word.

Because of the winds that swept up the pass throughout the long winter, the frozen snow was packed to the consistency of sand and neither snowshoes nor skis were needed. Jones set a strong, ground-covering pace across the plateau and as the terrain shelved up, switched to alternating the rest step with trail stride every five minutes.

By 0500, the top of the pass was in sight although still a thousand feet above them and dawn was an hour and a half away. The wind, as it swept out of the Arctic and down across the vast Russian steppes for hundreds of miles to the mountain barrier of the Tien Shan, where it was compressed as it forced its way through the high passes, was, luckily, behind them and tended to help rather than hinder their progress.

The same wind blew incessantly, rarely varying more than a few miles an hour from its average speed of twenty knots. But vicious storms were common throughout the long winter and then the wind speed might exceed eighty miles an hour. For now, it blew steadily against their backs, urging them on while at the same time chilling each man to the bone in spite of their protective clothing. To keep moving and exercising was the only way to keep from freezing to death when out of the shelter of trees or tents. In spite of the compression that raised the wind's temperature as it blew up through the passes, the equivalent temperature, combining ambient temperature and wind speed, was still well below 0° F.

Musart Pass was typical of the high Tien Shan. A wide pass, it was some three miles from side to side at the base. The approach from the northwestern slopes was exceedingly steep, almost fourteen hundred feet per mile. Halfway up the slope, it looked to Gillon, seeing it for the first time in the strong moonlight, as if it were a spillway into a vast bowl and he was trapped on the underside, struggling to reach the rim.

High ridges of stone lined the approaches on either side, but even though some of them reared a thousand feet above the floor of the pass, they were dwarfed into

104

insignificance by the immensity of the mountains around them. The way was smooth and the snow level, covering every possible obstruction to a depth of several feet. The terrain under the snow would be a coarse gravel, he knew, and there was no possibility that any living thing, plant or animal, could survive the continual winds. And in spite of its being hard-packed, a sudden spurt of wind could still whirl icy streamers from the surface that eroded the exposed skin like a sandblaster. Without snow masks and goggles they would have risked blindness.

For one eternal hour they plodded upward, strung out like bugs on a string, their trail stride having completely given way to the rest step. At eleven thousand feet Jones called a brief halt and they huddled together as best they could to escape the incessant icy searching of the wind. To talk was impossible and they squatted behind their packs like exhausted animals, breathing heavily into gloved hands. Gillon felt as if his lungs were constricted by a steel band that tightened with each successive step until it seemed as if his ribs would collapse. His back and legs were weak with tension and fatigue and it required a conscious effort to move each foot forward again and yet again. In spite of the aspirins, nausea tore at his stomach and every now and then he would be jerked to a halt as one of the men behind him paused to retch and vomit. Each time, Gillon signaled Jones by yanking the line and Jones stopped to wait impatiently for the second tug from Gillon that started him forward again like a machine. Only one other time in the long hours of steady climbing did Jones pause to rest. Incessantly, he pulled them forward by his own sheer determination.

For a long time, the top of the pass seemed to come no nearer and Gillon was reduced to the old climber's trick of forbidding himself to look at the crest again. He concentrated his whole being on shifting first one leg forward, pause, then shift the other again and once again in the incessant, maddening rest step that continues to carry you forward long after you would have sworn that you had no strength left at all. His back and hips were on fire from the weight of the pack, and the carbine, light as it was, dragged down at his right shoulder until it was all he could do to keep from throwing it away. Then the thirst, the terrible thirst of high-altitude exertion, began to make itself felt. At these altitudes and in winter the humidity is close to non-existent. The continual gasping for breath exposes the membranes of the mouth to the air, which greedily extracts their moisture. That, coupled with intense exertion, dehydrates the body quickly and it becomes impossible to force water into tissues in sufficient quantities to replace that lost to the air. Intense exertion at high altitudes then becomes a race against fatigue and dehydration, complicated by lack of oxygen for starved body tissue.

The darkness in those places shadowed from the moon, drifted away into a grayish sea that obscured the ridges on either side of the pass. Gillon gradually became aware that the slope had changed and when, forgetting his promise not to look up, he raised his eyes, he saw that the endless expanse of white was no longer above them but was now slipping away beneath his feet to a distant line of dark rock below. He glanced back over his shoulder and, in the gathering light, could see the straggling figures of the others strung out behind on the line. Their movements as they staggered up the killing slope were reminiscent of dangling fish.

Jones had stopped. Gillon closed the twenty-foot gap between them and they both sank down in the snow breathing heavily, and waited for the others to come up. For several minutes there was only the wind and the sound of their gasping before Dmietriev trudged up and collapsed beside them.

'Downslope . . . three miles . . . or more,' he rasped finally, 'trees begin.'

Jones nodded but said nothing, rubbing his forehead as Rodek and Leycock straggled in. It was too cold to rest for long.

Gillon watched as Jones got to his feet. They were all staggering, but Jones more so than the rest of them. That blow must have been more severe than they had suspected, Gillon thought, and Leycock caught his eye and nodded at Jones, but there was nothing that either of them could do for him and they both knew it.

As they started forward again, Gillon detached himself from the safety line. The others did likewise and he coiled the rope, tied it off and slung the bight over the upright portion of his pack frame. He watched the others file past, then turned to examine the pass and the high ridges on either side. The top of the nearly twelve-thousand-foot-high pass was no more than a few hundred yards wide. Looking back down the way they had come, he was even more impressed by the fan shape of the pass, resembling nothing so much as the spillway of a millrace. The two ridges that had paced their climb closed in around the top of the pass, broken only by a quarter-mile-wide gap at the top – the pass itself. The ridge to the right fell away to the west while that on the left loomed above the point where they stood. Overhanging its lip was a huge brow of snow, undercut by the wind. Because of the darkness, it had been invisible from below and Gillon was grateful for that. He would have had serious doubts about ascending the pass with the wind blowing as hard as it was and that massive pile of snow hanging above their heads like the sword of Damocles. The whole area had obviously been carved by a massive glacier creeping slowly down from the north, eons ago. Gillon tried to imagine the immense tonnage of ice that it would have required to fill the thousands of feet and cubic miles of mountain valleys and ridges until it finally overlapped this ridge, cut its way through the solid rock and carved out this pass before spilling over into the interior of the Tien Shan. It was beyond comprehension and, shaking his head, he started down after the others.

The snow on the south side of the pass was not packed, as the wind was less intense on this side. As they proceeded down undulations of the gentler slope, the snow deepened until they were plowing up to their knees. Jones brought them to a halt and they donned snowshoes. From there on, their progress became easier and the three miles to the heavy forest at eight thousand feet were sure to be completed by dawn. A few minutes later, the old familiar lacing pain began to grow inside

107

his thighs, arcing over to join beneath his crotch, as the unnatural, wide-legged stance forced by the snowshoes dragged at his unaccustomed muscles. Within an hour, Gillon knew the pain would be unbearable; every step would be a grinding, stabbing pain until the muscles grew numb with tension. And by nightfall, the pain would begin again as the cold cramped his legs. Gritting his teeth, he ignored the pain and struggled on.

As they trudged down the slope, the light grew apace until short of the tree line, the first rays of the sun could be seen above the peaks to the east. Gillon glanced around. He had been dragging his parka, weighted with the ski pack, in an effort to wipe away any tracks. The drag was doing its job and the steady wind would finish it. There would be nothing for low-flying search aircraft to see.

The sky was turning from its overcast gray to blotches of clear blue as the cloud cover began to break up, when Jones led them into the first of the pines, scrubby spruce that indicated they were below ten thousand feet once more. Gillon slapped the snow from his parka and halted long enough to slip back into it, retie the ski pack, then hurried on to catch up. The trees, sparse as yet and low growing, barely reached above his head but they would serve to hide signs of their passage.

They trudged on for another hour while the forest thickened and rose about them. As they marched on, Gillon noticed that the snow was becoming deeper and deeper and the saucer-like depressions around the tree trunks were more pronounced as they moved toward nine thousand feet, where the differential between day- and nighttime temperatures was great enough to allow intermittent thawing and freezing. They crossed one wide expanse of open slope, hurriedly, half sliding, half running on their snowshoes. There were no egg-carton marks as yet – hollows carved into the snow by the sun. They would come as the season advanced.

Jones brought them to a halt at 0900 hours, well inside a thick stand of towering spruce that closed in overhead to obscure any sign of the sky. The slope widened to an almost horizontal ledge at this point, then dropped sharply downslope for a hundred feet. There would almost certainly be a stream, frozen long since and covered with snow at the foot of the bluff. The trees were thick-boled, shooting as straight as shipmasts for eighty feet to one hundred feet. Virgin timber, Gillon suspected; natural selection had spread them widely in their contest for sunlight, and the underbrush, buried under several feet of snow, provided the site that Jones had chosen with a feeling of total silence, almost cathedral-like in nature. Except for the monotonous wind, there was not a sound to be heard in the immensity of the forest. Gillon stared off across the open space cut by the buried stream to see nothing but more trees forming a seemingly impregnable barrier a hundred feet away. To his left, the small canyon narrowed less than a hundred yards upstream to form a convenient crossing point.

Jones called to him and Gillon walked back through the trees. He had been less than twenty feet away, but so thick was the forest that the others were invisible and the sounds they made in setting up the small camp were completely obscured by the peculiar muffling quality of trees. He thought, as he walked through the forest, of his almost superstitious love of trees; the feeling that, among these giants, he was safe and could depend upon them for concealment and protection.

Jones was sitting on his pack, the map spread in front of him on the snow, while the others stood about waiting. He glanced up as Gillon joined the circle.

'This looks to me to be a good place to spend the day,' he began without preamble. 'We'll start again at 2100 . . . that'll give us about two hours of travel before we need to stop and eat. We'll sleep during the day tomorrow and by dawn on Thursday, we should be there. Also, if that damned caravan is still behind us, the jog to the east tonight will take us well out of their line of march. These trees are thicker than I thought but if the rest of you are as bushed as I am, we could stand the rest.'

Dmietriev nodded, indicating that Jones's plan made sense to him.

'I am afraid that the Chinese will be out after us in force. I think we need to put a guard at the top of the pass . . . anyone coming up the pass can be seen for miles and that should give time for the guard to ski down to warn us.'

Gillon grunted acknowledgment and Jones nodded. 'Good idea. Any volunteers?'

Rodek stepped forward without hesitation and as Gillon started to get up, Leycock pushed past him.

'Rodek and I'll go. My skiing is pretty good. How about his?'

'Sergeant Rodek was the Soviet Army cross-country champion two years ago,' Dmietriev answered solemnly. 'He is an excellent skier.'

'All right.' Jones nodded. 'If both of you go, you can spell one another and get some rest. I wish we had thought of this earlier. It would have saved you a long climb back.'

Leycock shrugged. 'It's not so far and with the snow-shoes, we should make pretty good time.'

'Don't forget to drag your tracks,' Stowe said suddenly, and without another word turned and walked over to his tent. Jones watched him for a moment, started, as if to say something, but thought better of it. Only Gillon noticed the slight head shake that Jones gave before he too stood up.

A few minutes later, Leycock and Rodek had marked their maps to show the location of the rendezvous in case they became separated from the main party, shouldered their packs and disappeared into the trees. Dmietriev, Jones and Gillon watched them go, then separated to set up their own tents.

CHAPTER NINE

Gillon finished rigging his one-man tent and crawled inside to arrange the sleeping bag, admitting to himself as he did so that he really did not envy Leycock and Rodek the long hike back to the summit of the pass; in fact, he had been downright relieved when Leycock had volunteered so quickly. Sitting on the edge of the bag, he tied the tent flaps shut, leaving a small opening for ventilation, pulled off his boots and slipped them between the nylon sheet ground cloth and the bag, near the foot, beat the snow from his outer clothes and slipped under the down cover. He was exhausted, more so than he would have believed possible after all of the rest he had gained during the previous two days. Aircraft pilots required oxygen at ten thousand feet and for all intents and purposes, they were sitting still. He downed more aspirin tablets, recalling his advice to Jones a few minutes before and the argument that had ensued before he would take them. Over Jones's objections, he and Stowe had forced an examination of his head. But, beyond a nasty-looking purple and black bruise that extended below the hairline, there was nothing to be seen. Only X-rays could show if there had been a bone fracture but he was certain that Jones had suffered a fairly severe concussion at the very least.

Between them, they had overridden his objections, splitting the watch between Dmietriev, Stowe and himself to allow Jones the maximum rest possible. Stowe had volunteered to take the first watch, Dmietriev the second and he the last – and part of the sentry duty was to make sure that Jones stayed inside his sleeping bag until they were ready to travel again. Jones had finally conceded after a lengthy argument, but with, Gillon remembered, barely concealed relief. The three of them had then gathered out of earshot of Jones's tent to discuss his condition.

Stowe began, not callously, but with a hardheaded appraisal of their predicament. 'If I had to guess,' he said softly, 'I would say that his skull is fractured. It's obvious that he is concussed from the way he moves. The way he dragged us up that damned pass should have killed him.'

'Should have,' Gillon agreed, 'but didn't. As far as I know, there is nothing that you can do for a concussion except bed rest. And he sure as hell is not going to get that out here.'

'One of us could stay behind with him,' Dmietriev suggested hesitantly. 'The plan calls for us to go back out over this same pass.'

Stowe swore loudly and added, 'Nonsense! With the search parties the Chinese will throw into this area as soon as they spot the wreckage, you can't believe we're going to be able to come back out this way? Hell, there's not a chance,' he answered his own question. 'We have to go deeper into the back country and hope to hell that a pickup aircraft can find us. There isn't a chance that we can come back this way,' he repeated for emphasis.

Gillon knelt down and spread out his map and began to study it closely. There was twenty miles yet to the rendezvous. Most of it seemed to be downslope and he guessed that it would be either snowshoe or ski work, although he did not relish the idea of skiing unknown territory by moonlight. But Stowe was probably right. It would be foolhardy at best to try and return through the pass to the drop point on the plateau, where an aircraft had been scheduled to return in three days to pick them up. He shook his head and looked up at Dmietriev.

'Stowe is right. We have to go on farther into the mountains.'

Stowe looked smug at that and turned to stare in the direction that Rodek and Leycock had taken. 'We shouldn't have stopped here either. We should have kept on as long as we had the forest for cover. I don't like waiting here . . . if they come after us, this is a damned bad spot to be trapped.'

Gillon snorted. 'That's why Jones sent Rodek and Leycock back up to the top of the pass.'

At this challenge from Gillon, Stowe spun around, a sharp rebuke ready, but Gillon stared at him challengingly until he flushed and glanced away. Perhaps, Gillon thought, he remembered the incident on the plane or perhaps he had just decided to bide his time for a while longer; either way, he kept silent. It looked more and more to him that Stowe was pushing hard to take over now that Jones was seemingly incapacitated and Gillon did not know if he liked that idea at all. If anyone, Dmietriev was the more senior and the most likely candidate if, in fact, Jones was really so badly hurt that he could no longer lead. But ever since the landing, Dmietriev had been curiously hesitant, not at all the same strong-willed man he had seemed after taking over the aircraft, and he wondered what had happened to him. Gillon shrugged and stood up. Those were all problems for some other time. Right now, what he wanted more than anything else was some sleep.

'Well, we can wait until tonight to see how Jones is. It might not be a fracture after all. The size of that bruise shows that he got hit pretty hard, but that's all it shows. A blow like that would be enough to shake anybody up. The altitude and exertion on top of everything else certainly aren't doing him any good. It may be that all he needs is a few hours' sleep and he'll be okay.'

'Yeah, maybe,' Stowe answered doubtfully, and turned away. Dmietriev glanced from one to the other and then with a shrug went to his tent.

Gillon lay in the sleeping bag staring at the vague sunlight that penetrated the tightly woven nylon, thinking back over the conversation. Jones's face had had a grayish tinge as he crawled into his tent but Gillon wasn't sure whether it had been the light, his imagination or what. Either way, he knew that there was nothing to be gained by rushing Jones into total incapacity. He was the only one with a detailed briefing, and as far as Gillon was concerned, there was a hell of a lot more to what was facing them than he at least, had been told. He only hoped that nothing had been deliberately concealed from Jones. Outside the tent he could hear the restless crunch of snow under Stowe's boots as he paced around the clearing. Gradually, the sleeping bag warmed and he fell asleep.

When he awoke to Dmietriev's call, the tent was deep in gloom and, wondering if he had overslept, he fumbled for his boots and chafed and rubbed them back into some semblance of softness, then slipped them down into the bag for a moment to rid them of their chill. The interior of the tent was icy cold and he shivered violently as he struggled out of the encumbering warmth of the sleeping bag and tugged on and laced up his boots.

Outside, he found that the sun had slanted so far to the west that it had dropped beyond the distant line of peaks. The cathedral-like atmosphere of the trees had disappeared, leaving behind a deep, all-pervading gloom that seemed half haunted. He slid back a parka sleeve to expose his watch and found it was close to 1600; he had been asleep for almost nine hours. Dmietriev came up to him and nodded and they stood for a moment without speaking, enjoying the comfort of each other's company in the lengthening shadows. Finally Dmietriev shivered, said good night and trudged off toward the snow-colored nylon mound of his tent. Looking around the tiny clearing, Gillon thought that anyone coming upon them would have to look hard to see the tents; bleached white as they were.

He stared about him once more, then crawled back into his tent and rummaged through the outside pockets on his pack for the Primus stove and the day's rations. Within minutes, he was sitting on the foot of his bag, crouched under the rain flap of the tent and watching the stove's almost colorless flame bring the double cup of water to a boil. He added the soup mixture, then sprinkled the contents of a package labeled beef stew into it. The soup was chicken noodle, or so the label read, but alone, or mixed with the beef stew, it would taste terrible. Gillon had yet to encounter a dehydrated food that tasted the way the label promised; all seemed to be chronically undercooked . . . as if manufacturers had never realized that at high altitudes water boiled at lower temperatures and what might taste fine in a sea-level laboratory was only so much over-spiced, half-cooked mush at high altitudes.

He put a second, double-sized cup of water on to boil as soon as the stew mixture had cooked to an edible, but lumpy paste and added a double portion of tea. That at least would make the meal worthwhile. And in spite of the taste, the appetite that high-altitude exertion always engendered in him was enough to cause him to wolf the food down.

Gillon washed the cups out with snow, wiped them carefully and stuck them away in the pack. At these temperatures about the only thing he did not have to worry about was dysentery from greasy pans. He stuck a few candy bars into his pocket and pulled the sleeping bag outside, turned it inside out to air while he struck the tent and in a few minutes had everything repacked.

Jones awoke an hour later and stuck his head out of the tent. Gillon went over to him immediately.

'Back inside,' he grinned.

Jones grimaced, struggled out and got shakily to his feet. Gillon could not be sure in the fading light, but it looked to him as if Jones was worse. His face did have a definite grayish tinge and his eyes were screwed up with pain. What little he could see of the whites was badly bloodshot. Involuntarily, Jones brought a hand to his forehead, wincing.

'Have Rodek and Leycock come back yet?' His voice was steady enough but Gillon grasped his arm and forced him back into the tent. He pulled his pack over and dug out the first-aid kit and handed him the packet of aspirin.

'You get two of those down you before we talk about anything else.'

Jones started to argue, then changed his mind and accepted the packet. Gillon handed him the canteen and watched him down the pills. As Jones handed the canteen back, he grabbed his hand and forced it open. Two tablets were resting on his palm.

'For God's sake! You *are* a baby. Take those damn things before I cram them down your throat.' Gillon broke into laughter and handed the canteen back.

Jones grinned sheepishly, took the canteen and washed the tablets down. This time he opened his palm and showed it to Gillon, then opened his mouth and stuck out his tongue.

'See, Daddy . . . all gone like a good boy.'

Gillon chuckled.

'All right, now that you've played doctor answer my question. Did they come back yet?'

Gillon shook his head. 'Nope, and they have two more hours to go.'

'Everything else quiet?'

'Yes,' Gillon answered with exaggerated patience. 'If not, we would have awakened you and asked what to do.'

'Yeah, I guess so.' Jones laughed. 'I suppose, too, that I ought to take what rest I can. The next two days are going to be pretty damned rough.'

Gillon studied him for a moment, noting that his eyes

115

were so red, they appeared inflamed. 'Do you really think that you can make it?' he asked seriously. 'I'm betting that you've got a concussion and possibly a fractured skull.'

'I don't doubt the concussion,' Jones said soberly. 'My head feels like it's stuffed to the splitting point. I got a concussion once playing football when I was a kid and my head feels now just the way it did then.

'But I'm certain it's not a skull fracture . . . I think I would feel a hell of a lot worse if it was.'

Gillon shrugged doubtfully.

'How about the others? What do they think?

'Think about what?

'Damn it, stop playing games. You know what I mean.'

'What makes you think they think anything at all?' he countered.

'Because,' Jones growled, 'they would have to be damned stupid not to! Look, the only thing that I'm worried about right now is finishing this thing up and getting us all back in one piece.'

'If you don't get back inside that tent and get some more sleep, you won't get anybody anywhere. Look, I'll make a deal. If you take it easy now, I'll go over the situation with you.'

Jones thought for a moment, then nodded and, wincing at the pain, crawled back into the tent. Gillon spread open the flaps and hunched down in the snow.

'Stowe is concerned about you. He thinks you do have a concussion and won't be able to make it.'

Jones snorted. 'Hell, that bastard just wants to run this operation.'

Gillon carefully refrained from agreeing and went on to describe the conversation they had held earlier in the day and Stowe's observation that they must head deeper into the mountains and call for the pickup aircraft to follow them in. Jones nodded soberly and Gillon knew that he had been thinking along the same lines. He finished with his own conclusion concerning Dmietriev.

Jones showed surprise at that. 'Dmietriev is supposed to be second-in-command of this idiot's delight. The Russians tried to hold out for direct command, but the

Agency wasn't buying. If you're right, that sure doesn't sound like the kind of man they would send along.'

'Well, I don't know about the politics involved, but from what he's shown me, not only does Stowe have him buffaloed, but he couldn't lead his way out of a paper bag if the exit was marked in neon lights.' Gillon thought for a moment, then added, 'Of course, it could be the altitude . . . maybe another day will make all the difference.'

Jones glanced at him sideways and muttered an obscene expletive. 'We'd better keep an eye on him in case he is cooking up something on his own. Anyway, it doesn't make a hell of a lot of difference, because I don't have a fractured skull.'

Gillon watched as he shifted to a more comfortable position inside the dim tent. Any movement obviously caused him a great deal of pain, because he moved stiffly, carrying his head in such a way that as little strain was transmitted as possible. After a moment he asked:

'Just out of curiosity, why did you decide to come along? After I saw you bringing in that beat-up barge I would have bet any amount of money that nothing could have dragged you along. You looked like the orneriest bastard I'd ever seen.'

Gillon chuckled. Around them the trees were blending into the soft darkness as the sun disappeared, submerging them in icy stillness. He could almost feel the temperature plummeting, as he had known it would.

After he had resigned from the service, he had never discussed the incident with anyone – he still carried the scars on his legs and, he supposed without much heroics, on his mind as well. He knew now that it was not as simple a matter as having something to hate . . . Communism versus the American way. To him, it was the idea that certain groups of men were able to direct the activities of other men, were able to gain such power that they would manipulate people as if they were numbers, playing pieces in some cosmic game, completely repressing or ignoring the humanistic considerations, the fears and sufferings, the essence of humanity in short. Perhaps it was that more than anything else that had led him, as a mercenary, always to the ranks of those fighting to overthrow an established government, in some unconscious search for a better way to govern. He really did not know, because in the three years since that incident on the narrow trail in Laos, he had shied away from thinking about it too deeply, and so it had settled immovably into the suspicion that all governments, of any kind, were innately untrustworthy.

He owed a debt to Jack Liu, that was beyond question. Liu had asked his help and he was bound to give it. But beyond, he was not really sure himself. Ignoring his own intense dislike of Communism, Jones's request – and Liu's too, for that matter – could also be reduced to the struggle between competing power groups. Gillon was sufficiently a realist to know that such power groups, no matter what they were labeled, had always and would always exist. He had also deduced that allowing the United States and the Soviet Union to obtain the information Liu claimed to have would assist in maintaining a balance of power between three of the five strongest powers on the globe. Whatever else may have been among his faults, Metternich had logically foreseen the consequences of powerful governments. The best way to prevent a war was still to see that both sides – or in this case, the three sides – were evenly balanced. Allow one to gain the upper hand, and war was the result. But he did not know if he wanted to tell Jones that or not. Jones would probably believe him, but his job was to make sure the United States got the information first and foremost. Then, if circumstances permitted, the Russians would be brought into the balance pan. Dmietriev certainly must realize this, and if not, then his bosses in Moscow did. If he wanted Jones's trust – and he had a feeling that that trust was going to be of overriding importance before they were through – then he would only tell him about Jack Liu . . .

Jones sat on the end of his sleeping bag, watching him, half lost in the darkness inside the tent.

Although Jones had promised himself that he would find out why Gillon had changed his mind so quickly that night, it was only an impulse that prompted him to ask Gillon then and there. As he sat in the semi-darkness, watching the play of emotion across his face, he knew that he was going to hear Gillon's reasons or, he amended to himself, what Gillon thought were Gillon's reasons.

Perhaps he needed to, Gillon was concluding. The psychiatrist who had talked to him in hospital in Japan had said that some day he would have to and, when Gillon had laughed at him, he had merely grinned back, a grin full of knowing. As he had told Gillon that day, sitting on the end of the hospital bed with the room full of early summer sunshine, one of those rare days in Tokyo when Mount Fuji was not hidden in the smog and dust: 'What has happened to you is neither unique nor that disastrous. You spend a few days going the rounds in here with me and I'll show you cases where, although they look perfectly sane and healthy on the outside, they'll never leave a Veterans Hospital for the rest of their lives. These are just kids, too, most of them not even old enough to drink. But, out there, one wrong word, one negative response in the wrong situation and they'll either go catatonic or turn into murderous maniacs. You've got it good, buddy. Your legs will heal, and the scars will disappear in a few years. But you've got to let it out someday before it tears you apart. Are you a Catholic?' he asked suddenly.

'What?' Gillon replied, startled.

'Are you a Catholic?' the psychiatrist repeated patiently.

'No . . . not since I was a kid anyway.'

'Too bad. The confessional is a clever gimmick . . . gives you a chance to bare your soul in relative anonymity. Sometimes you even get lucky and there's a sympathetic listener on the other side of the curtain. Maybe you ought to try it again . . . it's good therapy if nothing else.'

Gillon had merely shaken his head.

'Okay, it's up to you. But when the occasion arises, let it out.'

And so he told Jones what had happened to him on that day, while the arctic wind whipped about them and flapped the sides of the tent. Gillon no longer felt the cold, only the heat and the dust and the pain in

119

his legs as he talked, not sparing any detail, and when he finished, Jones was silent.

Gillon stared down at the snow for a while and then stood up and wandered through the trees a few yards in the direction of the pass. He was grateful that Jones had said nothing; at the same time he was surprised to find that he did not feel relieved of a terrible burden.

At 1800, Rodek stumbled into the camp. In the light of Stowe's flash, his face was whipped and bleeding with the effort of the desperate dash down from the pass and through the forest in the darkness. Gillon helped him to Stowe's tent and wrapped him in the sleeping bag while Dmietriev got the Primus going to brew tea. Jones had fallen asleep again but the commotion awakened him and he joined them in the small circle of light pressed out of the darkness by flashlights.

Through chattering teeth Rodek spoke to Dmietriev in Russian for a long time. He waved away the tea Stowe brought until he was finished and as he talked, Dmietriev's face grew longer and longer. There was no hope for Gillon, Stowe and Jones; they had to wait out the end of the story. When he had finished, Rodek gulped the tea and sank back, exhausted.

Dmietriev poured himself a cup of hot water with shaking hands and sipped at it before starting; then he took a deep breath.

'Sergeant Rodek reports that a large force of Chinese ski troops are moving toward the pass. Leycock went down the pass to investigate. From what Sergeant Rodek tells me, Leycock almost ran into them but does not think he was caught or seen. He is sure that they will pick up our tracks because the winds have stopped blowing.'

Jones swore viciously. 'Damn it,' he finished. 'Wouldn't you know. All year long they blow . . . except when we need them.'

'Rodek came down to warn us,' Dmietriev continued, 'and Leycock stayed behind to keep watch. They estimate that the Chinese will be over the pass by midnight.'

'Are you sure it's not just that damned caravan they saw?' Stowe muttered.

Dmietriev started to retort, took a deep breath and asked Rodek another question instead.

'He says,' Dmietriev translated when Rodek had answered, 'that these were definitely soldiers and there were no animals with them. They saw the caravan march off to the east. They did not come up the pass.'

'Moonrise is at 2330 tonight,' Gillon said thoughtfully, ignoring the exchange between Dmietriev and Stowe. 'That means they will pick up our tracks just below the summit. In this pea soup darkness, they probably won't spot them any sooner. But they know damned well that if we are in the area, we've got to cross the pass.' Gillon stood up and paced around a moment. The others watched in silence until he stopped.

'Look,' he said, emblazoning his words with repeated stabs of his gloved hand at the air. 'They must just be guessing that we are in here so far. It looks like they searched the wreckage sooner than we expected. Now they know we weren't killed when the plane crashed. That plateau is the only sensible place to land if you come in by parachute, which we had to do since we weren't in the wreckage.'

'But why up the pass . . . ?' Stowe demanded. 'The wind must have cleared off our tracks down there . . .'

'Yeah, it would have. But once you stand on that plateau, the only way off, unless you are a mountain goat, is up and over the pass. Those ridges are impossible at this time of the year. So they come up the pass, guessing that as soon as it gets light, they'll spot our trail. They must be figuring to camp for the night at or just below the summit.'

'Okay, hot shot, so you got them psyched out. Where do we go from here? Sometimes . . .'

'Shut up, Stowe,' Jones commanded absently. 'What have you got in mind, Bob?'

Gillon squatted down and took Stowe's flashlight and shone it down onto the snow. With his gloved hand, he drew a picture of the pass, approximating the shoehorn shape as seen from above. To the left, he sketched the northward-trending ridge and on the right, the southern ridge.

'All right, it's this. When we started down this morning, I noticed a ledge of snow along the face of the left ridge. It's been undercut by the wind and thaw and it's about ready to come down.'

'How do you know that?' Stowe asked, interested in spite of himself.

'Between college and the Army, I spent two winters in the ski patrol at Mammoth. We used to go out in the mornings before the skiers hit the slopes and clear out dangerous snow packs. After two winters, I'm pretty sure I know when a snow ledge is ready to come down.'

'Ah,' Dmietriev breathed. 'I see what you are getting at. You mean to blow down that ledge and block the pass.'

'Almost right,' Gillon corrected. 'I'm suggesting that we blow the ledge down right on top of that bunch of ski troops. There's more than enough snow there to do the job effectively. It must be two hundred feet high if it's an inch, and by the time it gets through dragging all the snow that's already on the pass along with it, not only will it block the pass until the spring thaw, but it will take those ski troops out as well.'

Stowe threw back his head and laughed. 'What a ridiculous pipe dream. Do you seriously think you can get those troops out of the way with an avalanche? Nonsense.'

'I do,' Gillon replied softly. 'There is no chance that anyone caught in that pass with all that snow coming down on them will get away. And if they do, so what? The pass will be closed completely.'

'Yeah,' Stowe shot back. 'But if they do, we're the ones who've had it. If you want to take them out, then we set up an ambush at the top . . . and hit hard. That way we'll make damned certain!'

'And let the Chinese know for sure we are in here,' Jones put in quietly. 'Right now, they are guessing where we are . . . at best. If we ambush and shoot them up, we might as well hang out a sign.'

'I think you are right,' Dmietriev said hesitantly. 'If

it looks like an accident . . . well, then they might be inclined to treat it as such . . .'

'Oh hell,' Stowe snorted, but Jones interrupted him.

'I say that Bob is right. Bloodthirsty as it might seem, if we leave those troops alone, they are bound to catch us sooner or later. If we start shooting, some of them may get away and, in any event, tomorrow when the spotter planes are out, if they see bodies all over the slope, the whole country and half the world will know in a matter of hours that we hit them. If they see an avalanche, chances are they won't find any bodies until spring.' Jones studied each one of them for a moment before he said, 'All right, then we do it Bob's way. Sorry, Chuck, but the avalanche makes more sense to me.'

Stowe started to protest again but, realizing that Jones's mind was made up, subsided into silence without a word.

'All right, then.' Gillon took a deep breath. 'It won't take more than two or three small charges to loosen that ledge and drop it straight down the pass. Andre, what explosives do we have?' Dmietriev got to his feet, went to his tent and returned with several wax-paper-wrapped cubes of plastic material and handed them to Gillon.

'They are frozen, but that does not matter.'

Gillon took the cubes and laid them on the sleeping bag.

'Gelignite?' he asked

Dmietriev nodded. 'A very special type.'

Gillon stared at the paper-wrapped cubes. 'Hell, the temperature must be near zero. This stuff is too un-stable to carry around.'

Dmietriev grinned and shook his head. 'We do not have to worry about patents, so we changed the formula by reducing the amount of collodion cotton from four to two and a half per cent. This makes the nitroglycerin much more stable and prevents exudation.'

Gillon nodded doubtfully. 'I'll take your word for it. We'll use three to be certain and connect them with a fuse. What kind of igniters do you have?'

Andre reached into his parka and pulled out a handful of metal tubes, pointed at one end, with a terminal at the other to attach the leads.

'They are very sensitive and can be ignited electrically by screwing the lead into the bulb socket of a flashlight.'

'Clever.'

'All right then, take what you have to and get going,' Jones ordered. 'You should be able to reach the pass well ahead of the Chinese. How about climbing the ridge?'

Gillon thought for a moment, going over the shape of the north-western ridge in his mind.

'There is a sharp hogback just above the pass,' he answered slowly. 'I think we can get up that way. If not, we can go straight up under the snow ledge. It's riskier that way, but it can be done.'

He paused, loath to ask what he had to next, but there was no help for it. 'I'm going to need help. Rodek is exhausted and Leycock will be too tired to climb. I'll send him down as soon as we get up there. Stowe, you and Dmietriev will have to come with me.'

Dmietriev nodded but Stowe started to shake his head, then changing his mind, shrugged and got up, walked over to his pack, pulled the carbine out of its case and slung it across his shoulders without a word.

Gillon nodded approvingly. 'That's a good idea, just in case there is a surprise waiting for us. The moon should be up in a few hours, so we'll take the skis as well and on the way back, we can ski to the tree line.'

He turned to Jones. 'If you hear the avalanche go, get Rodek up and be ready to go.'

Jones nodded. 'All right. If you get back before dawn we should still be able to reach the rendezvous point by tomorrow night.'

Gillon walked over to his pack, picked up his carbine and strapped his ski case on. With the snowshoes in one hand, he walked back over to where Jones stood beside Stowe's tent.

'Look,' he said, keeping his voice pitched low so that the others could not hear. 'There's no need to keep a guard now. You get back into your tent and sleep until Leycock gets back.'

Jones shook his head and Gillon gave him a disgusted look.

'All right, Doctor,' he relented. 'Just be careful up there. And watch out for our independent friend. Don't take any nonsense from him. There just isn't room for two super chiefs on this crew.'

'I don't intend to. He and I have had one set-to and if it comes to that, we'll have another. Sooner or later, he'll learn.'

Jones clapped him on the shoulder and watched as they faded into the trees.

CHAPTER TEN

Night had clamped down heavily on the forest by the time the three men moved out for the pass, each using his flashlight carefully to avoid stray flashes of light that might betray them to the aircraft they could hear droning above. The low-branched spruce trees with their short, stiff needles lashed at unwary faces in the misleading light from the torches, and within minutes all three of them had pulled ski goggles and wind masks on for protection.

It took them nearly three hours of heavy going in the darkness to break out of the trees. There, Gillon found that the sky had misted over, dimming the stars that ordinarily would have been bright enough to allow them to travel quickly over the open snow. But a high ice layer had moved in to suffuse and dim the starlight enough to mask uneven spots and depressions in the snow, forcing them to a cautious pace. Here in the open they did not dare risk the use of flashlights.

By 2200 hours, they were in sight of the top of the pass, which appeared as nothing more than a great blot in the blurred sheet of snow. Gillon stopped several hundred feet short of the summit and whistled softly. Receiving no reply, he whistled again. They glanced at one another. Dmietriev nodded and they separated to provide a more widely spaced target as they moved closer to the top of the pass. On the south side, the side from

125

which they were approaching, the last several hundred yards were up a fairly steep incline and in the dim starlight it reared above them like a pale cliff. Gillon whistled again, his imagination pinpointing the spots on his body where Chinese carbines were zeroing in.

This time Leycock heard them and whistled back. As they trudged the last few hundred feet to the summit, muscles screaming with the agony that Gillon had anticipated that morning, he stepped from the concealment of a snow bank and stood waiting for them. As they came level with him, Stowe curled his gloved hand around his flashlight and shone the yellowish beam into Leycock's face. Even in the misleading light, Gillon could clearly see that he was exhausted. His face was gray and pinched with the cold and he shivered uncontrollably. Together, they completed the last few paces to the top. Gillon and Stowe went forward a few more feet to examine the sweep of snow below for any sign of movement while Dmietriev questioned Leycock.

There was nothing moving below as far as they could tell in the darkness, and they listened carefully as Leycock described his trek down the pass that morning and the long back trail that he had made before he stumbled onto the Chinese ski troops.

'Where was that?' Dmietriev demanded.

Leycock slung his carbine. 'About six miles below the pass. Rodek and I saw an aircraft, a two-engined transport, circling way off to the north. We guessed that it was about over the southern end of the plateau. It dipped down below the ridge and then we didn't see it again until it flew over that ridge just east of that peak over there.' He pointed into the gloom and added, 'You can't see it now. Anyway, it looked like it was taking off, but we couldn't be sure. So we flipped a coin to see who went down to take a look. I lost.' He chuckled.

'So then, I went straight down the pass after the aircraft disappeared and then to the left into the trees along the west end of the glacier. It was a longer route, but I didn't want to stay in the open . . . Anyway, about two hours after I started, I cleared a small ridge and spotted a line of troops heading in the direction of the lamasery. I wasn't sure about that; even with the glasses they were too far away. Anyway, I figured that they wouldn't find anything on either the plateau or at the lamasery and would make for the pass sooner or later. So I cut across that small valley at the north end of the glacier below the plateau and that's where I almost ran into them. There were about fifteen of them and I got out of there in one hell of a hurry.'

Gillon dropped the glasses, letting them dangle on his chest. Rubbing his eyes against the bitter cold, he asked, 'What was the wind like up here today?'

'The wind?' Leycock repeated stupidly. He massaged his face and took a deep breath. 'Oh . . . yeah, the wind. A good steady blow until about 1500. Then it died away to nothing. But I doubt if there are any tracks left to find, if that's what you're thinking. Anyway, I stayed well west of the trail that we took last night. Unless they are going to cross clear over, they won't find tracks, even if the wind left any to find.'

'How many did you say?' Stowe asked.

'I'd guess about fifteen altogether. I didn't stop to count them because they were strung out and I was worried that they might have some point men out that I hadn't spotted.'

Gillon felt rather than saw Stowe nod in the darkness. 'Then we had better get busy on your damned avalanche,' he murmured, pulling back his parka cuff to peer at his watch. 'It's going to be risky as hell since we don't know how many are out there.'

'Have you seen anything since you got back up here?' Gillon asked, ignoring Stowe.

Leycock nodded. 'Just once at sunset. About two miles below the base of the pass. I saw them just after I reached the top and Rodek went down. It looked like they had stopped to eat, because I thought I saw a flash-light.'

Gillon stared hard through the glasses once more but the darkness was so intense that they could have been a hundred yards from him and he wouldn't have seen them. Moonrise was still an hour away and if Leycock was right, he estimated that it would be a close race between the moon and the Chinese troops. At best, they

127

would have an hour of light in which to work. At worst, they would arrive together.

Behind him he heard Leycock ask, 'What avalanche?'

Stowe described what they had come to do and then in a brusque voice ordered, 'You had better get down below to the camp and get what sleep you can.'

Gillon opened his mouth to protest, then thought better of it. There was just the faintest hint in Stowe's voice that he was expecting Gillon to disagree.

"All right, get going then, and be careful,' he said. 'That overcast makes it damned hard to see.'

Leycock nodded. 'If I wasn't so tired, I'd stay here with you . . .'

Gillon thought for a moment . . . there was a graceful way out, he thought, one that wouldn't give Stowe an opening.

'Look, it would take you just as long to get back down to the camp if you started now in the dark as it would if you waited for moonrise. This overcast doesn't look like it is going to thicken any more than it already has, so why not stay here until then? You can spread your sleeping bag here and get some sleep.'

Leycock agreed heartily. 'Great idea. I think I will. I don't fancy that stretch through the trees in the dark.'

Abruptly Stowe turned away without a word and shrugged out of his pack. 'Let's get busy,' he snapped. Gillon smiled to himself and went to work.

Fifteen minutes later, they had laid out and carefully fused the three charges of gelignite taken from Dmietriev's pack. He was worried about the length of wire they would need, but it was much safer and surer than using timed or burning fuses. Together, the three of them circled back down the pass several hundred yards, using their flashlights freely once they had dropped below the top. If there were any search aircraft still out in the overcast, they had had it, but Gillon judged that a lesser danger than a broken leg because of the darkness.

They found that the northwestern ridge above the pass presented a long, gentle slope behind that enabled them to climb up almost to the overhanging snow ledge. They were completely shielded from the troops advancing up the far slope by the pass itself and Gillon did not hesitate to use his flashlight to study the final portion of the steep ascent.

'Okay,' he said, 'let's go.' Occasionally, Gillon was forced to stop and cut steps into the steeper portions, but the ascent up the final portion of the eight-hundred-foot-high ridge was completed easily enough by the time the moon's upper edge began to show fuzzily over the eastern line of peaks. As they trudged forward across the top of the ridge, testing the snow's firmness with their axes, the sweep of moonlight seemed to precede them, changing the dull, frozen surface to a softly glowing opalescence as it drove through the high ice cloud.

The snow ledge itself reared above them another two hundred feet and, as they climbed closer, Gillon spotted a jutting ledge of rock barely visible immediately below the base. The entire incredible weight of the snow mass rested its forward surface precariously on this thin rock outcropping. Above the ledge, the snow leaned out and over the five-hundred-foot or more drop to the northern slope of the pass. Gillon could picture the spring sun growing stronger and stronger until it melted away the underpinning and of its own accord, the immense tonnage of snow broke loose and roared down the pass to block it completely until at least early summer. Below the snow and the rock outcropping, a shelving snow-covered expanse of rock ran below the base of the snow mass from where they stood. Wider at their end, it sloped at a thirty-degree angle for fifty yards and then fell away abruptly to the pass.

Gillon had Stowe and Dmietriev stop while they were well back on the ridge and he went forward carefully on snowshoes. He shuffled forward until he dared go no further, then turned to study the underpart of the snow ledge. It reared above him in the moonlight, a harsh white cliff now that the moon had risen high enough to clear the peaks. He could see where the snow rested on the rock and the wide melt channels that had already been carved by the sun. Two one-pound charges of gelignite equally spaced along the base of the ledge should certainly be enough to break it loose as one mass to bring it down into the pass. He would use three to be certain. The trick would be in getting in underneath to the rock ledge without triggering the avalanche. Fortunately, the intense night cold would help to stabilize the mass, although where the melt had run, the snow would be as slick as glass. Nevertheless, he thought, he should be able to reach it by climbing up the slope to the rock ledge. If he placed the charges well back into the snow, the rock ledge would lend added compression to the powerful explosive and muffle the sound until the snow was well on its way.

But he did not like the look of the slope below his feet – the frozen melt water and the steepness of the runoff. He shrugged. There was nothing for it but to try. He turned carefully by shifting his snowshoes a few inches at a time and trudged back to where Stowe and Dmietriev waited for him.

He chose Dmietriev to plant the first charge, the one nearest the ridge on which they stood, basing his decision on the fact that Dmietriev was several pounds lighter and had had more direct snow experience than Stowe. He gave Dmietriev careful instructions on how and where to plant the charge and then went to work to lay out his own climbing ropes, showing Stowe how to anchor the line with his ice ax.

'Yeah, yeah,' Stowe nodded with a trace of impatience, but Gillon continued remorselessly until he was certain that Stowe understood exactly what he wanted. If he slipped, he would go straight over the rock ledge. There would be only the line and Stowe's strength to save him.

Gillon led them down to the start of the snowfield. He indicated a spot, well back from the start of the ledge, had Stowe anchor his ax, then looped the line around it once and tied a double bowline in the forward end, through which he slipped his legs, and took a turn around his waist, fastening it into a crude belt. He stepped out of the bindings and jammed his snowshoes upright into the snow.

Stowe took his position behind the ax and began to pay out line as Gillon moved forward crabwise across the slope on his stomach, spreading his weight over as wide a surface as possible. After a few hundred feet, he risked a quick look behind to where Stowe and Dmietriev stood watching him. A trick of perspective seemed to curve the snowfield so that it appeared as if they were standing on the rim of a shallow bowl.

It took Gillon fifteen minutes to cross the thousand or so feet to the rock ledge, using his ice ax to chop hand- and footholds in the icy surface. The snow melt was a greater problem than he expected. It must flood down from the snow during the brief warm period around noon, he thought, creating the damnable glassy smooth surface. Once it caused him to miss a handhold when his glove slipped, but he managed to lash out with the ax, levering his arm from the elbow, to smash the pick end through the crust. He rested for several minutes, waiting for his heartbeat and respiration to return to a more normal rate. When he continued the climb, it was at a slower pace, never shifting now until he was doubly sure that at least one foot and hand were both secure.

The trip was not as bad as some rock climbs that he had made. The surface being more nearly horizontal relieved some of the tearing weight on his arms and the balls of his feet, but the icy wind that eddied about him, clutching and tearing with frozen, plucking fingers to drive the pain of restricted circulation into his extremities, was more severe than any he remembered.

His ax finally struck rock after what seemed like an interminable period of climbing and he paused for a moment before pulling himself up the last few feet to the rock ledge. Then carefully, an inch at a time, he drew his feet up under him and, using the ice ax as a crutch, stood up.

The rock ledge was only a few inches wide and the snow pack curved outward until, seven or eight feet above the ledge, it leaned beyond, forcing his head and shoulders outward as if trying to overbalance him. He was sure that he looked like some old-time movie hero stuck on the ledge of a skyscraper, Harold Lloyd perhaps; only here, there was no window to duck into; only the thin nylon line that stretched behind him in a long curve to where Stowe knelt in the snow, keeping it taut. If he slipped or fell, he would slither two hundred feet in a long arc down the glassy snow pack and the jolt when he reached the end would not only break bones but would probably snatch the rope right out of Stowe's hands. Savagely, he thrust the thought from his mind and concentrated on inching along the ledge until he judged that he had reached the two-thirds point.

The narrowness of the ledge posed yet another problem. It had widened for a space but then had narrowed again until he found that he could barely move a foot an inch at a time. He did not dare risk a look at his watch, but the steady climb of the moon above the peaks east told him that he was taking longer than he had reckoned. Unless he planted the charges, and soon, the soldiers would be over the pass.

Abruptly, the rock ledge gave out and his foot tipped over into emptiness and he lost his balance. Gillon scrabbled hard at the icy surface, arching his back against the front of the snow pack until he could jam his ice ax to provide a tenuous hold. He rested a moment, gasping in the thin air until here gained his breath, and looked around. He was short by several hundred feet of the point where he had planned to lay his first charge. As well as he could reconstruct the face of the snow mass in his mind, he was sure that he was about two thirds of the way across. That was far enough, he decided, and backed up several steps to firmer ground. The narrowness of the ledge and the overhang of the snow pack made it impossible to swing the ice ax with enough force to carve out a hole for the charge. Swearing at the perversity of fate, he kicked what snow he could away from the base, an inch or so above the ledge, until he had a shallow hole. Carefully, he stooped down, clutching the handle of the ice ax. It would not hold him if he fell, he knew, but just holding onto something gave him a feeling of steadiness.

He fumbled the packet of explosive out of his parka with his left hand and pushed it into the hollow, wishing to God that he had something that would serve to anchor it. He thought of his knife but its thin, sharp blade would never hold in the snow. He studied the packet, turning it into the moonlight to make sure that the igniter was still in place and that the single wire led out properly from the packet. To make sure it would not be yanked loose from the charge, he wrapped several turns around the packet, then with the spool of wire in one hand, he began to inch back along the ledge, hoping that the friction as the wire unwound would not yank the whole thing loose.

He backed for what seemed like an eternity, moving one foot to his right to feel for the ledge, plant down securely, dig his toes into the soles of his boots and hope. The trek was made worse by the fact that he could not turn his head to see where he was going. When he could no longer see the point where he had laid the first charge, he stopped, took a deep breath and leaning as far out from the wall as he dared, turned his head, scraping his chin across the rough ice.

The ledge was a bit wider here, allowing enough room to use the ice ax. He cut the hole deep, tunneling back as far as he could reach, and scraped the snow carefully out into a pile on the ledge. He checked the second charge as carefully as he had the first, stooped down and thrust it into the hole, then packed the snow back in until it was filled. Breathing easier now that the charges were laid, he tested to see how firmly the charge was planted, found it satisfactory and began inching back along the ledge until he could see the snow pack three feet below. He inched backward another few feet until, with the ax resting on the ledge for support, he could ease down onto the snow.

He rested there for a moment. Far to his right, Dmie-triev was working his way along the snow ledge to where Stowe waited. The planting of explosive on that end of the ledge had been completed, he realized.

Taking a deep breath, Gillon eased himself down onto the snow and began the crawl back, using his boots to kick holds. After several minutes, the line began to go slack and Gillon muttered curses at Stowe for his in-attention. He stopped, balancing precariously on the steep slope, and gave the line several hard pulls, but it failed to attract Stowe's attention. Still cursing but with more feeling now, he kept on, but within a few minutes, the line had gone so slack that he was becoming en-tangled. He did not dare shout at Stowe to attract his attention . . . the sound could very well carry all the way down the pass and warn the approaching soldiers. He gathered the line into coils and slung it over his shoulders; hardly a satisfactory solution but better than becoming so entangled that he lost his grip.

Just as he reached the lower limit of the arc, the hold that he had kicked into the snow a moment before collapsed. He felt himself begin to slide and feverishly he dug in hard with his right hand and stiffened his left foot, but under the sudden weight that hold collapsed as well. His hand plowed the thin crust of ice and he began to slide backward at a faster rate. The slack line looped around his shoulder snapped taut and he lost his grip on the ice ax. He slid down toward the dark edge of the snow pack, gaining speed with each second. He dropped the spool of wire, wondering idiotically that he had had enough presence of mind not to hang onto it any longer, thus tearing the charges loose. Far up the slope he heard Dmietriev's thin cry and saw Stowe's shadow racing down the slope. Good God almighty, he groaned, that bastard had lost the line.

His apprehension exploded into fear that verged on the blind edge of panic and he lunged forward with his right arm to retrieve the ice ax, fastened to his wrist by a nylon thong. But encumbered by the coil of rope around his shoulder, he could not reach it. He rolled hard onto his right shoulder and managed to turn over onto his back, from where he could pull his arm down until the ax was in reach of his left hand. In desperation, he grabbed the wooden stock, rolled again and swung the ax high in an overhand arc to bury the blade deep in the snow. The ice crust was extremely thin, almost a glaze this near the edge and the ax ripped through it as if it were so much paper. Gillon managed to kick his boots into the crest, plowing up plumes of snow that buried him almost to the waist but at the same time, slowing him enough to grapple the ax head down under his chest. The chisel blade dug deep into the snow, the pressure of his body forcing it deeper and deeper until just as his feet thrust out over the edge of the snow pack, the ax head brought him to a stop. A moment later, the nylon climbing line snubbed up sharply, then wrenched at his arm painfully. The temptation to lie still a moment with the stiff feeling of the hard snow and the painful jab of the pick side of the ax head pressing into his chest to remind him that he was still alive was great, but the rope was insistent and he struggled until he could crawl forward up the slope. As soon as he was well away from the edge, he waved his hand above his head and the line slacked free. Grunting with pain, Gillon freed the tight coils from his shoulder.

As he climbed back up the slope, he began to shake. The delayed reaction of adrenaline shock in response to the near fatal incident turned quickly to anger. He remembered Stowe's barely concealed impatience as he went through the instructions with the rope, explaining in detail the importance of keeping proper tension on the line at all times. It was Stowe's carelessness, inexcusable carelessness, that had almost cost him his life.

The snow surface grew firmer as he drew away from the edge. Gillon got to his feet and, kicking steps with his heels, climbed carefully until he reached the point where the slope flattened. He stopped here a moment to rest and saw that Stowe was gazing off down the pass as if completely unconcerned by the fact that he had nearly killed him, and suddenly that anger exploded and Gillon rushed across the snow. He vaulted the low ridge that separated the snow pack from the firmer ground of the ridge and dove at Stowe, smashing into him in a flurry of snow. Stowe just had time to turn and see him coming before he went down. Gillon struggled to his feet and swearing incoherently drove a fist at Stowe's face. Stowe deflected the punch and struck back, but Gillon followed through with an elbow that caught him on the side of the head, knocking him flat. Then Dmietriev was between them both, pistol in hand. He drove Gillon, still raging, away from Stowe.

'Stop it, both of you,' Dmietriev hissed through clenched teeth. 'If either of you ever does that again, I'll kill him . . . kill him. Do you understand?'

Gillon started forward but Dmietriev cocked the pistol. 'Stop or I will kill you . . .' he warned, and from his voice Gillon knew that he would and without hesitation. He stepped back, breathing hard, and stared at Stowe.

'You almost . . . killed . . . me.'

'It was an accident,' Stowe replied coldly. 'The line slipped through my hands when you fell.'

'Accident hell. Just plain rotten carelessness and stupidity. Nothing else.'

'Silence!' Dmietriev snapped. 'You will both be silent! This is neither the time nor the place to debate accident or carelessness.'

Gillon knew he was right and, with an immense effort of selfcontrol, choked back his anger. He turned without a word, picked up the rope and handed it to Dmietriev. Stowe climbed to his feet.

'If he goes near that line, shoot him.' Gillon jerked a thumb at Stowe.

'Where are . . . ?

'To get the fuse.'

Without another word, Gillon walked down to the ridge and climbed over onto the snow pack. He edged out onto the icy part of the pack and, using his ice ax, chopped a series of parallel steps across the shallowest part of the slope. If he was guessing right, the fuse would have unrolled its full length and should be somewhere straight ahead. The moon had risen higher until it was now well clear of the peaks. Its bright light flooded the snowfield, making it difficult to see through the glare.

It was nearly ten minutes before his groping hand brushed the wire. He dug his feet in securely and took a turn in the line around his wrist, leaving plenty of slack so that he would not accidentally pull the charges free. A gentle tug told him that at least the second charge was still secure.

With a smooth overhand motion, he began pulling in the loose end of the fuse line. It came freely enough and he coiled it around his hand and elbow until the free end snaked up. Breathing easier, he recrossed the slope.

Gillon, Stowe and Dmietriev crouched beneath a rock outcropping fifty feet above the pass and well away from the path the avalanche would take. The position provided an uninterrupted view down the pass in both directions. On the southern side, he could just make out Leycock's form through the glasses, as he zigzagged down the slope toward the trees to warn Rodek and Jones to be ready to move. On the north slope, the Chinese troops were visible in the bright moonlight, a third of the way up the pass. Stowe nudged Dmietriev and pointed. Dmietriev raised his glasses and stared in the direction of the pointing finger, then nodded, muttering to himself in Russian.

Stowe and Gillon had maintained a strained silence throughout the past half-hour during which they had circled down the ridge to the top of the pass. They had awakened Leycock, and Gillon had sent him down to warn Jones and Rodek. Then they had crossed the top of the pass and climbed the north ridge to the ledge on which they were presently sheltering against the stiff wind that had arisen in the past hour.

Try as he might, Gillon had been unable to fathom Stowe. He was certain that Stowe realized that his carelessness had almost cost him his life, yet his attitude suggested that he was totally unconcerned. Gillon debated the problem in his mind as they waited. Was Stowe really lacking in concern, or were his actions deliberate? If, in fact, he really did not care, then Gillon wanted to be rid of him now, before he did kill someone. The way he felt right now, he might even volunteer to shoot him. And, if his actions were deliberate, then Stowe was a plant, pure and simple. Yet he could not reconcile that possibility with Stowe's apparent concern for Jones after the Chinese general had hit him with the pistol. He shrugged and went back to studying the pass. The problem would have to be ironed out with Jones, and soon.

The Chinese troops, obviously fresh and used to the high altitude, were making excellent time. Through his glasses, he could make out the tiny dots that were the soldiers against moonlit snow. His plan was to set off the charges after the soldiers had passed the halfway point. There would then be no chance that any of them could reach the bottom and safety on their skis. Any higher and the pass narrowed to such an extent that they might be able to reach the high ridges along the sides. He said as much and Dmietriev grunted acknowledgment; for once Stowe did not argue, but agreed readily. The three men looked at one another; then each, knowing what had to be done, turned away.

Dmietriev attached the fuse to the flashlight, working slowly and deliberately, and when he had finished, glanced expectantly at Gillon. Gillon watched the soldiers for a moment, until he knew he must delay no longer.

'Ready?' he asked.

'Ready,' Dmietriev repeated. Stowe shifted position, but said nothing.

Gillon nodded and continued to watch through the binoculars. The troops were spread out in a line approximately seventy feet long. They were not roped together but trudged steadily on, heads down and concentrating on their footing. Each man carried ski poles, which he used to aid himself in the climb. Skis strapped to their backs appeared as outlandish feathers above the cowled heads.

'What are you waiting for?' Stowe muttered. The lead man was almost even with the rock projection to the right side of the pass that Gillon had selected as the marker. He took a deep breath and beside him felt Dmietriev tense.

As if warned by some extrasensory feeling, the lead man stopped and raised his head to scan the top of the pass.

'Now,' Gillon exhaled, and Dmietriev pressed the button.

For an instant nothing happened and Gillon looked at Dmietriev as he calmly pressed the button a second time. Snow erupted in triple fountains above them and three distinct booms rolled down the pass.

Gillon pressed his eyes to the glasses again and caught the trapped figures in the circle of moonlight. The lead man was staring wildly around him, pointing at the snow pack that had just begun to shift. As if in slow motion, the troopers began to run, some back down the pass, some toward the nearer, right-hand side. Gillon knew they would never make it. One figure, more clear-headed than the rest, was already fastening skis onto his feet.

Gillon swung around in time to see the leading edge of the snow mass dissolve into a vast spray. It hung for

138

an instant in midair, then with the grace and beauty of an ocean wave in crystal form, it began to fall in a long curve of ice until it touched the slope below. There it rebounded high into the air to touch down again further downslope, until within seconds, the whole snow pack was flowing downhill as if it were a giant tsunami, sweeping all before it. Gillon followed it until the leading edge gathered in the first of the fleeing figures and boiled them under. Only the man on skis, now well ahead of the raging wave, stood any chance at all. Gillon watched in an agony of doubt, fear, guilt and at the same time, a fierce elation at the thought the man might survive, might outrace the deadly mass of snow filling the pass with thunder.

The trooper was losing ground but still there was a chance. Dmietriev was already sighting his carbine, even though it was an impossible shot; then the soldier made the mistake that killed him. He should have waited a few seconds more before starting his turn to the side of the pass but the thunder of the snow behind must have driven him to panic and he attempted a *stem christi* at too high a speed. His downhill ski pole turned under the impact and he went down in a flurry of snow. The avalanche roared over him in an instant, leaving behind only a vast sea of moving snow. A moment later, the avalanche spilled out into the wide entrance as avalanches had done for millions of years and the immense sound died away. Gillon stood up, shaking violently, aware of the sound and its power only now that it was gone.

CHAPTER ELEVEN

Sunset of the third day in the Tien Shan. Jones held up his hand and brought the party to a halt just inside a thick stand of trees lining the rim of a well-hidden, narrow canyon. Gillon glanced over his shoulder to see Stowe raise his hand to signal the two Russians and Leycock, who were out of his sight in the trees. Overhead, he could barely hear the distant aircraft. All day the persistent whine of searching aircraft had been with them but the dense spruce and pine forest through which they were traveling had concealed them well, making it possible for them to move by daylight. Consequently, they had made up the time lost at the pass, and the rendezvous, set for dawn on the fourth day, would be kept.

Jones swept the canyon and the forest beyond with binoculars and while he was thoroughly engrossed in his examination, Gillon took advantage of the moment to study him. If ever a man had traveled on sheer will-power alone, Jones surely had. Following the long hours of rest, he seemed to have recovered somewhat and for two days now he had pushed them on, resolutely ignoring all appeals to consider his own health. Although they had covered nearly thirty miles through the high mountains on snowshoes and skis in the two days since the avalanche, Jones had become progressively weaker, stumbling several times in the late afternoon. For the last mile of travel, he had leaned heavily on Gillon for support, cursing his own weakness over and over under his breath until Gillon told him to shut up.

Gillon shoved his ski poles into the snow, shrugged out of his pack and plodded across the knee-deep snow carrying his own glasses to where Jones stood. The slope, falling away steeply at their feet, was relatively free of vegetation, but for scattered underbrush thrusting branch tips above the snow blanket. The bottom of the canyon showed a thin depression running through its center. Probably a small stream, Gillon thought, long since frozen and covered over with snow. Aspens lined either bank in thick stands and straggled up the eastern slope to blend with the spruce and fir that reached to the rim.

The aspens were so dense that in places it was difficult to see the snow in the fading light through their bare branches. Gillon traced the stream's course upstream to where it curved sharply and disappeared around a bend. Somewhere beyond that point, he knew, was the rendezvous. Jones had confided to him last night that they were to march along the stream bed for three miles, then wait for Jack Liu in a stand of trees, a stand that was to be identified by its mixture of pines and hardwood, the only one of its kind along the stream bed.

'Let's get a camp set up,' Jones said abruptly, as if to cut off the discussion of his health that he knew Gillon and Stowe, trudging up behind, were about to begin. He turned away and shuffled back to the clearing, where Leycock and Dmietriev were coming in. Gillon and Stowe stared after him for a moment, then both shook their heads and followed.

A quick, hot supper, cooked over Primus stoves, was eaten in silence. Without allowing any argument Jones set the watches, took the first one himself and built a small fire for warmth. They all knew that it was useless to argue with him by now and within minutes, all had turned in while Jones began to pace slowly through the camp.

Gillon awoke an hour later. He lay still, his fingers curling around the butt of his pistol beneath the rolled-up parka that served as a pillow, wondering what had awakened him.

'Gillon . . . !'

The whisper was repeated again, this time with a ferocity that surprised him. In his half-awake, half-asleep condition, it was several seconds before he realized that Jones was outside the tent.

'Jones . . . ?' he whispered back.

'Yeah . . . get dressed and out here, quick! Bring your snowshoes.'

Gillon needed no more urging than that and a few moments later, he pushed open the tent flap and wriggled out. He glanced at his watch, illuminated by the feeble light of the fire; 2000 hours, he shook his head. What the hell was Jones up to? he wondered.

Gillon slipped around the side of the tent, taking care to be certain that Dmietriev did not see him. Jones saw him coming and motioned to him to be quiet and follow. Once away from the firelight, it was pitch black. Gillon banged into a tree and, cursing under his breath, felt his way along, wondering what the devil was going on. A few moments later, a hand grasped his wrist and a tiny circle of light showed at his feet.

141

'Get your snowshoes on,' Jones whispered.

He knelt and snapped on the snowshoes, completely puzzled now by Jones's actions. Jones grabbed his wrist again and for the next half-hour, they moved quickly through the forest, the narrow beam of the flashlight leading the way until finally, Jones edged into a small clearing and stopped.

'We should be safe enough here,' he said quietly, and dropped down onto a fallen log.

The fast pace Jones had set through the trees coupled with the grogginess of insufficient sleep had left Gillon irritable and exhausted. Nevertheless, he sat down, laid the carbine across his lap and unfastened the snowshoes so that he could sit comfortably. 'What's all this nonsense . . . ?' he started. But Jones held up a hand.

'Wait now . . . give me a chance to catch my breath.'

He flicked off the flashlight and total darkness enveloped them. For several minutes they sat in silence while the thin noises of the forest gradually became audible around them. Distant cracks as live wood contracted in the cold; a faint stirring of wind among the snow-laden branches and occasionally, a soft plop somewhere as a branch dropped its burden of snow. Gillon was impressed with the absence of animal noises. There were no animal sounds at all; any that could survive nine-thousand-foot altitudes in winter were usually hibernating animals.

Jones finally broke the silence. 'I wanted to get you out here so that I could fill you in on what's happening,' he began, keeping his voice low, barely above a whisper. 'I figure that I can trust you more than any of the others.'

Startled at the unexpected admission, it took Gillon a moment to recover. 'Why?' he asked flatly.

'All right, if you want to know why, I'll tell you,' Jones answered without hesitation. 'Dmietriev I can't trust because he is a Russian and I know damned well he has his own set of orders that supersede any of my instructions if things should get tight. That's a fact of life, like it or leave it. Same for Rodek, and besides, if he speaks English, he isn't letting on. Stowe, never! Stowe is a born troublemaker and if we ever get out of

142

this thing, I'm going to fix it so that he never leaves a desk again. Dmietriev told me about the trouble you two had up in the pass. Stowe has been around long enough to know better.'

'Seems like we have two troublemakers then . . .' Gillon interrupted.

'If you mean Dmietriev, forget it. He told me because he's worried about his neck, naturally. You were in charge, Stowe should have obeyed without question. I don't know if he lost that rope accidentally or not, but when we get out of this, I'm going to find out.'

Both of them were silent. 'What about Leycock?' Gillon asked after a moment.

'Leycock would normally be my second choice. His record is damned good.'

'If it's that good, then why me?'

'Because without you this mission doesn't stand a prayer. If you aren't along, Liu doesn't hand anything over but trouble. And if you think there is a chance of shooting it out with them, forget it. We wouldn't stand a chance.'

'Glad to see you recognize that. Liu is one of the most careful men I've ever met.'

'So I picked you for that reason and for one other . . .' Jones paused a moment, as if trying to decide whether or not to continue.

'I don't mind telling you,' he said after a moment, 'that this damned head of mine is about to split. Look, let's get this over with in a hurry. There's something else we need to talk about and we have to get back before they find out we're missing.'

Gillon heard a rustle of papers and Jones turned the flashlight on again, shielding the bulb with his gloved hand so that only a glimmer of light showed on the map.

Using his finger, Jones traced the long route they had followed from the plateau on which they had landed, up and over the pass and down through the forest to their present camp. 'There is a chance that Liu and his people won't make the rendezvous tomorrow. If they don't, we have an alternate setup, here, fifteen miles southeast.'

Jones drew a wavering line across the steep ridge on

the far side of the canyon, then over several more lower ridges northwest to where it met a small valley less than twenty miles from the plateau.

'We make a circle . . . the idea is that from the alternate site, we can go back to the plateau, where the Russians can get an aircraft in to pick us up. Otherwise, if Liu and his people do make it tomorrow morning, then after we pick up the information he has, we march due east for eight miles' – he indicated the route on the map – 'to this area in the foothills of the Khalik Tau, above the Yakanash River.

'That radio contact with Ala Kul last night indicated that the Russians expect to have no trouble in getting a plane in at Khalik Tau or onto the plateau. So if Liu isn't waiting for us tomorrow, we radio Ala Kul and make tracks for the alternate point.'

'And if Liu isn't at either one?'

'Then the Chinese have got him,' Jones said with finality, 'and we get out as fast as we can . . . to either one of the landing sites. If we find we can't reach either one, then we are on our own and we run for the border as best we can.'

Jones paused. 'There is one other thing you ought to know about as well. The information that Liu has for us is just a little bit more important than just photographs and instrumentation data on the nuclear warhead test series.'

'Well, how about that?' Gillon's tone was sarcastic but Jones ignored him. He was not in the least surprised. Since the trouble at Ala Kul, he had begun to suspect there was more to their mission than he had been told.

'The data actually contain the locations and targets of the nuclear missile hard launching sites which the Chinese have set up in the past year along the Mongolian border.'

Gillon whistled. 'Do the Russians know?'

'Let's say they haven't exactly been told that much, but I'd be damned surprised if they didn't know. Incidental to the targeting information is the nuclear test data that the United States wants. It's in our interest to see a power balance maintained between China and

144

Russia . . . one of the basic reasons behind the Sino-American talks, although neither side will ever admit to it. We want the locations of these missile sites in Russian hands. You know the theory behind the balance of power,' Jones stated rather than asked. 'If one side gains a preponderance of power over the other, then they will be tempted to capitalize . . . if you'll pardon the pun . . . on it, which in this case could mean pre-emptive strikes resulting in all-out nuclear war. Nuclear war in Central Asia could be just as destructive to civilization as a nuclear war between the United States and the Soviet Union.'

'So now we're saviors of mankind,' Gillon answered sardonically. 'Look, I agree with you, it would be down-right dangerous to let China and Russia sling H-bombs at each other. But except for raising the radiation levels a bit, they aren't going to really hurt anyone but themselves . . . unless one of the other nuclear powers is stupid enough to take a hand.'

'Or either China or Russia figures they are about to and decides to hit first.'

'Yeah,' Gillon replied after a moment, 'there is that.' He shifted into a more comfortable position on the log, suddenly troubled by what Jones had said. All of a sudden his carefully cultivated and very comfortable cynicism had been cut to pieces. He hadn't thought that far along about the consequences of a nuclear war between Russia and China.

'You started to say that there was another reason you picked me?'

Jones played with the flashlight a moment as if gathering his thoughts, then laid it on the log to illuminate the map. 'Yeah, there is. As far as we know, the Red Chinese have no active interest and no agents involved in that two-bit war you left a few days ago. The decision to contact you was made minutes after Liu's message naming you as the contact. I was at Orly in Paris waiting for a flight to Moscow when the call came through to go and get you and six hours later Phan and I were waiting on that dock for you to come in. Except for an hour or so in the camp and the time in the barracks at Ala Kul you haven't been out of my sight since.'

'Meaning?' Gillon was puzzled.

'Meaning, I think you are the safest . . .' A branch snapped close by and Jones grabbed for the flashlight. A single shot cracked out of the dark forest and the flashlight went spinning into the snow. He had just enough time to see Jones lean forward as if completely exhausted and fall forward into the snow before he instinctively threw himself backward off the log into the underbrush. A moment later, a spray of bullets swept the clearing. He crawled madly into the trees for several feet, jumped to his feet and took four long steps to his right and stopped. He pressed hard against a tree trunk and let the night surround him, straining above the sound of his own convulsive breathing to hear the soft swish of branches or the sharper crunch of snow. After a moment, his mind began to work again. He judged that he was less than twenty yards from where he and Jones had been sitting, but now to the left of the point from where the shots had been fired. Jones had been the first target and that had saved his own life and whether it was because Jones was the leader of the expedition or had been holding the flashlight, Gillon did not know. He had been scared before, scared many times, but never this badly. He had had to fight to hang onto his sanity, fight to prevent himself from being overwhelmed by panic and racing away into the forest as every muscle, every nerve in his body was urging him to do.

And he couldn't stay here; already there were sounds of brittle tree branches snapping as if someone were moving closer to him. If he stayed where he was, they would find him sooner or later. If he tried to run for it, he knew damned well that without his snowshoes, which were still stuck in the snow beside the log, he would only flounder helplessly in the deep snow until run down. And besides, in the dark and confusion, he was no longer certain in which direction to run. Gillon ground his teeth together in an effort to control his ragged breathing and forced himself to think.

What had Jones been carrying? A rifle, maps? Probably nothing more. The maps were not worth going back for . . . he could remember the place names and his own map was a duplicate and there had been nothing on them to indicate their route of march or the two rendezvous points. Anything else that Jones knew about the mission that Gillon did not, was locked away in his mind – a mind that was no longer in existence. Whoever it was, might as well have those maps too, he thought. They seemed to have everything else.

Moving cautiously, careful to stay well back into the shadow of the tree, Gillon peeled back his cuff and looked at his watch. About five minutes had passed since the shots were fired. Whoever had shot Jones was either endowed with superhuman patience or else was gone and Gillon really did not believe that. Would they have heard the shots in the camp? he wondered, and decided not. They were at least two miles away and the trees would have suppressed the sounds over that distance. Also, a new thought occurred to him; if the killer had been one of the team, he would never have risked the shots within hearing of the camp. The killer would have been too readily identifiable by his absence.

His dilemma was compounded by the fact that he had not the slightest idea where he was in relation to the camp. Jones had taken a roundabout way through the forest to confuse anyone following. But it had also thoroughly confounded him. Gillon was not even sure in which direction the camp lay. He could, he knew, find their tracks in short order with his torch, but that would only invite a quick rifle bullet.

The soft squeak of snow beneath a boot sole snapped him instantly to full alert; even his breathing was suspended to a shallow draught. Years of fighting in the jungles of Africa and Southeast Asia had taught him to use all his senses in situations like this and, except for the snow, it was no different now than the many jungle ambushes he had led in the past.

He listened with his whole body for the next footfall. Instead he heard a soft voice speaking a high, singsong language . . . Chinese. My God! he thought. Of all the damned luck. Chinese troops. They must have been in

147

the area and heard them talking or had seen the flashlight.

Gillon unslung his carbine, crouched and moved quickly to his right, then as quietly as he possibly could, retraced his steps toward the clearing. A few moments later, he gently pushed aside the underbrush.

What he saw chilled him to the bone. Four Chinese ski troopers were shining flashlights down onto Jones's body while a fifth man, an officer, examined a blood-streaked map. As he watched, a sixth soldier pushed out of the trees and joined them. He said something and pointed to Jones's body. They all laughed appreciatively. Each was wearing a white snowsuit and hood, had skis strapped to his back and was wearing snowshoes. Each carried an AK-47 carbine and one man wore a radio. As Gillon watched, the officer spoke to the man with the radio and he took the handset and pressed a button.

Without seeming to hurry in the least, Gillon edged his carbine through the branches and shot the man with the radio through the chest before he could speak the first words. The others looked up, startled at the sound of the carbine, and Gillon sprayed the area with the carbine set on full automatic. Two other soldiers went down under the onslaught and a third, turning to run into the trees, stumbled as one leg buckled under him. The officer sprinted for the trees and disappeared. The sixth man had flopped down into the snow and Gillon saw him snatch at something inside his jacket. Guessing what it was, he threw himself headlong out of the thicket and rolled beneath the protection of a fallen, snow-covered tree. Something crashed into the brush to his right and exploded, smacking him soundly with the concussion as several pieces of shrapnel thudded into the wood. Gillon thrust himself away from the protection of the tree and scrambled to the edge of the clearing. One of the flashlights had fallen into the snow, providing just enough light for Gillon's night-adapted vision. The soldier who had thrown the grenade was holding a second in his hand, peering warily around, while the one who had been hit in the leg was staring at the trees, his carbine ready. The one with the grenade was clearly the more dangerous; he sighted in, fired twice and saw

148

him slump into the snow, the grenade falling from his hand. The wounded soldier swung the carbine around and shot twice in his direction before the hand grenade erupted. The other soldier must have already pulled the pin and was waiting to see in which direction to throw it. Stupid, Gillon thought, viciously. Stupid. He risked another look but both soldiers were dead. Shrapnel had caught the wounded soldier full in the side, spreading a dark patch beneath his body.

Gillon backed carefully out of the brush until he was well away from the clearing, then moved around to the far side in the direction taken by the fleeing officer. He squatted down just inside the trees. The grenade blast had destroyed the flashlight and there was only the faint starlight in the clearing to make the bodies identifiable as something other than forest debris. As he studied the clearing, he knew that he could not allow the Chinese officer to get away. He had to find him and stop him before he found someone to pass his information along to. If he didn't, then all of them were finished including Jack Liu. Without wasting any more time, Gillon entered the clearing, retrieved his snowshoes and hurried back to the trees.

The dull gleam from the clearing furnished him with a point of reference and he crawled carefully forward. In the almost total blackness, he moved more by touch and instinct than by sight. The mass of heavy-needled branches above now blocked any trace of light from the sky and Gillon was certain that even if the moon were directly overhead, its light could not have penetrated this depth of primeval forest.

Gillon felt his way forward, attempting to ward off the low-hanging branches that whipped and bit at his face. After what seemed like hours, but could only have been twenty minutes or so, he pushed out into another clearing. This one seemed to be several hundred feet in diameter and starlight glimmered lightly enough on the snow for him to make out the far side, where the trees began again, as thick and impenetrable as ever.

He had hoped for just such a clearing and quickly oriented himself by the constellations. He found that he was moving in a northerly direction opposite to that in which they had been traveling for the past two days. It seemed a safe bet that somehow the Chinese patrol had cut their tracks and followed them toward the campsite. It had been just his and Jones's rotten luck that they had come upon them first.

He knelt in the snow for several minutes, trying to think things out. The intense cold, coupled with the long day of snowshoeing over unfamiliar terrain in the high altitude, had left him exhausted and aching in every muscle. Yet he knew that he could not stop now or for hours yet to come. If he did not stop that Chinese officer, they would all be dead or captured before tomorrow was out.

If he assumed that the man was not running in panic – and somehow that seemed a very safe bet – then his objective would be to join a larger party further north. He knew that if he were to travel due south from where he now stood, that eventually he would come out on the edge of the canyon and since he could not be more than a mile or so either east or west, it would not take him long to find the camp. So now that he knew where he was, maybe he was in a better position than the officer, providing he took advantage of it.

The Chinese officer would have to be traveling slowly, as he would not dare to shine a light. He would of course assume that Gillon had not been killed, or else one of his own soldiers would have fired shots as a recall signal. Since they hadn't he would assume they were dead. Therefore he would play it as if Gillon were following him.

The deathly cold was almost paralyzing in its vehemence and he rubbed his forehead and cheeks vigorously where he was beginning to lose feeling. He pulled the snow mask out of his parka and slipped it on. It was certain death to stay in one spot without shelter for long and with a tremendous effort of will, Gillon got to his feet and, staying close to the tree line, began to circle the clearing, bending low over the snow to see the ground in the dim starlight. He was looking for tracks, hoping that the officer had crossed the clearing. After a short time, he ran across a set and the quick surge of excitement died stillborn when he realized that they were his own. Thoughtfully, he took out his flashlight and compass. Shading the lens with his gloved fingers until only the merest shaft of light shone through, he took a bearing, then faded back into the woods, moving due east, the hooded flashlight casting a wide but faint circle of light onto the snow. He was taking a desperate risk, he knew, but there was no other choice. After 350 paces, he stopped and retraced his steps carefully, searching the ground as a double check once more until he reached the clearing. There he paused, then shook his head and started due west. Three hundred and fifty paces in the snow was a quarter of a mile; three hundred on level ground. At the 267th pace to the west he spotted them; a double set of crisp indentations that indicated a man moving carefully in the deep snow. Without wasting another moment, Gillon turned and trudged back to the clearing. Skirting the edge and staying well into the trees, he stopped only long enough to check that he was moving to the northwest, in the same direction as the tracks, and with the flashlight well shielded, moved off at a trot.

Forty minutes of fast travel put him nearly two miles north of the clearing. He was sure that the officer would not have changed his cautious mode of travel . . . at least until he had gotten well clear of the trees. The forest had thinned considerably, as he had remembered, and with the moon rising now above the mountain peaks that formed the horizon to the east, he knew he would have no trouble spotting anyone moving across the open expanse of snow, the only route that led back up and over the ridge and the one which they had crossed during the afternoon, risking the chance they would be spotted. It had obviously been a bad risk.

Gillon, winded and his face an insane rictus of pain, clutched at his side and forced himself up the shallow slope at a dead run until the tops of the trees were below him. Then he sank down in the snow and leaned his head on his carbine to catch his breath. After several minutes his breathing began to ease and he became aware that he was terribly exposed on the slope in the light of the full moon. He burrowed back into the snow for both concealment and warmth, pulled his white hood down over his head and waited.

For one entire hour Gillon shivered uncontrollably until he was reduced to a semiconscious state in which only the intensity of his concentration kept him awake. Even so, it was several minutes after he caught the first flicker of movement before he realized that it meant anything.

The moon was well up, flooding the slopes with pale light. Something was moving purposefully toward the ridge where Gillon watched and waited. He had already decided that he dare not risk a rifle shot, as he had no idea how far away any larger parties of Chinese soldiers were. But if they were within hearing distance – and on a still night like this and clear of the trees, sound would carry for miles – they would be down on him quickly.

Accordingly, he waited until he was certain that the figure moving towards him was the Chinese officer, then he scrambled down the slope while the other was still in the forest, and took up a position just inside the trees and near where he figured the other must pass. Wishing to God that he had a silenced pistol, he waited.

Ten agonizing minutes passed before he heard the crunch of snow beneath boots. Moving quietly, Gillon slipped closer toward the sounds. He would only get one chance, he knew; one and if he missed, he would be dead, now or later. The man had shown that he had his wits about him and did not panic easily and with this in mind, Gillon approached him with the utmost caution. He was moving downslope now, a relatively steep slope. He had the advantage of terrain and surprise, plus he was somewhat rested while the other man was not and even now was stopping every few paces to catch his breath. Gillon first saw him clearly while still some twenty yards away. He appeared completely unaware that Gillon was near since he was not troubling to conceal his movements and his rifle was slung across his back. Gillon moved quietly until he was directly in his path, but concealed behind the trunk of a fair-sized spruce. The moon was shining across the man's shoulder silhouetting the tree but at the same time causing his shadow to lead him by several feet.

Gillon watched, judging his location by the progress of his shadow. Now he could hear his deep, racking sobs for breath, his breathing so terrible that it was a high-pitched whistle. The shadow came level with the tree trunk, then moved ahead to merge with the darkness. Gillon had estimated that the shadow was ten feet long . . . four or five steps . . . one . . . two . . . three . . . his knife was cradled in his hand, held low against his thigh . . . four . . . he exhaled carefully, emptying his lungs . . . five!

Gillon sprang from behind the tree, left hand, the empty hand, arcing up for the man's breastbone. The Chinese, caught by surprise, still was able to react fast enough to fall back a step, his right hand snapping from the elbow at the same time to deflect the blow, as Gillon had known it would. His own right hand snaked beneath the upraised arm and the knife slammed into the solar plexus. The Chinese stared at him a moment, closed his eyes and swayed forward without a sound against him. Utterly shaken, Gillon stepped back and let him slip down. He turned away and, after a bit, vomited hard into the snow.

The sky was shifting from black to meager gray as Gillon edged along the lip of the canyon, searching for signs that marked the spot where they had made camp well back into the woods. It had taken him three hours to drag the body deep into the forest, wipe out all indication that anyone had passed that way, and travel back along the way he had come, dragging a thick spruce branch to wipe out his trail. He reached the clearing an hour before dawn. Jones's body was still lying a little apart from the four soldiers. He dragged each of them deep into the trees and covered the bodies with snow, the only burial possible. He found the sixth soldier nearly thirty feet away from the clearing; he had not been killed immediately by the exploding grenade after all but, wounded as he was, the cold night had finished him. Gillon took his cap and rifle, then covered him with snow where he lay.

Then he had marched due south by his compass until he came to the edge of the canyon. Figuring that he was still east of the camp, he had gone that way for nearly two miles before he was convinced that he was mistaken. Two more miles west along the canyon rim, then another mile and he finally cut two sets of snowshoe tracks leading back into the trees.

A few minutes later, he whistled on the edge of the camp and found Dmietriev on watch, completely unaware that he and Jones had even been gone. Gillon was scheduled for the last watch and Dmietriev had been about to wake him.

Gillon handed him the cap and the rifle and described what had happened as briefly as he could, that Jones had been killed and that they were being followed by a patrol of Chinese mountain troops. Fending off Dmietriev's questions, he roused out Stowe, Rodek and Leycock and while they packed, told them as much as he thought warranted, mentioning nothing about the alternate rendezvous. At his suggestion, Leycock broke out the radio and in a few minutes, Dmietriev recorded a brief report in Russian describing Jones's death and the presence of the Chinese in the area. Leycock switched the radio on and inserted the tape cartridge. A high-pitched squeal sounded when Dmietriev pressed the transmit button and the message was sent in less than a second . . . far too fast for the Chinese to have obtained a fix, even with automatic triangulation equipment and assuming that they knew the exact frequency.

They waited the required five minutes for the Russian control station to clear the report, then signed on again. This time Dmietriev asked that an aircraft be standing by at the first landing site five miles east at sunset. Confirmation came through immediately and with it the bad news that weather was moving down out of the Arctic, pushing a high front loaded with snow into the Tien Shan. They could expect a further drop in temperature and heavy snow tomorrow night. The aircraft would be waiting for them at 1700 hours. Gillon nodded and Leycock signed off. Not giving them even a minute in which to question him, Gillon snapped out a series of orders and five minutes later, they had broken camp and were snowshoeing through the trees to the canyon's rim.

CHAPTER TWELVE

Shortly after dawn it had begun to snow, hours earlier than the prediction had led them to expect. Gillon stood beneath the branches of a tall spruce and stared up at the dark sky and worried about the pickup aircraft. They had covered the five miles from last night's camp to this spot overlooking the rendezvous site in three hours and immediately dispersed into the cover of the forest. The site had been empty on their arrival and an hour later, he had finally called Rodek in to make a wide sweep of the area for several miles around. There had been no need to caution him to watch for parties of Chinese ski troops; in the brief explanation that he had given before they broke camp, the four men had been disbelieving then angry in their first shocked reaction to the news of Jones's death. Stowe, as expected, had been the most vociferous. But none of them had objected when Gillon had begun to give orders and although Stowe had hesitated, even he had obeyed with alacrity. So far, he had been able to avoid any direct questions as to what he and Jones had been doing away from the camp.

Gillon had no doubt that his reign as group leader would last only until one of them – and undoubtedly it would be Stowe – balked. In the meantime he had to consolidate his position as much as possible if he was to retain any backing at all. The last thing he wanted was Stowe to start giving orders with his usual thoughtless rush into everything. He felt that if he could give a believable reason why he and Jones had left the camp that he might be able to depend on Dmietriev's backing, since he had, so far, shown absolutely no inclination to push himself forward. And if Dmietriev supported him, he felt certain that Rodek would follow as well.

Leycock, however, was the unknown factor. Leycock like Stowe and Jones was a professional intelligence operative and how he would feel about Gillon, an

155

amateur, giving him orders, Gillon could not even begin to guess. There had been a certain amount of antagonism between Leycock and Stowe so far and he was fairly certain that Leycock would not react kindly to Stowe taking on Jones's role. And like Dmietriev, he had shown no inclination to question any of Jones's decisions.

The one thing that they, as a group, must not allow was a breakout in discipline. Someone must make the decisions and the others must carry them out immediately and without question if they were to survive. They could not, under any circumstances, waste time arguing the merits of a decision. There was no doubt in Gillon's mind after last night that they were being pursued closely by Chinese patrols. One moment's inattention, one hour's delay and they could all be killed or captured. The one unfortunate thing was that there had not been time to take the others to the clearing and show them the bodies. The Chinese AK-47 and the cap had certainly shaken them up, but other than that, they had only his word for what had happened.

With these men, he knew that he could not force obedience; obedience only came from respect. Both would have to be earned and then would be given only as long as merited. Each and every one of them had certainly studied in detail the numerous theories of leadership and could probably quote to him at length from any one of a hundred authorities. These were four men who would not be taken in by any sham on his part, he realized uncomfortably.

Rodek came in at 1700 hours to report no sign of anyone in the area. He was dead tired and Gillon ordered him down for as much rest as he could get. He called in the others after that, having already decided long since that they had no other choice than to head for the alternate rendezvous site. From what Jones had told him, he knew they would have to be there by noon tomorrow or Liu and his people would have disappeared. Liu was playing this whole thing extremely close and Gillon was fully aware that he had to follow Jones's plan exactly.

For a short time this morning, he had considered chucking the whole thing, but there was nowhere else to go. It was fifty miles from where they were now, to the border, over some of the most rugged mountains in the world, and with only a two-day supply of food remaining they would never make it. Having come to that conclusion, he was angry with himself that he had not thought to search the dead soldiers for more food to add to their fast-dwindling supply.

Two days. Two days and they would have to be out of the Tien Shan, and with this snowstorm coming up he was not sure that they could do it. They were facing a march of fifteen miles yet tonight . . . fifteen miles in a heavy snow over completely unknown territory and in the dark as well. There was no hope for it and he trudged back to where the others waited.

Ten minutes later, a radio message had been sent to Ala Kul canceling the pickup and they moved out to begin the long trek to the alternate rendezvous point.

Gillon kept them all moving until nearly midnight. The snow had thickened to the point where even if it had been full daylight, they would have been little better off. The only thing in their favor was the fact that they were above ten thousand feet and the trees were sparse enough not to constitute a major hazard. All five men moved forward on snowshoes bent under the weight of the packs and their own exhaustion. One foot was thrust forward after another until finally legs rebelled and buckled, refusing to go further.

Leycock was the first to give out. He sank down into the snow and hollered for the rest of them to stop. Gillon judged that they had come nearly eight miles if his navigation by compass and map was correct. He shuffled back to where Stowe was waiting and double-checked his calculations against those Stowe had been making independently. Both sets differed by less than a mile and Stowe studied Gillon for a moment with what could almost have been respect.

'Surprised?' Gillon could not resist asking.

Stowe grunted and turned away. 'Let's go see what the hell's the matter with Leycock.'

Grinning, Gillon nodded and followed him back to

where Leycock was sprawled in the snow, leaning against his pack and massaging his legs.

'Damned muscle cramp, I guess . . . sorry, but I can't go any farther tonight.'

Gillon flashed his light around, but the steadily falling snow muffled everything beyond a few paces.

'All right. We might as well stop here as anywhere else. We've covered ten miles. We can do the rest easily enough by noon . . .'

He broke off as Leycock began to cough hoarsely and knelt down to shine his flashlight into his face. Except for the drawn, gray skin and bloodless lips suggesting exhaustion, Leycock seemed to be all right. His own legs were quaking to such an extent that he doubted that he could go any further himself.

The others agreed in relief and went quickly about rigging their tents.

Gillon helped Leycock and then made sure that he crawled inside his sleeping bag before he left him to set up his own. Then, before he could abandon himself to the sleep he desperately needed, he forced himself to make the rounds of the other four tents to make sure that each man had properly rigged his tent and was inside his sleeping bag, where he would not freeze to death. Guards, he considered, were an unnecessary precaution this night. There was absolutely no chance that anyone could have followed them in this heavy snow. Satisfied that he had done all he could, he crawled into his own tent.

The persistent buzzing of his watch woke him to a dawn equally as dark as the night and full of slanting, wind-whipped snow. The winds had gathered on the mountains during the night and were now raging down on the forest like an evil presence. Gillon went around to each tent, coaxing its occupant from an exhausted sleep, until they were all awake.

They ate a meager hot breakfast and shortly after 0600, were on the way again, the sky and the forest around them beginning to take on form and substance as the sky lightened. All morning they pushed on and Gillon was troubled by a vague urging that something

158

was wrong. It certainly, he thought bitterly, could not be said that their luck had changed unless it was to worsen. He wondered if their chances of leaving the Tien Shan were not approaching zero; if the Red Chinese did not get them, the weather would.

Then one of those atmospheric surprises common to the Tien Shan, common in fact to all temperate mountain areas where frictional heating often occurs as the winds surge through the high passes, happened. The wind, which had been steadily rising since dawn, threatening to turn into a major blizzard, dropped away to nothing. One minute it was whipping snow off the surface, the next, it had become only the faintest whisper of a vagrant breeze that now and then eddied the snow without disturbing its almost vertical fall. Within an hour, even the snow had diminished to flurries.

Ever since they had begun the trek to the alternate rendezvous, they had been climbing steadily; now the tall dense stands of timber had been left behind and Gillon realized that under the snow cover lay alpine meadow. The cloud cover remained thick and gray, cutting off the mountain peaks, and the long, upward slopes sweeping ahead of them had taken on the same funereal color, so that it was impossible to tell where snow ended and cloud began.

They struggled up the last ridge shortly before noon to see the terrain falling away to what appeared to be the mouth of a canyon still two miles distant and nearly a thousand feet below. It had begun to snow again, a mild snowfall that floated down gently. Clusters of stunted, wind-twisted trees marred the otherwise virgin snowscape on the slope. To the east, a line of dense black scrub pine furred the lower, far side of the valley and grew in strength until they overlapped the ridge. According to the map, that ridge then gave onto a series of valleys stepping successively down to six thousand feet to divide the slopes of the Tien Shan from the western foothills of the Khalik Tau range that stretched away east to Mongolia, separating the Dzungarian Plain from the Taklamakan Desert.

Gillon took the binoculars out of his pack and began to study the ground between the slope and the canyon.

Even at midday, the light was dimmed by the threatening clouds and the foreshortened circle of white was lacking in detail, so that it was difficult to tell if what he was seeing through the lenses actually existed or was a product of his vertiginous mind. After a few moments, he lowered the glasses and whistled softly.

'Damn, you can make yourself sick doing that,' he muttered.

A glance at his watch showed less than thirty minutes remaining till noon. He calculated that they could reach the canyon in fifteen to twenty minutes on skis and he decided that a quick lunch was in order. They broke out cold rations and ate what they could of the half-frozen, tasteless paste and washed it down with water that was barely above freezing.

'Okay, gentlemen.' Gillon grinned at them. 'Into the jaws of death . . . etc.'

'Tennyson may be appropriate,' Leycock grinned, 'but you could have picked something a little more cheerful.'

Gillon snorted and led them off down the slope. Now that the wind had diminished and the snow had stopped Gillon was certain that he could detect a drop in temperature. He half suspected that they were in for their coldest night so far if the pickup aircraft didn't get in. They were beginning to feel and show the effects of high-altitude exertion; dehydration, lack of energy, slowness of thought coupled with less than adequate sleep. The toll taken on their bodies had been fantastic. If the temperature dropped much lower, Gillon seriously doubted their ability to survive.

But at the moment, there was the mild challenge of an easy downhill slope, a fresh powder beneath their skis and the prospect that they would be out of the Tien Shan by tonight.

The snow whispered the way snow does only when it is fresh and the air is crackling cold. Gillon led off in long, exhilarating sweeps that took them easily but swiftly down the slope to the valley floor. As he came down the last bit of the slope he leaned sharply into the turn and thrust strongly for the canyon gaping open before him.

160

As with the main rendezvous of the day before, this one was also set in a canyon. Seen at its wide northern end, it appeared to wander for several miles. Gillon looked around him as he pushed for the canyon; peaks seen indistinctly through the snow towered around them, lining the sky on three sides with jagged teeth. He guessed they were no more than a mile or two distant and probably climbed to yet another three to four thousand feet. The valley was really a Y; leading down from the north from the head of a large glacial field, it had probably once been a spur of an immense glacier. One branch of the valley ran east and the other north by northwest. The meeting place was located just inside the eastern branch and if the map was correct they had less than a mile now to go. There were none of the large twenty-thousand-foot peaks visible to the southwest, although if he remembered the map correctly, some twenty miles away was the main spine of the Tien Shan. Between this valley and the main section of the range, lay a series of deep river valleys.

As they closed in on the canyon, Gillon became aware of an unaccountable tension beginning. He wasn't sure yet but it appeared that the canyon closed at the far end. The map had not suggested that it was a box canyon . . . which did not surprise him, as the maps were lacking in dependable detail and this region had not been seriously explored since 1903. Still, he did not like the idea of skiing into a box canyon in spite of the fact that it was impossible for Chinese troops to have tracked them during the snowstorm. Even if they were equipped with the latest in personnel detection devices, infrared, ultraviolet and chemical detectors, all would have been useless in the bad weather. Still, he was uneasy and he brought the group to a stop. 'This is a box canyon,' he announced flatly.

Dmietriev pushed ahead a few paces and used his binoculars to examine the walls and the portion of the canyon floor visible to them. Leycock and Stowe leaned on their ski poles, watching curiously, and Rodek unslung his carbine from his back and reversed it across his shoulders so that it lay against his chest, ready for instant use.

161

Dmietriev fell back. 'You are right. It is a closed canyon.' He paused a moment to stare around, then muttered half to himself, 'I don't like the feel of it.'

Gillon rubbed his forehead. 'I can't imagine Liu ever selecting a place like this but that's what Jones's map showed.'

'Well, hell, man, if that's what the map showed, then this must be the place. The Agency doesn't make mistakes.' Stowe's voice was mocking, but it held some of the same apprenhension that Gillon felt and he let it pass.

'Not much chance that they could have followed us last night . . . or today either,' Leycock observed half-heartedly.

Gillon studied the sparsely wooded ridge to the east with his glasses. It was heavily forested near the crest, enough to provide sufficient cover . . . He pointed in that direction.

'As long as we are still out of sight from inside the canyon, let's go up that ridge. We can take a good look at what . . or who . . . is down there before we decide to go in.'

Stowe started to object, 'For God's . . .' His hand was upraised and his mouth open but he never completed the sentence. Rodek lurched, and pushed him down. An instant later, Gillon heard the distant, flat crack of a rifle. Rodek half turned, clawed feebly at his chest, gasped and collapsed like an empty bag, one leg beneath him and his arms thrown out at odd angles. For an instant, they remained frozen in shock, then Gillon shouted and without thinking shoved off toward the canyon. He thrust desperately into the snow with the ski poles and ran for the canyon's mouth and its insignificant safety. He risked a quick glance over his shoulder and saw Stowe struggling to his feet and far behind him two long lines of white-clad ski troopers slicing down the same slope they had just negotiated. Tiny plumes of smoke showed for a second but skis are not the steadiest platform for accurate shooting at long range and he never saw where the bullets went. Rodek's body lay huddled in the snow where he had fallen. Stowe shoved him half over, hesitated a moment, then was skiing after them. With a sickening feeling, Gillon knew that Rodek was dead.

He concentrated on his skiing now, thrusting steadily with the poles to increase his speed to the maximum possible down the slight grade. They had half a mile to go and already the Chinese, fresher and stronger, had gained considerably on them. The sound of rifle shots was becoming more frequent, an indication that the distance was closing. Gillon risked another look behind and estimated that there were close to thirty troopers behind, divided into two groups; the group to their south was the closest and stood an excellent chance of cutting them off before they reached the illusory safety of the canyon. If they reached the canyon, they might put up a good defense for a while in the trees that he could now see clustered along the bottom but ultimately, when their ammunition gave out, the Chinese troopers would hit them from above as well as from ahead. There was nothing, he knew, to stop the soldiers from climbing that same ridge that Gillon had considered, crossing along the top of the canyon and swooping down on them from above.

. . . Nor, for that matter, was there anything to prevent them from doing the same thing. He tried to recall what lay on the far side. As best he could remember, the ridge gave over to a river valley that was unnamed on the map. He recalled that it fell away gradually for nearly two thousand feet to the east. The sides of the valley were sure to be thickly covered with the usual spruce and pine and perhaps if they could make the top of the ridge, they stood a chance after all. Gillon was only sure of one thing at this point and that was that he did not, under any circumstances, wish to be caught inside that canyon!

Abruptly, he made up his mind and shot off to his left, yelling for the others to follow. He risked one fast glance behind as he completed the turn and saw that they had all managed to keep up with him. Dmietriev, Leycock and Stowe may not have known what he was up to, but it would not take them long to figure it out. In the same glance, he had also seen that the Chinese had been taken by surprise and had not yet started the turn. They had gained a few seconds by surprise and those few seconds had opened a wide amount of distance between the hunted and the hunters. They were, in effect, bisecting an angle between the two flanking groups of Chinese with a line that did take them closer to the northern group, but as they were further behind to start, it made no difference.

The snow had begun to swirl faster and Gillon knew that the wind was increasing in spurts and gusts. Each time that it did so, it mixed newly fallen snow with that swept off the surface into a meager ground blizzard. It would not slow either group, Gillon knew, but it would cause the Chinese to save their ammunition.

A few minutes more and the race would really become critical, he realized. They would be starting to climb the ridge while the Chinese came on at full speed. By the time they had gone more than a few hundred feet the Chinese would be close enough for accurate firing. He fought down the fear that realization inspired and when he felt the slope beneath his skis begin to slant up, swung to a stop.

Dmietriev and then Stowe flashed past. Leycock started to swing to a stop beside him but Gillon waved him on, shouting for him to go further up the slope. Then he dropped to one knee, unslung his carbine and checked to see that the magazine was fully loaded and the two spare magazines handy in his zipped parka pocket. Then he waited, his hands shaking badly with the cold and tension for the leading Chinese troopers to come into range. If he was lucky, in the gusting snow and his white coverall, they might not have seen him stop.

But whether they did or not, they came on as if convinced of their invincibility. Gillon raised the carbine, steadied the sights on the leading figure and squeezed off a shot. The range was still too great and he lowered the carbine and waited a moment before trying again. The second time, he missed again. The third time, he saw the man's hood snap off his head but still he came on, probably not even aware that he was under fire. Pick one and keep shooting until you hit him, he had been taught, and he raised the carbine again and squeezed off the fourth shot. This time, the man went down abruptly, disappearing into a rolling flurry of snow.

Gillon shifted to the next figure and was surprised to see just how close he was. He took a deep breath and fired and missed. The second shot, however, must have hit the man low in the leg, because he crashed downward, somersaulted with his momentum and lay still for a moment before crawling rapidly away from the line of fire.

The rest of the soldiers were now too close and to discourage them before they ran right over him, he flicked the selector lever to full automatic and as he came to his feet, sprayed the carbine at the four leading men. One went down and the other three dove off to the right, kicking up flurries of snow, and dropped to the ground. Behind him he heard Leycock's carbine start up and not waiting to see its effect, he began side stepping up the slope as fast as he could move.

Several hundred feet higher he passed Leycock, lying prone in the snow, firing carefully and calmly. Gillon went past a few hundred feet further and stopped, reloaded his carbine and yelled for Leycock to get moving. The nearer line of troopers had all dropped down into the snow and were firing steadily up the slope but in the wind and snow their shooting was anything but accurate.

Gillon looked for Stowe and Dmietriev as Leycock went past and spotted them near the crest, but still a hundred yards below the tree line. Dmietriev was waving down and Gillon waved back, fired a fast clip and followed Leycock once more.

Snow swirled around them in gusty blasts completely hiding them from the troopers below for minutes at a time. It was only a matter of time until somebody was hit. The slope, which had looked so gentle from a distance, was treacherous; it was steep and covered with bare outcroppings of rock that were hidden in the general whiteness; all of this was now painfully apparent. What was worse, none were suitable for cover, but all imposed obstructions. The gusty wind and whirling snow were for Gillon almost heaven-sent.

Racing up the slope, he came level with Leycock and

165

shouted for him to stay where he was. Gillon jammed his carbine butt first into the snow and stripped off his skis. He broke them down and slipped them into the straps on his pack. It took only a few seconds to don the snowshoes, even while struggling in the snow to maintain his balance.

'Get your snowshoes on,' he yelled to Leycock, and snatched up his carbine and fired a burst downslope to discourage any pursuit that he could not see. Leycock did as he was told and a minute later was half shuffling, half running toward the crest as the wind died as suddenly as it had begun and the snow's curtain lifted for a second.

A thin whine, outraged screams of anger rose fitfully from the clustered soldiers as they caught sight of Leycock racing up the slope, and Gillon smiled for the first time in days. The troopers' rage told him that they had only skis; skis that forced a sidestepping climb up a slope, a slow and exhausting gait. Leycock had reached Stowe and Dmietriev and the three of them began to fire downslope to cover him.

The leading trooper was barely visible in the heavy snowfall less than fifty yards distant when Gillon slung his carbine and started up the slope after Leycock. Snow spurted around him twice and, so encouraged, he sprinted away on a long reach diagonally up the slope, directly under the fire from above. Within a few minutes, his overtaxed lungs were at the bursting point and he was gasping deep, sobbing draughts of air. Blood pounded so hard in his temples that he wondered if he were on the verge of a stroke, but even so, he dared not slow. Gillon knew that he had cut the margin too fine and now he was going to pay for it; it came to everyone sooner or later, he thought, sooner or later all of the chances, all the miscalculations caught up with you and combined into one overriding mistake and you bought it. He had experienced this feeling twice before, on the Laotian border and in the delta off the African coast. Both times something had intervened to cancel the mistake . . . *luck*. If you were good in this business of war and violent death, and Gillon knew he was, you fought against it right down to your dying breath and then some, if you could manage it, because luck was just that and no more.

The probing fingers of rifle fire began to search again and tiny spurts of snow plumed around him. The roar in his ears was so loud that the sounds of both firing and wind were completely obscured. For some reason, he thought of Jones. Jones had been a professional, a better one than he, and yet he had been shot dead in one of those situations that no one could have foreseen, a million to one odds that those troops had come on them in the middle of the forest . . . a forest several thousand square miles in extent.

Then as suddenly as it had begun, the firing stopped and Gillon realized simultaneously that he no longer knew where he was. He crouched down, gasping the thin air while he stared around at the swirling wilderness of white. The snow had thickened until it had closed right down, obscuring everything beyond a few feet. As the pounding in his ears began to die away, he heard the high-pitched whine of wind increasing in force.

The world had suddenly been reduced to this narrow circle of white barely ten feet in diameter. Once he thought he heard a shout, a high-pitched voice far down the slope, and groggily he pushed himself to his knees and struggled upright onto the snowshoes. The Chinese troopers would be spreading out in a long skirmish line across the face of the slope. They would move straight up the ridge toward the crest, expecting any moment to be fired upon and therefore ready for the first sign of movement.

Gillon forced himself to move upslope as fast as his aching lungs and the terrible stitch in his side would allow. The high blood pressure induced by the heavy exertion had left him with a raging headache and nausea.

It took Gillon nearly an hour to climb the remaining four hundred feet to the top of the ridge, a terrible hour of stumbling over hidden obstructions, avoiding snow-covered boulders and brush that clutched at the frames and webbing of the snowshoes; an hour of pain and nausea in the thin, cold air. Intermittently, he heard shouted orders and once the sound of a whistle as troops were mustered, but all sounds came from below. He still had the advantage of snowshoes over their skis and he could move twice as fast, but as exhausted as he was, he knew that they were about even.

Gillon reached the top of the cliff by the simple expedient of tripping on the abruptly level ground. He rested where he had sprawled for several long minutes before the iron bite of the cold and the snow drove him to his feet. He had no idea where he was in relation to the others. When the snow had closed down, he had been moving diagonally across the slope and now he was unsure whether or not he had passed their last position. He knelt in the snow and listened intently for several minutes but only the steady keen of the wind was audible.

A figure materialized suddenly, carbine swinging toward his face. Gillon stumbled aside on the snowshoes, and fended the blow on his right arm, left hand snatching the knife from the sheath behind his neck. Before he could strike, he was face to face with Stowe. Stowe fell back and lowered the carbine.

'For God's sake, we've been searching all over hell for you . . .' Stowe shouted to make himself heard above the wind. 'We thought those bastards had gotten you.'

Gillon shook his head. 'Not yet . . . where are the rest?'

Stowe took him by the arm and led him along the rim of the canyon to where Leycock and Dmietriev were sheltering just inside the fringe of pines.

A hurried discussion of the position convinced them that they did not stand a chance if they remained where they were. It would not be long before the Chinese troopers gained the top. In the brief argument over which direction to take, for once Gillon found himself in agreement with Stowe. They must head back into the mountains as quickly as possible. Liu and his people had not kept either rendezvous and so it was a safe bet that the Chinese had intercepted them.

Either way, all ideas of completing the mission were now irretrievably lost; on that they all agreed. Their overriding concern was now to get themselves out alive, a feeling to which Gillon heartily subscribed. Roped together once more to avoid losing each other in the heavy snow, the four men headed in the direction of the Khalik Tau.

Gillon led them deeper and deeper into the forest as the hours lengthened. The ground had begun to slope steadily downward toward the first of the low-lying river valleys well to the east of the rendezvous locations. Occasionally they crossed wide clearings in the trees but could see nothing but swirling snow around them. Not once did the snow ease and Gillon knew that the snow-fall of the night before had only been a prelude to this blizzard. He was also aware that they were now down to one final day's rations and unless the snow let up soon there would be no chance of getting a plane in to pick them up tonight. If that happened and the Reds picked up their trail again, they stood a good chance of never leaving the Tien Shan alive. Only once during the long afternoon did they stop and then only long enough for Leycock to rig the radio and Dmietriev to report to Ala Kul that Rodek had been killed and that they were being driven eastward by Chinese ski troops. Of the last, Gillon had absolutely no doubt. The Chinese, now that they had been seen, would never end the hunt until they were killed or captured. Gillon knew that they would certainly guess they had gone over the ridge and into the valley rather than attempt to skirt the ridge above the canyon and double back. It was the only way open that allowed even the meagerest chance. Even now, he was sure that at least one party of Chinese troops was pushing on fast to be down into the valley ahead of them when the snow should let up. He also knew that as soon as the weather moderated, more troops would be parachuted in to surround them. They were, in effect, in the center of a slowly tightening noose and their only hope was to outrun the far side.

Dmietriev signed off and while Leycock replaced the radio, Dmietriev translated the message.

'There has been no word at all for two days from our contact. Moscow reports that a battalion of ski troops has been moved into this area and that a second battalion is also being brought in.'

'Oh, Christ,' Gillon muttered.

'The weather report is equally bad. That high pressure area has moved down out of the Arctic sooner than they had anticipated. We can expect snow and blizzard conditions for at least another two days. They suggest that we hide somewhere until the snow stops.'

'Nuts,' Gillon snorted. 'We do that and with one whole battalion already looking for us . . . we wouldn't stand a chance.'

Dmietriev shrugged. 'Perhaps . . . but then, in this snow, they will not find us anyway.'

Stowe had been listening to the argument and now he leaned forward and stared hard at Gillon. 'Dmietriev is right. We need to find somewhere to camp . . . the gooks won't be able to find us in this snow.'

'You keep thinking of them as *gooks* and we'll be dead before you know what's happened,' Gillon snapped back. 'These aren't guerrilla soldiers, half-starved and as much concerned with finding something to eat and a place to sleep as finding us. These are trained mountain troops. You saw how neatly they sprang that ambush on us a couple of hours ago . . . they may not be able to track us during the blizzard, but it won't take them long to find us after the snow stops. If we don't get as far away from this area as possible, we'll never get out alive.'

'He's right,' Leycock said unexpectedly. 'Don't forget one thing. No one has heard from this mysterious contact we are supposed to meet. In both Moscow and Washington . . . and probably Peking, and every other goddamned capital in the world . . . they know by now that there was no one at either rendezvous site to meet us. As far as they are concerned, the mission is a failure. And if you think they are going to exert themselves to get us out . . . you're crazy.'

'That's nonsense,' Stowe interrupted. 'The last thing in the world the United States wants is for us to be caught here . . .'

'Exactly,' Gillon interrupted in turn. 'Think it out, man! We've failed, the mission has failed. No one gains anything? Of course the United States doesn't want us caught . . . but the Russians, there's another matter. If the Chinese take us, then the Russians have a propaganda victory at least. Americans captured by Chinese soldiers while on espionage mission in Chinese territory. Think how that'll sound. The Russians will have gained, even if no one else does.'

'Wait just a moment . . .' Dmietriev began angrily.

'Shut-up, Colonel . . . can't you see it? You are as expendable as the rest of us. There never was a Colonel Andre Dmietriev with the GRU . . . or at least there isn't now. If we don't get out of here alive or without being captured . . . you have suddenly become one very *un*-person.'

Gillon watched the Russian's face, as he spoke, go from anger to thoughtfulness to apprehension. Certainly well acted, Gillon thought. And he had no doubt that if things worked out as he had just described, that Dmietriev had already thought them through and arrived at the same conclusion . . . in fact, Gillon suspected, Dmietriev's orders probably covered just such a contingency. But he wondered. Just what arrangements had the Americans made to counter any such Soviet duplicity? There was no honor among thieves, or among governments who thought they were competing for survival, for that matter. Whatever the arrangements were, they had died with Jones.

A heavy silence fell over the four men as they considered the implications of the latest turn of events. The snow swirled wildly through the trees in time to the wild keen of the wind. It settled on the folds of their snowsuits and the mounds of their packs, on their carbines and faces until eyelashes and eyebrows, moustaches and beards were covered with white frosting.

'We have no other choice but to keep moving,' Gillon said finally. 'The border is thirty miles west, straight-line distance from where we sit . . . and you can bet your boots that the Chinese will have a good half of their available forces between us and the border, just watching for us to try. Half of the rest will be concentrated in a line north of us to the next nearest border crossing and the rest will be marching as fast as they can to get around in front. There is absolutely nothing to be gained by going any further east . . . twenty miles more and we run out of mountains and in the high desert

171

they'll pick us off in no time. So we go south in an end run and hope that their football strategy is damned rusty.'

The others slowly nodded agreement in silence and once more they started out again.

Gillon led the way, compass always in his hand, as they negotiated the thick forest and occasional change in terrain. By late afternoon, the downslope became definite once more and Gillon was sure they were nearing the Chiran-toka River.

As they descended, the forest grew thicker until, at times, it was almost impenetrable. The terrain here was rugged in the extreme, full of glacially deposited boulders and fallen trees that often forced extensive detours, until Gillon was no longer sure of anything but that they were still moving downslope. As they descended from the ten-thousand-foot plateau, breathing began to come easier and as Gillon had counted on, they revived somewhat to remain just this side of exhaustion awhile longer. If the slope had been uphill for any distance, he was certain they would have all collapsed within an hour.

The one point in their favor, he realized, was that they were professionals; each of them had been in similar situations before where they were required to exert themselves to the utmost, long after other men would have collapsed. They knew, each and every one of them, that the stakes were no less than their lives. And while they might differ as to the approach to be taken in extricating themselves from the depths of the Tien Shan, they would each push on until exhaustion forced total collapse. Not until then would they stop. Gillon knew this and was depending first on their strength, and secondly on their desperation to keep them going. There was also the chance that by now, the blizzard had become too much for the pursuing troops and that they had holed up. He had meant every word he said to Stowe about not underestimating the Chinese. But that did not prevent him from reckoning on *their* underestimation of them to save their lives.

At 1800 hours, they stopped and cooked a hasty, hot meal, rested for thirty minutes and continued the march

172

into the night. The trees had thinned considerably by the time they reached the mid-slopes of the valley, making travel somewhat faster. Gillon calculated that it was still eight miles to the river; his goal was to cross and march deep into the forest on the far side before they stopped for sleep.

Silently they marched on, and in the faint light from his shielded flash, the vague slope to the land was no longer apparent; there was only the white, continuously moving circle of hypnotic light that preceded them, broken occasionally by a tree trunk or the top of some bush barely thrusting wiry branches above the snow. His snowshoes followed the trailing edge of the circle of light, which itself was guided by the compass needle, and Gillon pushed on, knowing that he was half hypnotized by its bobbing glare, but not caring because it made it that much easier to drag himself forward.

There was no longer any doubt in Gillon's mind that Jack Liu and his people were dead or captured and that they were now completely on their own. His analysis of their situation earlier was, he knew now, the only accurate one. Unless they could be picked up without exposing the hand of the Soviet Union in this whole affair, they would be abandoned. At the very least, the Soviets would gain the disintegration of the Sino-American rapprochement.

He wondered as they trudged along just how the Reds had taken Liu. However it had been, it would not have been an easy task. The wind swirled the icy snow crystals around him, but for just a moment, he felt again the sun beating down on his back and tasted the dry, gritty dust and felt the grinding pain in his legs. For three hours they had taken turns in relays, pounding away at his leg muscles, and the cramps that twisted and tugged at his strapped legs were almost more than he could bear. Every fifteen minutes, they stopped while an officer, a tiny old man with a wispy moustache and a pleasant smile, asked him politely in French if he had reconsidered and would now tell them where the ambush was to take place. Each time he had shaken his head, his mouth, nostrils and eyes full of the talcum-like red dust that covered the narrow trail on which he

lay. The sun and the thirst and the fact that he knew
that they would go on like this until he was dead . . .
made it a certainty that he would talk eventually. They
were clever at their trade, these Pathet Lao regulars.
They knew how to adjust their torture to avoid pushing him into insanity with pain, knew how to keep him
balancing on the edge of agony until he either told them
what they wanted to know or died. And Gillon knew
that he would never last long enough to die; no one
could, unless he was insane to begin.

Time after time they had stopped and he had shaken
his head and the officer had dribbled a bit more liquid
from the canteen near his face so that he could smell
the water as it disappeared into the dust.

Then had come a moment when the rifle butt had
not fallen. He had been counting the blows, thirty per
minute, and then they changed off to the other leg.
Fifteen changes and the officer asked his question and
the water dripped into the dust near his face. They had
not varied the routine in three hours. He had raised his
head in puzzlement, but could no longer see clearly, and
for a long moment, the officer's twisted face had con-
fused him. Then he heard the snapping of small-arms
fire and thudding feet around him. He saw camouflage
uniforms running from the growth along the trail and
Jack Liu was in front, pistol in one hand and knife in
the other. The pistol fired twice and he fainted.

When he awoke, it was long after dark and he was
being jolted through the jungle on a stretcher sling. He
could just see the faint outline of the carrying pole and
then moonlight flooded everything as they crossed a
clearing that marked the beginning of the hills. The
swaying of the stretcher made him sick and he vomited.

Someone whispered and the column halted and he was
laid carefully on the ground. The moonlight was bright
enough to show that it was Liu bending over him.

'How are you feeling, Bob . . . ?'

In answer, Gillon choked and gagged once more and
Liu put an arm around his shoulders and lifted his head
to ease the reflex. After it had passed, Liu wet a cloth
and bathed his face, then carefully poured water into
the palm of his hand and urged Gillon to drink.

174

'Can you hold out until we reach the camp . . . ? I'll be able to get some morphine for your legs . . .'

Gillon tried to answer but found that he could not work his lips enough to form words, nor could he force any sound at all past his aching throat. He nodded his head and Liu spread the cloth over his eyes and ordered the column forward once more.

For hours they traveled, but always uphill. He floated in and out of consciousness and he thought he remembered a period of delirium when he tried to call out for help, but he was never sure whether he managed any sound or not. For hours they traveled until at last he could no longer find the pale glimmer of moonlight through the cloth and he must have slept deeply then, because there was bright sunlight under the trees when he awoke once more.

An old Meo woman sat near him, fanning away the flies and when he turned his head to look at her, she stared back without emotion. The fan moved steadily, never missing a beat, and after a bit she went back to staring at the distant hills, ignoring him so completely that she might have been fanning herself.

His head was propped on a hard pillow and he could look around him. After a few minutes, everything slid into focus and he recognized their base camp high in the hills near the North Vietnamese border. After a few minutes, an American walked across the compound toward him. It was no one that Gillon had ever seen before, and although dressed in a pair of khaki slacks and open-necked sport shirt, the pistol strapped to his waist indicated that he was well aware that there was a war on. The man stopped beside his stretcher and stared down at him, a friendly grin on his face.

'How you feeling, buddy?' He did not wait for an answer but squatted down, raised the blanket and studied Gillon's legs.

'Not too bad for the beating you took,' he answered his own question. 'Not bad at all. You go out today and they'll be able to give you some decent care in Tokyo.'

'How bad are they?' The words came out in an awkward croak but Gillon was surprised that he could speak at all, the way his throat ached. The memory of the trail and the long trek came back in an instant's searing pain.

'Like I said, not bad at all. Your legs are going to be as tender as hell for a month or so, but I don't think there'll be any permanent damage.'

The intense blue sky and the heat were combining to rob him of consciousness again and for a long time afterward he was never sure whether he had heard the story from the CIA doctor or had dreamed it all.

He had been leading a scouting mission, ahead of his band of Meo tribesmen, up near the border. Liu was one of those nameless and unidentifiable people who came, stayed awhile and disappeared, all ostensibly working for the Laotian royalist government, as was he, but usually as a matter of convenience only. A Chinese had appeared one day, introduced himself as Jack Liu and presented all the proper credentials. Since then, he had become an invaluable member of Gillon's unit and a close friend. This particular day they had received word that a combat unit, fresh from rest and refit in North Vietnam, was moving down one of the thousands of pathways that made up the Ho Chi Minh Trail. Gillon's assigned task was to intercept, destroy and return with prisoners for interrogation. Accordingly, they had moved out and set up their ambush. Gillon and one guide had moved carefully up the trail to try to obtain a firsthand look at how large and well equipped was the force they would be facing. Either the guide had betrayed them, or else had been taken by surprise and killed, as Gillon suddenly found himself surrounded by black-pajamaed Pathet Lao troops.

Perhaps, Gillon thought long afterward, someone else would have figured that Gillon had been taken and made to talk . . . it being axiomatic that anyone captured by the Pathet Lao would talk or die. By rights, Liu should have withdrawn and quickly, before he found himself the victim of a similar ambush. Instead, Liu had sent the main body back toward the hills in an apparent retreat, but had moved quickly with a handful of men across and around south of the trail until he had found Gillon. A surprise attack had killed or routed the Pathet Lao. Later that day, a helicopter flew him out to an airfield in Thailand and the next thing he remembered was the soft freshness of the sheets in the Tokyo hospital. He had not seen Liu since that night on the trail. In spite of that, he knew Liu had risked his life for him and that was a bond not easily forgotten. Yet tonight it had been broken for him and there was nothing, not a damned thing, that he could ever do about it.

Shortly before midnight, they reached a depression in the snow that became a wide, flat surface and he knew they had reached the river. They had come down through thick stands of aspen, clambered over a sharp dip and edged out onto a smooth surface nearly a quarter of a mile wide. On the far side was an identical dip and again, more aspens. The ground climbed sharply upward to the beginnings of the spruce forest. Barely able to keep his eyes open and his feet moving, Gillon trudged on without thought of rest now, knowing that if they stopped, they would never go on again.

For another hour they climbed higher and higher until the ground crested and flattened. Gillon paused, breathing heavily, and shone his flashlight around. They were deep into the trees again and he was certain that they had passed beyond the tightening circle of Chinese troops. If his assumption was correct, then they stood a chance once more.

They stumbled on until they found a small clearing. In the swirling snow, the flashlight was insufficient to show details, but even so the clearing appeared suitable for their needs. Tall spruces rose straight from the floor of the forest to hide their crowns in the gloom above. Gillon guessed that they roofed together about sixty feet or so above the ground and that would provide all the cover from air search they would need.

'Here!' he gasped out, and like automatons, the others dropped their packs, broke out the tents and in minutes were collapsed inside and dead to the world in their utter exhaustion.

Gillon trudged into the trees for several yards, forcing himself to take the elementary precaution of searching

177

the immediate area. He was not sure what he would find or that he would be able to do anything about it if he did, but the precaution had to be taken. The cold had settled down until he was certain that it was well below zero; he guessed that the wind was blowing at speeds close to twenty miles an hour and the combined effects of wind and temperature produced a chill factor of between forty and fifty-two below zero Fahrenheit. To try to mount a guard in their weakened condition would only have invited a quick death by freezing. Gillon gave up halfway around the circuit and found his way back to his own tent. He had just enough strength left to strip off his boots, brush the worst of the snow off his suit and crawl into the sleeping bag before he collapsed.

CHAPTER THIRTEEN

Gillon fought his way out of a drugged sleep like an exhausted swimmer struggling for the unobtainable mirror surface. He opened his eyes to a diffuse light filling the stuffy tent. Above his face there was a sheen of frost crystals on the nylon underside where his breath had condensed during the night and frozen into tiny stalactites. It was daylight of their fifth day in the Tien Shan, he realized finally. His watch showed 0800 hours: long past the time that they should have been on the trail. He struggled out of the seductively warm folds of the sleeping bag and crammed his feet into the half-frozen boots that he had forgotten to tuck underneath the sleeping bag the night before.

Pulling his parka on he crawled reluctantly from the tent into the bitter cold, cold so intense that it snatched his breath away and he had to cover his mouth and nose with his gloved hands. In the half-light, the forest was low and menacing. Only the tops of the four tents showed above the newly fallen snow; at each end warm air from the interior had seeped out during the night to create saucer-like depressions around the tent flaps. Gillon reached back inside for his snowshoes and strapped them on, chafing his frozen boots as he did so to soften the leather.

At least two additional feet of snow had fallen after they stopped for the night, certainly more than enough to cover any last trace of their passage from the pursuing Chinese ski troops. He crumbled a handful of snow between his gloved fingers, judging the consistency of the fine, frozen powder to be perfect for skiing. That of course could work against them, he realized. It would be just as perfect for the Chinese.

Remembering the steep ridge they had climbed last night, he figured that it was less than half a mile back. If he recalled correctly, the slope to the ridge was bare of trees near the top and might just afford him a vantage point from which he could survey the river valley below. He took his bearings with the compass and set out through the trees.

As Gillon trudged on, his boots warmed and the cold ache began to leave his feet. In spite of six hours of uninterrupted sleep, he was still exhausted. It was an effort to move one snowshoe forward after the other. They had been very near the point of collapse when they had stopped; closer even than he had realized. Looking back now over the previous day and night's march, Gillon was convinced that if they hadn't stopped when they did, they would have collapsed within another hour and died from cold and exhaustion. He knew that it was only the warmth of the tents and the sleeping bags that had saved their lives. In mountains this high and this cold, the human body was horribly vulnerable; the slightest miscalculation of resources could easily cost your life.

There was a curiously muffled quality to the forest, weighted down as it was by the thick blanket of snow. Even the wind had died away and the snow-laden spruces stretched quietly toward the gray sky. The pristine whiteness of the newly fallen snow was marred only with grayish shadows left by the snowshoe webbing. Shortly, the ground began to slope and the wall of trees before him thinned perceptibly. Gillon moved carefully now, using the trees for cover as he approached the ridge.

179

A few moments later, he broke out of the trees to find the ridge covered with scrub bushes and several feet of snow. He took off his snowshoes and thrust them into the snow beside a tree, then with his binoculars, he crawled forward until he could peer over the broken and jumbled rock of the crest and down into the valley.

The view was breathtaking, even in the flat light of the overcast morning. The ridge fell away steeply to the river nearly a thousand feet below, where a barely discernible fringe of snow-covered aspens marched along both banks, outlining the white thread of the frozen river itself. The whole snowscape before him was painted in shades of gray and white as if done by a master Japanese artist. Peering down on the frozen river, it was inconceivable that they had accomplished the climb in the darkness and the howling blizzard. Spruce and cedar reached skyward, yet the tops were still several hundred feet beneath him.

Gillon searched the valley with the glasses until the cold finally drove him back from the edge. He had seen no trace of movement. In spite of the fact that the sound should have been audible for miles at this altitude, he had not heard a single aircraft engine. The absence of aircraft could very well mean that the Reds were searching farther to the northwest for them, concentrating on the canyons and plateaux around the rendezvous sites and west toward the Khalik Tau. If so, then they had managed to travel far enough south . . . at least fifteen miles, he estimated . . . during the afternoon and night to break completely out of the closing ring.

Gillon fastened on the snowshoes and started back to rouse the others. He wanted to circle back to the north, where the map showed a level area large enough for the pickup aircraft to land. Every mile farther from the search area and toward the border increased their chances of survival, chances that yesterday afternoon had been nonexistent. By tonight, they would be out of the Tien Shan and back at Ala Kul . . . providing they managed to elude the Chinese search parties for the rest of the day. He hurried back through the trees, following his own trail.

Less than two hundred yards from the camp he came

across a set of snowshoe tracks crossing his own at right angles. As an iron hand of fear clamped down on his chest, he knelt slowly to examine the tracks. They showed plainly that the other traveler had milled around a moment while he examined Gillon's trace, then had gone off to the east. Thirty yards away, the tracks joined a second and third pair.

The snowshoes were the oval bear-paw type and none of them were wearing bear-paws; all had the long, narrow trail shoes. Gillon got up slowly, his heart pounding hard in his chest. As he glanced toward the trees, a single white-clad figure materialized, cradling a carbine in his arms. The two men stared at each other in surprise and before Gillon could move, more figures stepped out of the trees into view, all with weapons leveled. Behind, he heard the soft crunch of snow and he realized he had been neatly encircled.

Gillon was painfully aware that except for the pistol, zipped into the inside pocket of his parka, he was unarmed. The carbine was still in his tent and his throwing knife was of absolutely no value. The troopers closed in remorselessly, faces hidden by the hoods of their snowsuits.

'I guess some people will just never learn not to walk into traps.'

Gillon heard the voice and for a long moment the meaning of the words did not register. Jack Liu stopped in front of him and pushed back his hood to reveal a wide grin.

'Christ, buddy, how many times do I have to pull you out of trouble before you learn?'

Gillon gave a shout of laughter and they rushed at each other, chortling like two fools.

'How in the hell did you find us?' Gillon managed to gasp out after a moment. 'I would have bet that no one could have followed us through that damned blizzard?'

Liu grinned, waved at the others and started walking toward the camp. Still shaken by surprise, Gillon fell into step beside him, unable to believe that Liu was still alive and that he had managed to locate them after all.

'I've got to admit, no one else could have. I just

figured that if I were you and I managed to get myself out of that ambush, that I'd just keep on going up and over that canyon wall and down the other side as fast and as far as I could go. So then it was only a matter of figuring out just how far west you would go before you realized that there was no percentage in heading into the Khalik Tau. When the snow really hit, I figured, not knowing the country, that you all would hole-up until the snow quit. So to get ahead of you, we camped at the river and this morning climbed the ridge, where we could watch for you. If we hadn't spotted the tracks you made a while ago, we'd still be waiting for you to cross the river. I thought you might get that far, but it never seemed possible that you could climb the ridge in the dark.'

'What the hell,' Gillon chuckled. 'We iron men are capable of magnificent and outstanding feats.'

Liu laughed and translated for the rest of his men, following behind, and they laughed in appreciation. A moment later, the group broke into the clearing. Stowe had just crawled from his tent and was peering about him at the forest as Gillon had done an hour earlier. The expression on his face as the Chinese troopers came out of the trees was one that Gillon would not have missed for anything.

'Hold it, Chuck,' he shouted. Stowe had started to duck into the tent for his carbine. He stuck his head back out and Gillon waved. Reluctantly, he crawled from the tent and stood up.

'These are the people we've come to see,' Gillon yelled, waving a hand to take in the troopers clustering around the tents.

Within a few minutes, the Chinese strike team's rations – almost as meager as theirs – had been pooled and were cooking over the small fires. While they ate, Gillon and Liu laughed and joked, slapping each other on the arms like two schoolboys, in their relief at finding each other alive.

'When we didn't see you at the main rendezvous and were ambushed at the alternate site, we figured that you had bought it,' Gillon summed up. 'We decided that the

182

best thing left for us to do was get out as fast as we could.'

Liu slapped Gillon's leg fondly. 'It's a damned good thing that you did. Otherwise, we would have tramped way out here for nothing.'

'Moscow claims to have lost contact with you,' Stowe broke in. 'Is that true or are they feeding us a line . . . ?'

Dmietriev glanced warily at Stowe, shook his head and returned his concentration to the ration pack. Liu studied him a moment before he answered.

'Yes, it is true that they did lose contact with us. The Reds were waiting for us at the main rendezvous . . .'

He stopped at the look of surprise on Gillon's face. 'They were waiting for you . . . how the hell could they be . . . ?'

Then it dawned on Gillon. The group of soldiers that had killed Jones had not been searching for them, they must have been on the way to the rendezvous to set up the ambush and stumbled across the two of them as they talked in the forest.

'They were waiting for us as we came down into the valley,' Liu answered. 'But we must have arrived before they were set. We spotted them moving into position soon enough to pull back but a squad sent around to cut off our retreat caught us in the open. I lost my radio operator and the radio.'

'I'll be damned,' Gillon breathed. 'So that's why . . .' He got up and motioned Liu away from the fire, ignoring the suspicious stares that Stowe, Leycock and Dmietriev gave him. Liu got to his feet and followed, a quizzical look on his face.

'Look, the night before that, Jones and I had gone out into the forest so that he could brief me in detail without the others overhearing. The Chicoms spotted us and shot Jones but missed me. I assumed they were the bunch trailing us . . . but maybe they weren't after all. We set off an avalanche down Musart Pass that we figured wiped out any pursuit for at least two or three days . . .'

'Jones was . . . ?' Liu asked.

'The jerk in charge of this collection of idiots,' Stowe

183

answered, walking over to join them. 'He managed to get killed early on . . . saved himself a lot of trouble.'

Gillon turned slowly, barely able to control his rage. 'You bastard,' he whispered. 'I've had about all I'm going to take from you. Open your mouth one more time and I'll shut it for you for good.'

Stowe stepped back, shifting his weight onto his rear leg in a defensive stance, and smiled thinly at Gillon. Gillon was half hoping that he would take up the challenge, while at the same time fully aware that this was neither the time nor place to fight. But Stowe relaxed and grinned at him. 'Whatever you say, boss, whatever you say.' And walked away.

As Gillon turned, Liu stepped back; his right hand was resting casually on his holstered pistol. He made as if to say something then thought better of it.

'A real winner,' was Liu's only comment, and Gillon nodded, still angry but now with himself, rather than Stowe. 'We had better break out the radio and report in. I want to get a plane in by tonight to take us all out.'

As they started toward the tents, Gillon yelled for Leycock to follow and he trotted up, grinning from ear to ear.

'Hot damn, maybe we can get out of this overgrown icebox and get a decent night's sleep tonight.'

His enthusiasm was infectious and Gillon's anger at Stowe's obstreperousness was vanishing. He grinned at Leycock and slapped him on the shoulder. In the last few days, he realized, he had come to depend more and more on Leycock. He was willing where Stowe was sullen, decisive where Dmietriev was hesitant. He had noticed that in their marches, Leycock always brought up the rear and his constant joking and encouragement kept the other two from straggling.

Leycock crawled inside the tent for the radio. A moment later he backed slowly out, turning to look up at Gillon with a stricken face. Gillon stared at him in puzzlement until he realized that Leycock was holding out the canvas-covered radio pack. The front flap was folded back and the faceplate of the transceiver was cracked and the metal top dented badly. When Leycock threw the power switch, there was no answering hum.

* * *

The closely spaced contour lines on the map began to build a mental picture of the terrain as Liu's finger traced out their route. The more Gillon thought about it, the less he liked it. It took them too close to the Khailik Mebuse Col and he was certain that the Chinese Reds would have stationed a sizable body of troops there to prevent an escape attempt at that point; a point only eight miles short of the border. It was far too dangerous; not only would troops be patrolling that area but aircraft would be concentrated heavily in the vicinity, especially as it became clearer that they had escaped the tightening net above the Chiran-toka.

'But that is just it, Bob.' Jack Liu tapped the map with a finger to emphasize his point. 'It is the most unexpected thing that we can do. First of all, we will be at least three miles south of the col in heavy forest . . . the only open ground is along the south branch of the Musart River. Secondly, the slopes of the Tengri Khan are the most obvious place to cross . . . therefore they will never figure that you would try, even though they will guard the pass carefully in case you do.'

'Try that again,' Leycock muttered. 'I'm not sure that it made sense.'

'Look,' Liu said patiently. 'This is like a chess match . . . the object is to figure out what your opponent is thinking and use that to beat him. Look at it this way. The Khailik Mebuse Pass above the Tagrak-Yailak Glacier is the shortest way to the border. But it's all open country and they would find you easily. So some smart general will reason this way: The Americans are too smart to make such an obvious move. But, because it is so obvious, we will not waste many troops in guarding it closely . . . so it becomes the best opportunity for the Americans and therefore we will put a very strong guard on the passes to catch them when they do come.'

'Of course . . .' Leycock broke in, but before he could go on, Liu motioned for him to wait.

'The next question to ask is where will those soldiers

be? . . . in the col, of course,' he answered his own question. 'They will watch the col above and not the forest below. Therefore, the way to the glacier will be wide open and you should be able to cross the glacier at night or under a heavy cloud cover that would keep aircraft away. The border is only a few miles away there.'

Gillon said nothing, waiting for him to continue, and Leycock nodded to indicate that his question had been answered.

'Okay,' Liu said. 'If we are agreed to go south of the col, then by nightfall, I can turn you over to a caravan and start you on your way.'

'Caravan,' Gillon yelped. 'A caravan of what . . . ?'

'A caravan of Kalmuck traders.' Liu grinned in delight at the reaction he had evoked.

'Listen,' Gillon broke in, 'we ran across a caravan the first night. They were heading for an abandoned monastery below Musart Pass, where we had holed up for some sleep.'

Liu nodded. 'I know the place. It used to be a stop on the caravan trails. It was abandoned for some reason before the turn of the century. No one seems to know why.'

'Do you suppose it's the same caravan?'

Liu nodded. 'I don't doubt it. It's the only caravan that moves this early in the season.'

Gillon shook his head. 'I'll be damned. It seems like this would be one of the most deserted areas in the world. But every time we turn around, we fall over somebody else. We couldn't figure out why a caravan would be traveling at night and so we beat it in case their intentions were not peaceable.'

'This particular caravan always travels at night until they get well into the range. They have a long way to go and the competition is stiff. In fact, not even the government knows that they are on the move. They go south every spring to the Atabashi range in northern Afghanistan for the summer rendezvous. The Communists on both sides of the border have pretty well discouraged the caravans and ruined the caravan routes. They don't like the idea that so many people can come and go across a border without being controlled.'

186

At that Gillon sat up. 'Without being controlled . . . what do you mean by that?'

'Aha. Now you're interested, hey? These people have been traveling these routes for nearly twenty-five hundred years. A little thing like governments and armed soldiers are not going to stop them. So both Red China and the Soviet Union have made a deal with the remaining caravan masters. If they will register their caravans and routes, they will not be taxed heavily and will be allowed to cross the border at selected points. And that's fine for some of these people. But others are less civilized. They do not like governments and do not recognize their right to tell them where they can and cannot go. These Kalmucks are strictly traders. They start their annual trek about this time each year. It takes them two months and they arrive in mid-June, just as the fair begins.'

'How do you know they will take us in?' Gillon asked.

'The caravan master owes me a favor, a damned sizable favor. So there is no need to worry about that.'

Gillon sighed. 'Okay, so where do we meet this paragon of stealth?'

Liu grinned and pointed to the map. 'About eight miles south of the pass, there's a flat meadow at eight thousand feet. If my guess is right, we should meet them here at sunset.'

'And from there . . . ?'

'And from there, the caravan moves southwest, crosses the north and south forks of the Jam River and, staying on this side of the border, marches to the Kok-shal River. From there, they go upriver and cross into the Soviet Union in the Atabashi Mountains and finally into Afghanistan. But you won't dare stay with them that long. Once the Reds find you're not inside their net or at one of the logical border crossings, they'll start searching in earnest for that caravan. When they find it, they'll search it from top to bottom. So you are going to leave the caravan about three days' march south, cut back north until you reach the southern slopes of the Tengri Khan. You'll cross the Tagrak-Yailak Glacier and the border will be right in front of you. From there on you are on your own.'

Gillon was silent for a moment, studying the map. Leycock and Dmietriev watched for his reaction. Stowe had been squatting on his heels, staring around at the soldiers as if it did not matter one bit to him what they did. Now he asked suddenly, 'What do you mean, we're on our own? Where the hell are you going to be?'

Liu stared hard at Stowe a moment before answering. The silence stretched out uncomfortably while the two men watched each other.

'We have other plans,' Liu said finally. 'We'll discuss them later.'

Gillon knew by the tone of Liu's voice that he would say no more at the moment and there was no use in pressing him. He stood up quickly to head off any further protest from Stowe.

'All right, Jack. There doesn't seem to be any other way out of here . . . and you know this territory better than any of us. Let's go find your caravan.'

'Wait a minute,' Dmietriev objected, and remained where he was as Leycock got slowly to his feet.

'Yeah, let's wait a minute,' Leycock said quietly.

'Get up!' Gillon snarled at Dmietriev, ignoring Leycock. Startled, Dmietriev made as if to rise, then sank back onto his heels. Gillon took a step forward.

'I said get up.'

Dmietriev glanced from him to Leycock and then to Stowe, who was watching with a grin. Dmietriev started to shake his head, then thought better of it and got to his feet, face red with anger.

'I said we follow the plan Jack's laid out . . . it's the only chance we have to get out of here. Anyone who doesn't like it is on their own.'

'And that means,' Liu said slowly, 'that I'll shoot anyone who stays behind so the Reds can't find out what we're up to.'

Dmietriev nodded curtly and stamped away to his tent. Leycock followed thoughtfully and with a glance at the ring of Chinese troopers, Stowe went after them.

Gillon took a deep breath. He had weathered that crisis, but he knew a next one would not be so easy.

The combined group trailed through the forest, two point men skiing ahead while the main party followed on snowshoes. Liu had detailed two men to lag behind to watch their rear and periodically, they came skiing up to report while two more were dropped back to replace them.

'Took us about a month during the first winter to work out this technique,' Liu explained to Gillon. 'We learned a lot those first months . . . and it cost us a lot. We came in with twenty-five men. Now we have sixteen. But we lost only two men this winter; one got separated from his patrol and froze to death, and the radio operator who was killed yesterday. The others were all lost last winter . . . and all because we hadn't learned to take the right precautions.'

The group, numbering twenty men, drifted through the forest like so many ghosts. It was impossible to wipe away all traces of their passage but each man knew to avoid contact with tree branches where bent or broken needles would tell a sharp-eyed scout that someone had passed; that you stepped lightly both to conserve energy and to soften the impact of snowshoes or skis. Behind the party came three men equipped with drags fashioned from parachutes and filled with snow, which they pulled along behind with ropes. The nylon pillows filled in the tracks; time and wind would level the surface.

Morning waned into afternoon and still they moved through the endless forest in the gray half-light that filtered down through the thick cloud cover. They were moving now down a definite slope and if the forest had been more open, they could have traveled faster on skis. But the trees were still too closely spaced for twenty skiers to move safely. The party crossed two large ridges, struggling up extremely steep slopes and then fighting to maintain balance as they came down the far sides. Gillon had about given up on the maps. They were accurate only as far as general direction and gross terrain features were concerned, but were worse than useless for estimating distances and altitudes from which he could calculate the effort that would be required along a given route.

They stopped in the late afternoon above a wide valley. The Musart River was somewhere to their left and it was in this area that Liu expected to find the caravan. Gillon was sitting somewhat apart from the rest of the group clustered near the edge of the trees above the gentle slope that led down to the river. All day long he had studiously prevented himself from thinking about the smashed radio and its implications. He had purposefully done so to allow his mind to arrange all the available data into some kind of sequence that would allow him to consider it as logically as possible. Sometimes it worked, sometimes not; he depended on unconscious thinking processes to automatically restructure a sequence of events and fit any odd pieces of data onto the framework of events.

So far, it had resulted in a confirmation of something that had been nagging at him since Ala Kul. He wondered just how-in-hell many people knew about this mission. The plane in Rome had been crowded with at least fifteen people; and then too, how many in the Soviet Union knew the details? Somehow or other, they had been betrayed. And as a consequence, three men were dead . . . Phan, or whatever his real name had been, murdered in Rome; Jones, shot and killed below the pass; and Rodek, shot at the alternate rendezvous. You could extend the shroud, he thought, to include the Chinese general, whose name he had forgotten, the three Chinese troopers and the two pilots killed on the airplane and the Chinese soldiers killed at the pass.

Somehow, the Chicoms had learned enough to anticipate every move they made. According to Dmietriev, who may or may not have been telling the truth, the Soviet Government had been taken completely by surprise at the sudden appearance of the Chinese Ambassador at the Kremlin, demanding that the government halt this mission. And there was the fact that the Chinese had known where both, not one but both, rendezvous points were.

Gillon had long ago learned never to trust anyone and never to let emotions interfere with decisions. Emotional decisions were invariably wrong, and he was learning that if there was a 'Murphy's Law' pertaining to espionage, it would be the classic first rule with a modification. 'If anything . . . or anyone . . . can go wrong, it . . . or they . . . will.'

190

Gillon shook his head. Hard fact was too scarce to reach any conclusions. All he knew at this point was that with the radio gone, they were completely isolated from all help. As best they had been able to figure, Leycock must have damaged the radio during one of the frequent falls they had all taken during the wind and blizzard of the previous night. When he had taken the faceplate off, Leycock had found two cracked circuit boards. In the middle of Central Asia, there was no way to repair the damaged printed circuits.

Gillon sighed deeply. That was that, then. Liu's caravan offered their only way out. Gillon was surprised to find how exhausted he was. His legs were as heavy as railroad ties and he wondered how much longer he could go on. Five days of constant travel through high mountains at altitudes above nine thousand feet had sapped them all. Their food supply, even when that of Jack Liu and his men was added, was at a dangerously low point. He had estimated roughly that they had no more than a one-day supply remaining for each man – a one-day subsistence supply of slightly less than 5,000 calories. At these altitudes and temperatures each man required 5,000 calories just to maintain himself. The heavy exertion of climbing and marching with thirty-pound packs added a requirement for an additional 5,000 calories, 10,000 calories in all per day.

It was this, the chance to gain additional food supplies, more than the relative security offered by the caravan of Mongol nomads, that had led Gillon to accept Liu's suggestion. He knew now, with their radio smashed beyond repair and Liu's gone as well, that a third factor had been added to the survival equation – weather, Chinese troops, and food. And the equation, rapidly being calculated, was not balanced in their favor – to say the least.

CHAPTER FOURTEEN

By early evening, they were moving in slow file through thinning trees. The heavy cloud cover had given way in the late afternoon to a broken wrack of cirrocumulus clouds promising more snow. The immense fir trees cast blue shadows for unbelievable distances in the waning afternoon sunlight. The air was intensely cold and their faces were blue and pinched and they shivered constantly, dissipating what little energy remained to them. Gillon estimated that they had traveled nearly twenty miles on skis and snowshoes that day and all during those long hours, they had not seen or heard any sign of pursuit.

At 1800 hours, Liu brought them to a halt in a small clearing and gave terse orders to set up a quick camp; then, calling to Gillon to get his skis and follow, he moved out of earshot.

'We'll go down farther into the valley and wait for the caravan. I don't know whether it will be through here tonight or tomorrow, but I'm pretty certain they haven't passed yet. We met them two days back, nearly forty miles north of here.'

Gillon nodded and took the skis out of the pack. He fastened the fiberglass shells together, locked them, then slipped his feet into the bindings and followed Liu down the slope. They skied for several minutes before Liu pulled up sharply beside a clump of bush projecting above the snow.

'If they come, they will follow along that line of trees down there.'

He pointed to a row of trees growing in a straggling line near the bottom of the valley.

Liu pushed off again down the slope and Gillon followed. They skied for nearly fifteen minutes, taking a roundabout path to avoid the remaining thicker stands of trees. Gillon found it exhilarating to be on skis once more after the muscle-wrenching drain of the snowshoes.

Liu held up his hands and began to slow. Gillon followed his lead and they came to a stop inside a stand of pine.

'We'll wait here . . . we've a good view of the valley in both directions.' Liu stepped out of his skis and began to tramp around in a tight circle to beat down the soft snow. Gillon did likewise and in minutes they had compressed a circle nearly three feet deep. Liu slashed some pine branches and piled them around the 'well' they had stamped out to create a fairly snug shelter from the stiffening wind.

'Goddam, it's cold,' Gillon muttered through chattering teeth.

'That's what worries me. In all the time I've been out here, I've never seen a blizzard without an intense cold snap following. And when that happens, usually another, bigger one is right behind. I pity anyone caught up in those peaks when the cold really digs in.'

Gillon turned toward the mountains rearing loftily behind them. The valley was swathed in deep blue, almost smoky shadows as the sun dropped lower. But the peaks to the north, peaks whose flanks they had just left, were glowing madly. The bottom half of the mountains was covered with black fir, patched here and there with white as open spots showed. But higher, above the tree line, the mountains were bleak and uninviting, ice-covered and glacial in aspect in spite of the sun's gold tinge, suggesting the coldness of a killer rather than the home of the gentle Chinese gods as the name Tien Shan indicated.

'You've got yourself a real problem with that crew, haven't you?'

Surprised, Gillon jerked his thoughts away from the peaks. 'Yeah, I guess I have. I wouldn't wish them on my worst enemy.'

'How did you get stuck with them?'

'It wasn't easy.' Gillon told him in greater detail how Jones had called him out into the trees that night to discuss the route and how he had been shot and killed. 'There wasn't anybody else who seemed willing to say, let's get the hell out of here . . . well, maybe Stowe would have eventually . . . but I'll be damned if I want my neck in the hands of that pompous jackass.'

Liu nodded silent agreement. 'It looks as if you are stuck with them then.' He was silent a moment, then looked up at Gillon. 'Unless, of course, you want them off your back.'

'How?'

'Easy enough. Dump them with the caravan and let them find their own way out. Without that radio, the only way is by foot. I figure to take my people south through the Tien Shan to Afghanistan following an old caravan trail. We'll cross into Kashmir and fly back to Taiwan from India.'

'That's going to be some trip,' Gillon observed. He knew he should have been surprised, but then with all that had happened coupled with two years of complete independence, he supposed that he had all along known that Liu would not stay with them.

'Hell, we've marched a thousand times that by now. And it's the only way, I think, that we have any kind of a chance of getting out of here.'

Gillon thought about Liu's offer. He knew that if he stayed with the other three, there wasn't much chance that any of them would get out alive. But, on the other hand, in his estimation, Liu had even less chance of crossing nearly six hundred miles of Chinese territory to the Pakistan border than they had of marching sixty miles to the Soviet border.

'So you don't want to cross the border with us, then?'

'Hell, Bob, it's not a matter of wanting to. I just don't think that twenty people . . . especially including you four, as inexperienced as you are . . . stand a chance of making it. The Reds are going to be watching too damned closely. But, if we all go south, then I think we can do it. The Reds certainly won't expect us to leave the Tien Shan. What do you say, are you coming with us?'

Gillon pushed back his hood and scratched his head. God, he thought, I'm dirty.

He shook his head. 'Sorry, old buddy, but I figure we have a better chance running for the border. Besides' – he grinned – 'I need a bath too badly to wait another three or four months.'

'All right.' Liu shrugged. 'It's your neck.'

Both men fell silent after that as they watched for the caravan. Gillon stamped his feet and flapped his arms in an effort to keep warm. The wind was beginning to gust up to twenty or more knots and even though the pines broke the initial force, it was still terribly cold.

The last tinges of gold had faded from the peaks when Liu touched his arm and pointed down the valley.

Gillon peered into the gloom but could see nothing. He warmed the eyepieces of the binoculars in his gloved hands and tried again. This time in the fading light, he thought he could see a line of dark figures. It was difficult to make out details, but he had the impression of a long string of animals, camels or horses, with smaller figures marching beside them that could only have been men. Liu watched for several minutes, then with a grunt of satisfaction, he took a flashlight from his pocket, pointed it toward the slope above them and flicked it on and off four times.

'That should bring the rest of them down in a few minutes.' And he went back to staring at the approaching line of men and animals.

'I just hope they are the right bunch,' Gillon said, and not without some apprehension.

'It is,' Liu replied quickly. 'Soldiers wouldn't travel with pack animals. They would come on skis or snowshoes, depending on airdrops for supplies.' He chuckled, half to himself. 'They've forgotten damned quickly what Mao Tse-tung said about living off the land. As they become more sophisticated, they become more cumbersome and we run them in circles.'

The caravan drew steadily nearer and a few minutes later Liu's men, as well as Dmietriev, Stowe and Leycock, filed up silently and distributed themselves among the trees.

'Expecting trouble?' Gillon asked.

Liu looked up at him quickly. 'No, but it's better to be prepared. Or at least that's what they taught us in the Boy Scouts,' he said with a grin.

'Boy Scouts . . . did they have Boy Scouts in China . . . ?' Gillon snorted.

'What China? I grew up in Anaheim. Belonged to Troop Two Forty-Six, Sunset District.'

'Oh.' Gillon nodded vaguely. He had known Liu for nine months in Laos. And not once did he give the impression that he had been raised anywhere but on Taiwan. His English was accentless . . . almost American . . . was American, in fact . . . but that was nothing out of the ordinary these days. The American Army was filled with so many colors and nationalities that it could sometimes be mistaken for a United Nations Army.

The caravan was close enough now that he could make out details through the binoculars even in the fading light. He counted nearly thirty men walking beside a motley collection of camels and horses in just the first section of the caravan before it faded out of sight in the trees. Everyone appeared to be on foot and Gillon was surprised to see that they were on skis or snowshoes. It had never occurred to him that these Norwegian and American Indian inventions would be used by Central Asian nomads. The ungainly camels, low-slung, swaying beasts, were much smaller than he had expected until he realized that they were the twin-humped Bactrian variety common to Asia.

'Come on.' Liu climbed out of the well and fastened on his skis. Gillon followed and, in the deepening dusk, they skied quickly down to the lowest part of the valley, a frozen watercourse now covered with snow, and swung to a stop to face the oncoming caravan.

Gillon knew that they had been seen as the last vestiges of twilight were behind them. But even so, the caravan gave no sign and came steadily on. When less than fifty yards separated them, Liu muttered for him to follow and skied slowly toward the man walking in front, well out of the path of the plodding animals, which strode along under their heavy loads, wide-toed feet sinking no more than a few inches into the thigh-deep snow.

As they approached the man to the side of the caravan, Gillon saw that he also was on skis. He coasted to a stop, unslinging a rifle as he did so and letting it rest casually in the crook of his left arm while he waited for them to come up.

The light was almost gone now and as the rank-smelling beasts plodded by, Gillon felt, rather than saw, every eye turn to them. There were, he realized, a good number of rifles watching for the slightest false move on their part.

Lui stopped and bowed in the Chinese manner to the man who stood waiting for them. After a moment, the nomad bowed just as deeply and the two men clasped hands and began to talk in a high-pitched yet guttural language, one of the many Mongolian-based dialects that abounded in Sinkiang. The man spoke to Liu but never once removed his eyes from Gillon. His face, what little Gillon could see of it under his cap, was dark-complected with a wide brow and heavy eyebrows over slanting eyes. A thin moustache straggled down either side of his mouth to meet a surprisingly heavy beard. He looked more Japanese than Mongolian, Gillon thought. The light, which in the open, away from the trees, had lasted a few minutes longer, was now almost gone. The darkness was too complete to make out any other details and Gillon waited, stamping his feet while the two men spoke, and watched the dim shapes of the pack animals and men file past.

After a moment, the nomad pushed up to him on his skis and peered into his face. Gillon met his gaze steadily and the man grunted, then was gone. Liu came back to where Gillon was staring after the man.

'I guess you've passed inspection. He's not happy about it, but he'll take you along. He expects you to stay out of the way, but if there is any fighting to be done, he wants you to pitch in. I told him that you are all very good fighters, that you personally were in Vietnam and then in Africa. That seemed to satisfy him.'

'Vietnam and Africa . . .' Gillon said in surprise. 'What do they know about Indochina or Africa?'

'Look,' Jack Liu said, his voice quietly serious. 'Don't ever underestimate these people. For over two thousand years they've managed to stay alive by using their wits. They know what's going on in the outside world. Right now he knows that the Reds will be looking for you as hard as they can because of the negotiations between the U.S. and China. He knows this will cause problems but because he owes me a favour, he will take you.

'Come on, it's too damned cold to stand around. The caravan is camping for the night in those trees. We are to follow behind into the camp. They'll give us a place to sleep and some food.'

Gillon nodded agreement and Liu led the way back up to the clearing, where he and Gillon explained the situation to the others.

197

'Damn,' Stowe said through chattering teeth. 'That's the most cutthroat crew I've ever seen. I hope to hell you two know what you're doing.'

'At least we will have hot food, and for a day or so a warm place to sleep,' Dmietriev murmured. 'In this cold, that's worth almost any risk . . . maybe you were right after all,' he finished, turning toward Gillon. A moment later, he was gone into the dusk, leaving Gillon staring after him, bemused.

The long file of men moved off at an easy pace after the caravan. The twilight had disappeared into darkness, in which the faint starlight did not penetrate the heavy pines. Liu was using a flashlight to guide their way but the bulb furnished only a dim, yellowish light. The intense cold, which Gillon estimated at close to twenty below, even without the wind, had nearly frozen the batteries.

The caravan stopped for the night well inside the forest, not far from the head of the valley. A half-hour of slow, shuffling travel was required to reach the shielded light cast by the watch fires.

A challenge hissed from the trees in the same high, guttural language and Liu answered softly. A moment later, three men materialized with weapons leveled. Gillon suspected there were more out of sight. One of the guards stepped near and shone his flashlight into each face before he was satisfied.

A single word started them forward again, through a screen of bushes and into a firelit area some forty feet in diameter. After the darkness of the forest, the light was blinding, dim as it was, and it was several moments before they were able to see the huddle of rounded felt tents called yurts which were spaced around the circumference of the open area. Liu came back to Gillon and motioned for Leycock, Stowe and Dmietriev and him to follow.

To Dmietriev he whispered, 'Say nothing about being a Russian. If they find out, they might hang your head on a pole. These people hate Russians even more than Chinese.'

Liu led them across the open area to the line of tents, where several Mongolians with slung rifles waited. They exchanged a few words with Liu. Liu started in surprise and began arguing angrily, but the men cut him off and stalked toward a yurt several feet away.

'All right,' Liu said wearily. 'It seems there's been a problem. The caravan master has been overruled. They are going to give us a chance to talk to the full council before a final decision is made.'

'What the hell?' Gillon roared. 'What is this? I thought you said everything was settled.'

Liu spread his hands. 'I thought it was too. But it looks like they feel the risk is too great. The council wants to talk it over.'

'And if they decide against us, what then? Do they shoot us first, or turn us over to the Chinese?'

A shadow of worry passed across Liu's face. 'Neither, I think. They have offered you hospitality by inviting you into their camp. According to their customs, they must abide by that offer. If they say no, they'll ask you to go . . . probably. But, you will be considered fair game if they meet you again. Also, they might try and contact the government . . . but that's doubtful since it would give them away as well.'

'Great idea you had there,' Stowe sneered. 'Unspoiled nomadic natives helping the white hats. Crap! Let's get the hell out of here before they decide to shoot us all.'

'You can't leave now,' Liu said. 'Look around. There must be twenty guns watching us right now. I did these people a big favor last winter and they pay their debts . . . so the only thing to do is to find out what's making them so edgy.'

Gillon snapped, 'Let's get at it then. If they turn us down, I want to put as much distance between us as possible before the sun comes up.'

At the very thought of having to travel more that night, his knees began to shake. He knew they were in no shape to do so; their food was almost exhausted and so were they. The intense cold and Liu's speculation that it was the prelude to the major blizzard to come made him doubt strongly that they could survive.

'Okay, let's go then.' Liu nodded. 'All of you, keep your mouths shut. I don't think anyone here speaks

English, but you can never tell. I'll do the talking . . . understand?'

They all nodded and Liu led them to a large yurt that had been erected on the edge of the cleared space. It was fully six feet high in contrast to the low profile of the other yurts scattered about. Gillon was surprised to see that it had a door, rather than a hanging flap of felt; a much scarred wooden door, but a wooden door nevertheless. It was beaten and weathered and tied into place with ropes, but it served its function.

One of the guards shoved it open and motioned them into the smoky interior. A bluish haze filled the dome to trickle lazily out a round hole cut into the top of the tent. A small fire of dried camel dung flickered in a small brazier in the center of the yurt. The floor had been covered with reed mats, which were already becoming saturated with slush and melted water from the snow beneath. The floor squished unpleasantly at every step. An old man was spreading what looked to be plastic tarpaulins and as he shuffled about he waved them impatiently out of the way while he completed the task. Over the tarps he dragged some none-too-clean sheepskins and, satisfied with his job, rubbed his hands briskly together, stared at them with a sneer and disappeared through the door.

The five men gazed around them for a moment and then Liu began to walk slowly around the walls, studying them closely.

'Looking for microphones?' Stowe asked sarcastically.

'Shut up,' Gillon snapped.

'Crap . . . these gooks . . .'

Liu stepped quickly across the tent and shoved Stowe back with a stiffened hand. 'Shut your mouth, you fool!'

Stowe started to reply but an angry hiss from Gillon stopped him and he subsided into sullen silence.

Before anything further could happen, the door whipped open and five Kalmucks followed by the caravan master crowded in and silently took up positions facing Gillon, Liu, Stowe, Dmietriev and Leycock across the fire. Their faces, barely seen in the narrow gap left by close-fitting hats and jackets, showed nothing.

Twelve dark eyes stared unwinkingly, more than half shrouded in shadow.

'These people are Kalmucks . . . the fiercest and smartest of all the Mongolian peoples,' Liu whispered. 'The great khans were Kalmucks and they have never forgotten they once ruled the greatest empire in the world. So mind your manners.'

Gillon nodded. He was surprised to see that the jackets and leggings these men wore could have come from the military surplus shelves of any Western nation. All but one old man wore various shades of drab-colored, cold-weather gear. The old man, however, wore the padded or quilted clothing that Gillon had always associated with Mongolians. In addition to the padded jacket and leggings, his hat was the typical lined helmet with earflaps worn throughout Siberia and China. Gillon shook his head; the old ways were disappearing all over the world and even in the remotest backwoods of Asia, modern technology had arrived with a vengeance.

A moment later, the same old man who had laid the tarps and furs entered with a hissing Coleman lantern, which he hung from a peg hammered into the centre pole; he bowed to the six men seated on the far side of the fire and left.

'Now the serious talk begins,' Liu whispered. 'That old man with the padded jacket is the overall leader. Caravans like these are sent out from a winter village under a caravan master. But the elders still make all final decisions and even though the caravan master is the supreme authority on the trail, he can still be overruled in matters of policy not directly relating to the running of the caravan by this council.'

Gillon nodded, understanding now why the caravan master's decision had been overturned.

The old man spoke quickly to the others seated beside him, then turned to study the five outsiders searchingly. He asked one question and Liu squirmed uncomfortably before launching into a long speech that caused the elders to look at one another in surprise several times. Liu spoke forcefully and at length, and when he finished, it was on a challenging note. The old man answered in a brief speech, during which the caravan master squirmed angrily, then he sat back and waited.

Liu turned to Gillon and spoke past him to the rest, his voice pitched low, his face carefully concealing the trouble that Gillon saw in his eyes. 'Listen to me, carefully. Don't let anything show when I tell you what they said, do you understand? If they see the least bit of emotion, they'll throw us all out. Do you understand?' he repeated.

They all nodded and Liu stared hard at Stowe. 'Do you understand? We aren't playing around here. This isn't Washington behind some nice safe desk with a big map stuck full of pins.'

Surprisingly enough, Stowe nodded, his demeanor as serious as the situation warranted.

'Okay,' Liu said, relief evident in his voice. 'They say that they will not grant us a place in the caravan. They say it was foolish of the caravan master to do so in the first place. They say that they are at peace with the Communist government in Peking and they want to keep it that way. The elders overruled him and that's quite a rebuke and he doesn't like it. But he has no choice. He must do what they decide.'

'So that leaves us out in the cold, no pun intended.'

Liu shook his head. 'No, at least not for tonight. They'll let you stay until dawn, then will allow you one day's travel.'

'What the devil does that mean?' Leycock demanded.

'That means that they will not try and turn you in for at least twenty-four hours after you leave the camp. It seems that the Chinese have placed a pretty big price on your head . . . enough to keep this caravan and the village it comes from in luxury for twenty years. The Chinese are offering the equivalent of fifty thousand American dollars for your capture. So you can see, it's a mighty big temptation to them.'

Gillon rubbed the back of his neck. 'So, after we leave, we have twenty-four hours in which to get the hell out of this area. Do these people have a radio?'

'No, but they can build a pretty sizable fire and it won't take long for one of the search planes to find them. I'd say within thirty-six hours of the time you leave the caravan, the Chinese will know you've been here. Look, I've an idea. We aren't dead yet . . . I don't think they really want to risk giving themselves away if they can help it.'

Liu stared across the fire at the old man for a long moment and he in turn watched Liu without a trace of emotion. The inside of the yurt was growing steadily warmer as the fire in the brazier caught hold and burned more fiercely. Gillon was sweating copiously inside his cold-weather gear. He wondered how the Kalmucks endured the heat, but they gave no sign of being uncomfortable. In addition to the heat, the acrid smoke bit into his lungs and stung his eyes. At first the yurt had been a grateful change from the angry wind and cold outside, but now Gillon was no longer so certain which he preferred.

Liu talked for what seemed like hours and the five elders stared at him across the campfire, seemingly never blinking and never moving. Gillon found his head nodding once and he forced himself stiffly upright in an effort to stay awake. He risked a quick glance at the others and saw that they were all fighting the same battle. Dmietriev, seated next to him, was running with sweat and as he turned back, he caught the gaze of one of the old men sitting on the far right of the fire. He thought he saw a hint of amusement at their sweating faces, but the man's eye went quickly back to Liu. Laugh, you bastard, he thought.

Finally, Liu stopped talking. 'We may be getting somewhere at last,' he muttered to Gillon. 'I've found a bargaining point, one besides money. The Peking government, no matter how grateful they should ever be for their help, will never let them have more than small-caliber, single-shot rifles for hunting. These people think that guns are an invention of the gods. So, if we offer them rifles in addition to matching the fifty-thousand-dollar reward, they may change their minds.'

Gillon thought for a moment. 'Why not offer them AR-18s? That should impress the hell out of them.'

Liu nodded and spoke to the elder, who sat up quickly, his stiff face cracking with interest for the first time. Gillon unslung his carbine and tossed it over the fire to the old man, who snatched it gracefully from the air. He called out in Mongolian and a moment later, a young man entered the tent. The old man handed him the carbine with a series of quick instructions and he went out. A moment later, Gillon heard the sharp, fast-paced snapping of the carbine being fired and the young man came back into the tent holding the AR-18 in one hand and his own ancient shotgun in the other. He handed the AR-18 to the old man and nodded. Gillon could see the excitement in his eyes.

The elder pointed to Gillon and the man stepped around the fire and handed it back to him. Gillon ejected the clip, stuck it in his pocket and inserted a new one, slid a cartridge into the chamber and reslung the rifle, staring at the elder all the time.

'Ask him,' Gillon said to Liu, 'if two hundred of these rifles and a thousand rounds of ammunition each, delivered to him across the border in Afghanistan plus fifty thousand dollars is satisfactory payment for passage with the caravan until we reach the crossing point?'

Liu nodded and spoke to the elders once more. They argued in whispers among themselves until the old man waved a hand sharply and looked up. He appeared to be searching Gillon's face for any sign of deceit, then dismissed him abruptly, nodded to Liu and spoke at some length. When he finished, Liu translated briefly.

'He says, all right. They will be waiting for the delivery at a pass known as Dahnash-kol in mid-July. They will take *my* guarantee of payment . . . and you realize that if payment isn't made, I'm as good as dead?'

Gillon nodded. 'I'll see that the carbines are delivered. Don't worry about that. The only thing that would stop me is if we don't make it out of here.'

'Yeah, they recognized that fact right away. They figure it's their tough luck if you don't, but once you leave the caravan, they won't do a thing to help you. This isn't their problem and the rifles and the favor they owe me are the only things that persuaded them to help you.'

The five old men and the caravan master got to their feet and without a backward glance trooped out. Liu stood up and the rest of them got to their feet as well, stretching and shedding jackets immediately.

'This is where you stay for tonight . . . they want you where they can keep an eye on' you. My people are quartered with the rest of the camp and since we've spent time with them before, they won't guard us too closely. But they do,' Liu warned, 'put sentries around the camp at night. These hills used to be full of bandits and south, toward civilization, they still are. The guards are in two concentric rings and you would have no chance of sneaking past them. The penalty for a guard allowing anyone in or out without permission, is death by dismemberment and it ain't a pretty way to go. So they stay on their toes.'

The door pushed open and four Kalmucks stepped in carrying their packs and snowshoes, which they tossed onto the floor. One of them stared around at the men, uttered one word, spit on the floor, then stalked out.

'He called you barbarians,' Liu said wryly. 'The fact that you will equip them all with new weapons means nothing. They could just as easily have slit your throats and taken the ones you have now, but the headman has put them under orders not to do so. You have their hospitality and as long as you don't abuse it, they will leave you strictly alone. So don't expect any favors. If you can't keep up, or if you violate any of their rules, you've had it.'

'Nice people,' Leycock muttered.

'Don't forget, these people once ruled half the known world, the largest empire ever assembled. On top of that they've managed to survive war after war and attempt after attempt to kill them off. If they think they are kings of the world, you sure as hell are not going to change their minds. They'll use you only as long as they think there is something to be gained; once they get what they want, or figure that they no longer stand a chance, they'll throw you to the wolves.'

'Yeah . . . I guess you're right. But it doesn't make me feel any better. I don't like being anybody's poor relation.'

Liu laughed at that. 'A poor choice of words, my friend. You don't even rate as high as a poor relation.

They take care of their own. Strangers are fair game
. . : but only after the rules of hospitality have been met.'
Liu, still grinning, motioned to Gillon to follow him
outside.

Gillon nodded and pulled his parka on, tugged the
hood down as low as it would go and followed Liu outside into the mounting wind and cold. Gillon had forgotten, in the brief hour they had been inside the yurt,
just how cold it could be outside in the wind – and how
fresh the air could seem as well. Liu led him away from
the yurt toward the main fire, which was burning in
fitful gusts, yet still casting some warmth. Liu stopped
beside it and stamped his feet, swinging his arms at the
same time to keep warm.

'Damn, it's cold. I'm sure glad they decided to keep
us tonight.'

'Amen.'

Liu pivoted around, staring into the darkness, then
went back to swinging his arms, assured now that nobody was in earshot – even though the wind would have
made it impossible for anybody more than a few feet
away to overhear what he said.

'You know, old buddy, we haven't had time to talk
over old times,' Liu clasped his hands behind his back
and stared into the fire.

Gillon waited, wondering what Liu was leading up to.

'Of course,' he went on, 'that scene in Laos is not
something you can really look back on as a good time.
Not any of it.

'How are your legs? They don't seem to be bothering
you.'

Gillon shook his head. 'Okay. The doctors said that
only one bone was broken.'

Gillon half turned to face him, 'You know, I never
really did get a chance to thank you. By the time I knew
what was happening, you were gone and I always did
wonder where.'

Liu flashed him a grin. 'And now you know, don't
you? Two years,' he muttered half to himself. 'Two
years in this damned icebox. Freeze in the winter, roast
in the summer and run like hell all year round . . . but

206

this is it, the end of the tour. We are on the way out now and nothing is going to stop us.'

'Then what?'

Liu watched the fire dancing in the wind for a moment. 'I don't really know. I haven't thought much about it. I guess I'll go home for a while and try and figure out what I want to do with the rest of my life.'

'Where's home, now?' Gillon asked, and instantly regretted the question.

Liu turned his head and Gillon saw the puzzlement in his eyes, even though his face was half hidden by the hood. He shook his head. 'That too is a very good question. I don't know any more. When I was a kid, it was Southern California. After college, it was Taiwan. Now . . .

'What about you?' Liu asked.

Gillon laughed at that. 'Hell, man, I don't any more know than you do. Once I thought I did, now the only thing I know is that I don't know.'

'Asia has a way of doing that to you,' Liu said quietly. 'When you first get here, you think, man-oh-man, I know exactly what I'm going to do and it's right; there's just no argument about it. Then, after you've been here awhile and see some of what is really happening, you begin to wonder. You think . . . these people are getting killed in droves and they don't even know why. They go out without a whimper . . . have been for thousands of years. It's no different today than when Genghis Khan or Tamerlane came through here. Then we send our own people over and they get killed and don't know why either. No one out here knows Communism from a hole in the ground or democracy or anything else either, and you begin to wonder if it's worth all the pain and killing to try to teach them. Then after you've been here a year or two you are pretty damned certain that . . . like you said . . . the only thing you are sure of is that you aren't sure of anything any more. And you look back at home and you see the mess that's been made while you've been away: everybody afraid of everybody else, afraid of saying something because they might offend some minority group and consequently no one has enough guts to stand up and say, by God, this is wrong and let's fix it right, all the way right and not just some stupid half measure that will just cost money and make it that much worse.'

Liu fell silent and kicked at the snow for a minute. When he went on, it was in a quieter voice. 'You and I have both seen too much and done too much to ever rest easy again. I don't know where I'm going to go . . . hell, maybe, when you come right down to it, that's why I asked you to come.'

Gillon laid a hand on Liu's shoulder and gave it a gentle shake.

'Hell, maybe it's just as well we don't have time to talk about the good old days . . . I'd probably want to go out and shoot myself afterward.'

Liu laughed at that and the tension eased. 'Okay, let's talk about why we are really here . . .'

'Well, I figured it's not to stand around philosophizing while we freeze to death, you can bet on that.' They both laughed again and Liu became serious.

'You have got yourself a problem, boy, if you stick with these people. One of them is going to get you killed for sure. I have half a mind to not give you this packet, except that you're a big boy and you've got to make your own decisions.'

'Jones told me the other night,' Gillon said slowly, 'just before he was killed, that the data you have contain the location of the Chinese hard-launch sites along the Mongolian border. Is that true?'

Liu stared at Gillon speculatively. 'You believe that?'

Gillon shrugged. 'First, he told me that it was information and photographs on the latest nuclear warhead test series.'

'For God's sake, they could get that from satellites . . . they don't need us for that kind of work.'

Gillon shrugged again. 'Could be, but that's what he told me at first; maybe he decided by the other night that I was trustworthy.'

Liu chuckled. 'New in town . . . ? In this sudden burst of confidence, he didn't happen to tell you just who it is that's keeping the Reds on your tail, did he?'

'What are you talking about . . . ?'

'Damn,' Liu muttered wearily. 'Didn't you learn anything in Indochina? Just how in hell do you think the Reds have managed to keep up with every move you've made . . . ? One of those three clowns tagging after you has been telling them every time you blew your nose.'

'Well, I'll be damned . . .'

Liu laughed softly. 'Now is it all beginning to make sense to you?'

'You're crazy,' Gillon said feebly. 'Those people were handpicked . . .'

'So was Benedict Arnold,' Liu snorted. 'So was Kim Philby and so was Oleg Penkovsky. What the hell does that mean?'

And he knew that Jack Liu was right. Suddenly, it all fell into place for him – the odds against being accidentally discovered in all those thousands of square miles of forest and at night were just too long. But, if someone had followed them away from the camp, met with the Chinese soldiers at some predetermined spot, then led them back to the clearing where they killed Jones and tried to kill him – it could very well have been that their midnight jaunt had upset someone's plans. They were only a few miles from the rendezvous. If one of them was a plant, he may have figured that the other five could be dispensed with now that Liu was in the bag. But, because they had missed him, and he had managed to wipe out the patrol, the timetable had been offset to the extent that not only had they escaped the net, but Jack Liu's people had as well.

'Of course,' he muttered aloud. 'Now it all begins to fit together.'

'What begins to fit?' Liu asked with a trace of sarcasm.

'All right, so I'm dense, but you people play this game all the time. Somebody in the group is a traitor, a double agent, fink or whatever you call them.'

'Congratulations. You have just earned your bachelor's degree in spying . . . the hard way. Of course you have a double agent with you. Do you think they have aircraft with instruments that can see through blizzards and trees? How the hell do you think the radio got busted . . . that somebody sat on it maybe?'

Gillon was brought up short by that.

'Then maybe,' he said slowly, 'whoever he is, he's

overplayed his hand this time. The radio must have been smashed sometime during the night, when we were all sleeping . . . probably after he sent a message giving the Reds our latest position. Whoever did it could not possibly have foreseen that you would show up, because as far as he knew, as far as we all knew at the time, you had been wiped out. So now the Reds know that we outran their trap. But they don't know in which direction we've gone. When he wrecked that radio, he isolated himself as well.'

Liu nodded, grinning. 'That's my boy. Now you're catching on to how the game is played.'

'I see,' Gillon said slowly. 'So you've known all along?'

'Let's say that I suspected as soon as I saw the radio. You've got to admit, it was cleverly done. I imagine you all took so many falls during the night that Leycock would never remember the one that landed him on the radio. The damage wasn't much . . . just a cracked circuit board, but without a replacement, there's no way to fix a transistorized radio short of an electronics lab.'

'Well, since you have had a chance to watch us all day, any ideas as to who it might be? It wasn't Jones or Rodek, that's for sure, not unless their ghosts go around smashing radios.'

Liu nodded. 'If I assume that you are safe, that leaves one out of three . . . a Russian and two Americans.'

Gillon looked at him. 'Why assume that I'm safe?'

'Because who would know that I would pick you to be the contact? There wouldn't have been time to get to you.'

'That's what Jones said,' Gillon muttered.

'What?' Liu asked sharply.

'Nothing. Just reminding myself how dumb I am.'

'Who was on guard at the time you and Jones left the camp?'

Gillon winced. He hadn't thought of that. He was so damned tired that it was a miracle he could think at all. He forced his mind back what seemed eons past but in reality was only seventy-two hours . . . who in hell? . . . then he remembered Dmietriev's bearlike form outlined against the tiny fire they had built for warmth.

'Dmietriev,' he said finally. 'And one other thing . . .

his tent was right next to Leycock's last night. Nothing short of a bomb blast would have awakened Leycock . . . or any of the rest of us for that matter.'

Liu stared into the fire, thinking. Finally he said slowly, 'Dmietriev was in on the complete plan from the beginning . . .'

'That's what Jones told me.'

Liu nodded. 'All right, then . . . ?'

'Hell, it's pretty damned circumstantial . . .'

'Look, Clarence Darrow, this isn't a courtroom . . .'

'Yeah, yeah . . . but still.'

'Who brought the Chicom general . . . wouldn't he be a natural to stay with you to make sure they recovered this information?'

'They'd sacrifice a general for what you have?' Gillon asked incredulously.

Liu turned to him. 'For what I have, they would sacrifice half of China . . . because that's what it could cost them in the end.'

'All right,' Gillon said at last. 'So it's something more than launch site locations . . . what?'

'Oh, they are launch site locations, all right. But it's what's inside those damned launch sites that counts. How many nuclear bombs or warheads do you think the Chinese could manufacture and stockpile in five to ten years?'

'What the hell has that got to . . . ?'

'Everything,' Liu interrupted. 'The Russians have had nearly twenty-five years to build up a nuclear strike force. Do you think the Chicoms can compete, can even hope to approach the Soviets' capability, even in retaliatory power, in five to ten years. Red China doesn't have one tenth the Soviet gross national product, manufacturing capability and anything else that you need to run a nation complex enough and rich enough to manufacture nuclear bombs.'

'So what then?'

'So this then. Those missiles are loaded with BW weapons.'

Gillon stared at Liu in stunned silence. 'Bacteriological warfare!' he finally stammered out.

'Yeah,' Liu answered quietly. 'It takes one hell of a

huge national organization to develop nuclear weaponry, but a few biological laboratories supported at the cost of nine or ten million each can turn out weapons that could make even the H-bomb look like conventional weaponry as far as killing power is concerned.'

'Goddamn,' Gillon swore. 'It's never dawned on me that the Chicoms could be fooling around with that stuff. They don't have the technology or the background.'

'Well, don't let the old Chinese-style medicine put you off,' Liu said, sarcasm dripping. 'When you are as poor as China is in skilled professional manpower, even the psychological effect of sticking needles into your patients has its place.

'Look,' he went on. 'If there is going to be a war between Russia and China, where the hell are they going to fight it out?'

Without waiting for Gillon's answer, Liu went on, 'The action is going to take place along the Mongolian border. For the most part, that's wide, flat, semi-arid desert land. And the Russians are so far ahead of the Chinese militarily that if they decide they need another few million square miles of buffer zone, the entire Chinese Army will hardly slow them down.'

'Crap,' Gillon snorted. 'The Chinese can throw more men into the field than the Russians have in . . .'

'Use your head,' Liu snapped, cutting him off in midsentence. 'The Russians have 3,375,000 regular troops compared to China's 2,880,000. It would take the Chinese weeks to mobilize an effective reserve force. The Russians have fifty-two armored divisions to China's five. The rest of their infantry, all one hundred and two divisions, are completely motorized. There are, at best, thirty motorized Chinese divisions, all with obsolete Russian equipment. The Russians have ten thousand combat aircraft compared to China's twenty-eight hundred. The hour that the Russian air force begins preemptive strikes to knock out Chinese interceptors so that the helicopters and motorized infantry divisons can swarm across the Dzungarian and Mongolian plains, the Chinese know the war has begun . . . and ended. And what the hell are they going to do about it . . . march their infantry up to the front on foot to stop them? What front? The Russians will cross the Mongolian border and they won't stop until they have reached Szechwan Province to the south and occupied all of Manchuria in the north. The Chinese can play a great game at guerrilla soldiers with the thoughts of Mao to guide them, but to stand up to a nuclear-equipped, highly mobile army in an all-out, no-holds-barred war, not a chance. China needs some way to stop the Russians before they get started. Nuclear missiles . . . no.' Liu shook his head. 'They aren't in that league yet and won't be for twenty more years. But, germ warfare? That game they can play and match the Russians counter for counter.'

'How?' Gillon asked skeptically. 'BW weapons are just too damned unreliable. Some of those diseases they've developed are far too deadly for any effective vaccine to be developed. The user could lose his entire army because of an unexpected change in wind direction. And they still don't have a chance against the Russian cities. The Soviet anti-missile network might not be effective against the sophisticated American and British missiles, but it sure as hell will be against anything the Chinese will have for several years to come. It just doesn't make sense.'

Liu stared at Gillon quizzically. 'Have you ever seen the Dzungarian Plain?'

Gillon shook his head.

'Well, I have. It's half a million square miles of rolling, almost treeless plain. No water but a lot of mesquite, greasewood, sand and nothing else. It would be great tank country . . . if it didn't turn into mud periodically. But the high ground . . . ah, that's something else. The high ground makes perfect helicopter bases and helicopters can carry entire divisions across the plains and into China . . . as long as the Russians hold command of the sky. Hell, we proved the worth of helicopters in Vietnam . . . there's nothing like them for carrying out large and sudden troop movements.

'The Dzungarian Plain does have one advantage for the Chinese. Summer and winter, the winds blow north, constantly, never stopping. And that is what will make

213

the Chinese use of bacteriological warheads an excellent defensive . . . or even offensive weapon in case they decide that a pre-emptive strike is called for?'

Gillon could picture in his mind the Dzungarian Plain the way Liu described it. Vast, rolling brush- and scrub-covered country, a quagmire in the winter rain and snow, a dust bowl in the summer. But helicoptered troops would never be slowed by mud or snow. If Liu was right about the winds . . .

'All right,' Gillon said into an unnatural silence. For a moment, even the incessant whine of the wind had stopped – as if to punctuate Liu's story – and the lack of sound was foreign to the land of snow and wind and death, he thought disconnectedly.

'If that's what you have in the packet, then I can see why the Americans and Russians want it so badly.' Gillon stopped abruptly.

'You don't really want to do this, do you? he asked.

Liu grinned half to himself and Gillon knew he had been hiding what he would rather not think about. 'No. I don't. Communists or not, I'm Chinese and that means something to me that maybe only another Chinese can understand. But I guess I believe in the balance of power theory too. If China is allowed to install these damned things, God knows what they could let loose. There is a faction, small, but powerful, in the government which is capable of sometimes overpowering the military, who by and large are very conservative. It's these people who could unleash this nonsense in some do-or-die first strike. They got loose a few years ago and the country went through the idiocy of the Cultural Revolution. So the Russians have to know and have to be in a position to force the Chinese to withdraw these damnable things before they complete the installations.'

Gillon nodded. He knew little about the concept of bacteriological warfare but he did know that certain bacteria and viruses could be mutated in the laboratory to make them toxic enough to kill within hours, if not minutes.

'What organisms are they using?'

Liu shrugged. 'I don't know. It's all in the packet. I don't know much about that stuff . . . anthrax and

214

botulism probably. Someone told me those are the easiest to work with.'

'So then you are saying that the Chicoms will use the bacteriological warheads as tactical weapons. If that's so, then why the hell use missiles?'

'Because the troops they already have on the border are sufficient to hold back Russian border troops. That isn't the problem. It's the strike-force troops that will be brought up from the rear that will overrun them . . . courtesy of the helicopter. The missiles are for those troops and for blackmail against Soviet cities. One of those blasted things dropped anywhere near an inhabited area could start a plague. They won't need to aim for the cities. The suburbs, beyond the range of the anti-missile defenses, will serve just as well.'

Gillon knew that there was no need to discuss the matter further. Liu was right. The real danger in the Chicom plan lay in that unregulatable human factor, the possibility that some fool or madman might get his hand on the trigger. The danger was strong enough with nuclear weapons; but bacteriological warfare was immensely more dangerous.

'What do you say?' Liu asked softly. 'Give the packet to one of the others and come with us. Let those bastards in Moscow and Washington sort out their own mess.'

Stubbornly, Gillon shook his head. 'No. Give me the package.'

Liu reached into his parka, then hesitated. ' "Never was a patriot yet, but was a fool," ' he intoned in a somber voice.

Gillon snorted. 'There's no patriotism involved. I don't owe anyone a damned thing. And anyway, you're not the only one who can quote poetry . . . "plots, true or false, are necessary things, to raise up commonwealths and ruin kings." Dryden, wasn't it?'

'Damn . . .' Liu burst into laughter. 'All right. Like I said, you're a big boy. Take it.'

He tossed a slim creased manila envelope, stained with perspiration, to Gillon. It felt empty and he held it up to the firelight.

'Microfiche,' Liu explained, noting the way Gillon

215

was handling it. 'Take damned good care of it. More people than you know about have died for that . . . that and some stupid theory formulated by a power-hungry maniac in the last century to describe what any text on child psychology would tell you.'

Gillon tucked the envelope away inside his own pocket without comment. He had what he had come for and, strangely enough, he felt no elation. Their chances were very slim indeed of ever crossing the border to deliver it. If he wasn't such a damned fool, he'd take Liu up on his offer and march south with him. But he turned away and paced around the edge of the wavering firelight.

'No,' he said suddenly. 'If my double agent doesn't have a radio, then he has to figure some other way of getting word to the Reds; otherwise, he is just as trapped as the rest of us. The Chicoms don't know where we are now and your friends in the caravan don't want them to know. So our boy is stuck . . . for a while anyway. If it is Dmietriev, then he is going to have to make some move to attract their attention. All I've got to do is stop him before he does.'

'Yeah, that's all.' Liu shook his head. 'All right, I've tried.'

'Jack . . . look, why don't you come with us? That way, we'll all stand a better chance of getting out. The Russians are going to let you through . . . you're the one who got the packet.'

Liu shook his head. 'Sorry, but probablys and maybes aren't enough in my line. You go ahead . . . you'll stand a better chance in a small party. But I won't leave you flat. We're heading off to the southwest and we'll kick up enough of a fuss along the way to distract them.'

Gillon nodded, knowing that there was nothing more that he could say. Liu knew . . . or thought he knew . . . what he had to do. Liu stuck out his hand.

Reluctantly Gillon took it. 'What do you think your chances are . . . ?'

'One in a million, same as when we came in two years ago. They never change, but somehow we keep going.'

Gillon nodded and Liu gripped his hand, hard, then turned and hurried away toward a smaller yurt, in front of which several of his hard-faced Chinese troopers stood watching.

Feeling like a fool, Gillon forced down the lump in his throat and walked slowly back to his own yurt, thinking bitterly that in a few days they could all be dead . . . and for what? Some stupid pieces of information in a stupid game that would probably be public knowledge in a few months anyway. Was a few months worth their lives and the lives of all those who had already died in this elaborate chess match?

CHAPTER FIFTEEN

Gillon stood beside the yurt watching the spectacular display of color flaming over the eastern horizon above the peaks of the Khalik Tau. Long streamers of high cirrostratus cloud swept in feathery whorls across the sky, changing from rose to white as the sun heaved itself above the peaks. The valley floor was still enmeshed in night but the camp was astir with the activity of camels being loaded and yurts and equipment packed away. Three old men worked like frenzies packing crates and bags near the central campfire and Gillon spotted what he supposed were women carrying boxes toward the line of camels that had already been saddled and were complaining loudly as the loads were lashed securely onto their backs. Men, women and children wore the same heavy clothing, either the traditional padded jackets and pants or else the cast-off cold-weather clothing of a dozen different armies, and it was extremely difficult to distinguish between sexes at distances beyond a few feet.

Behind him, Stowe edged out of the yurt through the narrow doorway. He bent forward and tugged the white coverall parka over his head, then glanced toward Gillon.

'Morning.'

Gillon nodded and watched two small boys chase a bellowing camel in from the trees. The noise was unbelievable but he saw that in what appeared to be complete chaos, every action was performed with practiced purposefulness. The felt yurts disappeared quickly and shortly the women were at work sweeping the snow.

Gillon nodded at Stowe. 'If we want to eat, we had better get this thing packed up. Or else they may decide to leave us.'

Stowe stopped swinging his arms and stamping his feet against the brutal dawn cold and glanced around the campsite, noticing the activity for the first time. He turned to examine the yurt.

'Have you ever taken one of these things down before?'

'Nope, but it looks like it should be easy enough. The felt covering is tied to the curved risers and the floor is separate. I noticed that last night.'

Stowe wandered around the other side, then stopped to watch two women at work, as they struck a smaller yurt.

'Hey, look at that! The covering goes on in quarters . . .' Gillon walked around to join him and they both watched for a moment.

'Yeah . . . look, see if you can find any drawstrings inside where the sections meet while I pull the pegs out. We'll take one quarter at a time until we get this thing figured out. Oh . . . and get those other two clowns up, we'll need the help,' he called after Stowe. Stowe nodded and disappeared back inside. A moment later Dmietriev and Leycock stumbled out to stand shivering in the snow while they zipped up their parkas. The sheepskin floor coverings flew out after them. One roll hit Leycock in the back of the legs as he bent over to lace up his boots and sent him sprawling into the snow. Between Leycock's profanity and Gillon's and Dmietriev's laughter they made a fair start on dismantling the yurt.

Drawstrings on the inside held the four quarters tightly over the pole framework that came together in a cleverly fashioned socket at the top to form the smoke hole. The eight tent poles were then held securely in place by the tension of the felt covering. It took them twenty minutes of fumbling and false starts to dismantle the yurt and roll the felt quarters up tightly. By the time they had finished they had gathered a crowd of grinning men and angry women.

218

Stowe straightened up to see one of the women glaring at him. 'Oh, oh . . . it looks like we are in for some trouble,' he called to Gillon, and jerked his thumb at the crowd.

Gillon turned to look and the men broke into gales of laughter as one of the older women made an obscene gesture and spit into the snow at his feet.

Surprised, Gillon dropped the roll of felt he was tying off and the stiff fabric began to unroll. The old woman elbowed Dmietriev out of the way and spitting a stream of curses, snatched it up.

'It looks like we are breaking into someone's union . . .' Gillon started to say when he caught sight of the caravan master stalking angrily toward them. Still laughing, the men broke away to return to the camels but the women began shouting and gesticulating at Gillon. The caravan master pushed through, then with kicks and blows herded them back toward the camels. He returned immediately, shouting angrily, and Gillon understood at once. They were not to touch anything, they were to stay out of the way entirely. He put his hands behind his back and marched to the side, nodding his head to show that he understood. Somewhat mollified by this ready acceptance, the caravan master stopped shouting, shook his head and turned back to the camels. A few paces away, he turned and pointed toward the cooking pots, then at his mouth, then at the four of them and finally at the ground beside their half-struck yurt.

'What the hell was that last bit?' Leycock demanded.

Dmietriev, grinning for the first time in days, explained.

'He was telling us to keep our hands to ourselves and not touch any of his equipment. Then he told us that we were barbarians, not fit to live with civilized people and that we would be fed, but we would have to stay away from his people.'

'Do you understand that language?' Stowe asked in surprise.

'Mongolian . . . oh no. But the meaning was plain enough.'

'That it was,' Gillon said quietly. He turned away,

angry and somewhat embarrassed at the same time. Around the camp, the darkness was beginning to dissipate as the sun climbed higher over the eastern peaks. As yet, it had not reached into the valley, but the ridges to the south and west were sharply outlined in the reddish dawn glow. As the light brightened, he caught sight of a line of black dots crawling slowly over the crest of a ridge to the southwest. A sudden feeling of loneliness went through him as he realized that it was Jack Liu and his people. For one intense moment, he was tempted to throw the packet to Stowe and go after Liu.

'Come on,' Leycock said, breaking into his reverie. 'They're ready to feed us.'

Gillon shivered slightly, took a last look at the distant line of figures, then followed Leycock, Stowe and Dmietriev toward the central fire.

The sunlight had barely reached the valley floor when the caravan march began. Gillon had never imagined a caravan traveling through forest. Camels and caravans belonged to deserts, not high mountain valleys. But now that he was actually a part of a caravan, following one of the most ancient caravan routes in the world, he realized that the desert portions of the Asian route would be relatively short in proportion to the segments that would lead through temperate forests and high mountain passes.

According to Jack Liu, the route they would follow was one of the oldest. Centuries before, it had constituted the main road from Peking and Urumchi to the ancient Central Asian cities of Samarkand and Herat. From there, it led to Persia and finally Istanbul and Antioch, a total of nearly seven thousand miles. Now it was reduced to an almost unknown route less than two thousand miles long. But even so, an annual business only slightly less lively than that of the less ancient African trade routes was still conducted. Across the Gobi into the Khalik Tau range, down through its valleys to the southeastern flanks of the Tien Shan to the Pamir-Altai plateau, where it crossed the Soviet border a final time into northern Afghanistan; all but four hundred miles of the trail — the Gobi portion — was above six thousand feet.

The caravan was large and stretched so far ahead that Gillon, Stowe, Leycock and Dmietriev, stuck back near the tail end, where they could be conveniently watched, could rarely see the entire line. All the long morning and well into the afternoon, they marched at what Gillon considered to be an exceptionally fast pace.

They were placed so as to march abreast of the last few camels in the single file. The camel masters steadily ignored them except to shout curses if they came too near. Guards came and went on snowshoes or skis, always watchful. They were under the constant surveillance of at least two guards at all times. The one time during the day that a search aircraft flew at treetop level over the forest the caravan came to an abrupt halt while guards swept down the line warning all to remain perfectly still. The Kalmucks stood as carved from ice with practiced precision that told Gillon this was for them a routine drill. He was, however, not certain that he appreciated the five men who surrounded them with lowered rifles. The aircraft did not return and the caravan moved off, but the four of them remained subdued for some time afterward.

It was well along toward sundown before the caravan halted for the night. Near exhaustion, Gillon stumbled to a halt while the camel drivers led their animals off. Having learned that morning that their help was neither wanted nor solicited, he lowered his pack and sat down in the snow under the branches of a spruce. Leycock dropped down next to him.

'Christ! You'd think they would at least take these damned packs so that we wouldn't have to carry them.'

Gillon gave him a grin of sympathy and nodded. 'I suppose they have each animal loaded to the exact mark. Another thirty pounds each just might swamp them.'

'Yeah, I guess so. Did you notice that no one rides? Not even the women or kids.'

Gillon nodded, and too tired to carry on a conversation, closed his eyes and let his mind drift.

Stowe and Dmietriev trudged up, dumped their packs and sank down into the snow beside them.

'Goddamn, I'm bushed,' Stowe muttered. 'These are the marchingest people I've ever seen. I thought caravans only traveled about fifteen miles a day and stopped early. Hell, I bet we've covered at least twenty miles.'

Dmietriev leaned back, cradling his head against his pack with a deep sigh that blew a plume of frosted breath in a long, curling streamer. 'Perhaps they are anxious to be rid of us. If we have walked twenty miles today, then we are much nearer the border than I thought we would be.'

'Speaking of the border,' Stowe said, turning to Gillon, 'no one has asked yet, but did your gook friend pass on the information that we came for?'

Gillon bit back the sharp retort at Stowe's choice of words. He shook his head, wondering how the devil Stowe had gotten as far as he had with a disposition that automatically set your teeth on edge every time he opened his mouth. But he was too tired to argue and so he contented himself with a nod.

Stowe stared at him for a moment, then shrugged. 'We come halfway around the world, risk our lives climbing all over these goddamned mountains in the dead of winter, nearly get ourselves killed a dozen times and all you can do is nod.'

Gillon answered mildly. 'Right now, I care more about something to eat and a place to sleep. If this damn weather keeps up, none of us are going much farther.'

'I'll second that.' Leycock chuckled. 'Let's get something cooking before we do anything else.' He grabbed his pack and started to undo the straps. Gillon grabbed his arm.

'Wait a minute. Part of the deal that Liu worked out included food. Let them feed us, they've got plenty and we may need what little we have left. In fact,' he added, 'save whatever you can from dinner tonight, just to be on the safe side.'

Gillon's order left them all feeling uneasy as the women came up and silently began to pitch their oversized yurt.

Two more long exhausting days followed as the four

men plodded along in the wake of the fast-moving caravan. They ate mechanically the bland food that was furnished to them and at sunset collapsed into their sleeping bags only to rise before dawn to march through heavily forested foothills and mountain slopes. During the three days of the long march they covered nearly fifty miles, which took them along the high, wooded escarpment of the Tien Shan and down into the Jam River valley. On the evening of the third day the caravan halted on a ridge overlooking the river, which in spite of the fierce cold and high winds, still tumbled and flashed between snow- and ice-encrusted banks in its plunge from the Subarcho Glacier ten miles northwest to the desert sixty miles southeast. As soon as the yurt had been rigged by the women, they collected their food bowls and dragged their packs inside and slumped down on the soft sheepskins and ate silently, too tired even to talk, while the interior warmed slowly from the smoky fire. The only blessing so far had been the fact that Liu's expected blizzard had failed to materialize.

Gillon dug out his maps and studied the area between the valley and the glacier.

'All right, gentlemen,' he announced finally. 'Tomorrow we leave these marching fools.'

The other three sat up quickly, interest overriding their weariness.

'All right! Leycock chortled. 'It's about time. Another day of this and my feet are going to fall off.'

He crawled over to the maps and Gillon laid a finger on the ridge where they were camped. 'This is where we are now.'

'So where do we go from here?'

Gillon moved his finger, tracing out a route that followed the river upstream.

'We'll cross the river with the caravan, and follow it west to where the valley narrows as the river comes through this gorge. From there, we'll go southwest along the edge of the glacier to the Kara Bure Col. It's five miles to the border from there.'

Stowe bent over the one-inch-scale map, studying it intently, then shook his head.

'It looks damned rough. Nearly eighteen thousand feet . . .'

'Want to stay with the caravan?' Leycock asked.

'Hell no . . .'

'Then shut up.'

Dawn brought a pale band of cloud across the northern horizon. Gillon dragged himself, still exhausted, from his sleeping bag to the iron cold of the morning. He shivered and wrapped his parka around him while the women struck the tent and brought food to them before the start of the day's march. Gillon raised his binoculars and studied the river valley below. The ridge on which they were camped was heavily wooded but as the slope descended toward the river, some five hundred feet or more below, the trees grew sparser until they had almost disappeared along the stream bed. Despite the river's fury as it thundered down from a series of falls at the head of the valley, Gillon could see why the caravan route led this way. The river broadened a mile downstream, spilling out over a wide, probably marshy area. In places, the river rippled over the bottom at a depth of less than two feet. The current was swift, but its shallowness would make fording relatively simple. Gillon did not, however, like the hour or so of exposure that would be needed to take the caravan across. But there apparently was no other choice unless the caravan climbed some eight thousand or more feet and crossed the Subarcho Glacier itself. According to the map, the river narrowed again further downstream, probably growing swifter and deeper as it plunged through the foothills to the southeast before it disappeared into the salt flats of the Taklamakan Desert.

He turned away and saw the caravan master striding toward him. This was the first time they had been so honoured since their first morning with the caravan. Other than the women who rigged and struck the yurt and brought their food and the ever present, ever changing guards, they had been studiously avoided by the rest of the caravan. Gillon saw Leycock step out of the yurt and stretch widely, then, as he saw the caravan master coming toward them, stoop and turn to call to the others inside. Leycock then sauntered over to stand in back of and to Gillon's right. Gillon noticed that he had his carbine slung over his shoulder.

The caravan master, a short man, but broad and appearing even more so in his bulky cold-weather clothes, stopped in front of Gillon. His eyes flicked first to Leycock and then to Stowe and Dmietriev as they both emerged armed from the yurt.

The caravan master bobbed his head in the jerky half-bow that seemed to be a standard greeting. He pointed to Gillon, then to Leycock, Stowe and Dmietriev in turn and finally swept an arm around to indicate the caravan. He stopped and waited to see if Gillon understood. Gillon nodded to show that he did.

The caravan master muttered approvingly and pointed next to the sky and waved his hand from horizon to horizon to signify the path of the sun. Gillon nodded again and to cut short a lengthy pantomimed explanation, he stooped down and drew a long line in the snow with four dots following another line away to the west. He sketched in a curving track and pointed to it and the sun.

The caravan master again rumbled approval and pointed to Stowe's carbine. Gillon nodded and sketched a long line leading from the caravan to the southwest, drew three crescent moons and the stick outline of an airplane. The caravan master nodded, squinted closely at Gillon, then shaking his head, strode away, bellowing orders as he did so.

The four men, feeling somewhat superior, grinned at each other and wandered back to the yurt, where an old woman had just deposited a plastic pail of some steaming, incomprehensible, gooey concoction of grain and unknown meat. It tasted horrible, but it was starchy and filling and they ate, if not with relish, at least with appetite.

If they had waited even a few more minutes, Gillon thought later, they could have wiped out the entire caravan at one pass. It happened so suddenly that the caravan came to an abrupt halt, milling in panic as they were midway out of the trees. The high-pitched turbine whine was screened by the trees and the ridge behind and the Migs were on them without warning. At the first ear-splitting roar, Gillon glanced up in time to see the second Mig flare out over the tops of the trees. Its silver shape was nothing more than an impression before the concussion of the first bomb threw him into the snow. Through the reddish haze that covered his eyes, Gillon saw billowing clouds of snow and smoke spurt up along the line of march and the Migs were banking around for a second run. They were using bombs, he thought stupidly, hardly able to credit what he was seeing; anti-personnel bombs and the air was full of whirring shrapnel and the snow was already littered with bodies, women, children, men and animals. Other animals raced in panic through the trees. One horse sheered back along the line of march, caroming off trees in its frantic efforts to escape the deadly bombardment. Gillon watched, frozen, as the horse galloped toward him and then was gone into the forest. The Migs made a third pass and this time their machine guns stuttered and the snow and ground beneath were churned into mud as the metal carved trees into kindling and sent great, jagged splinters whizzing through the air.

The Migs disappeared as abruptly as they had come and without knowing how or why, Gillon was running back along the length of the stricken caravan. Bodies, some reduced to mere bloody bundles of rags, were scattered in the snow. Here and there, a dying camel screamed shrilly and kicked and thrashed in agony. Gillon moved helplessly, shouldered aside rudely whenever he stopped by the uninjured men of the caravan, who glared at him with hate-filled eyes before they turned away. Even if he could have spoken their language, he knew it would have been useless to offer the excuse that their own greed for the money and weapons he had offered was as much to blame as his presence.

A woman lay dead, her face a bloody mass where the shrapnel had slashed into her. It was impossible to tell who she had been or how old she was. A few feet beyond, a camel quivered, struggled one last time and fell back stiffly and slowly relaxed, its great, wide eyes hazing as it died. The smoke of the bombing lay heavily in the trees for a moment, then stirred sluggishly with the breeze. Gillon leaned against a tree, sick to his soul. It was as bad as any village in Vietnam or Laos . . . after a Viet Cong raid or an Allied shelling or bombing . . . the results were always the same.

He turned away and started back, moving with a purpose now: to find the other three. He searched among the huddled wounded where those who had escaped the effects of the bombs were beginning to bring some order out of the chaos of smoke and blood.

'Gillon . . . Gillon, where the hell are you?' A moment later Leycock was running toward him. 'For God's sake, I've been looking all over hell . . . are you okay?'

Gillon nodded brusquely. 'Where's Stowe and Dmietriev?'

Leycock rubbed his forehead as he answered and Gillon saw that his face was pale and the pupils of his eyes dilated. Leycock swayed and, for a moment, Gillon thought he had been hit, but he recovered and answered.

'I . . . I don't know . . .'

But Gillon did not wait for him to finish. He trotted off back down the line again, checking each body, each cluster of dazed and injured along the way.

For ten minutes they searched back and forth along the length of the caravan until Gillon stopped suddenly.

'Listen . . .'

Leycock stared at him, but Gillon was already running ahead to the edge of the trees. Leycock followed and when they broke out into the open on the rim of the valley, Gillon waved him to silence.

For a long moment, they stood silently, listening to the faint sounds borne on the wind from the southern end of the valley. Then Leycock recognized the thin whine of a gas turbine engine and the heavier beat of the helicopter blades above the whimpering of the wounded behind them.

'Helicopters,' Gillon whispered at almost the same instant. 'Helicopters, we've got to get out of here . . .' He swung around but Leycock stopped him.

'Dmietriev and Stowe . . . we can't just leave them . . .'

'They are dead,' Gillon snarled. 'What else? We can't find them. They are either dead or gone. Either way, there is nothing that we can do for them. If we don't get out of here now, we'll be dead too. How long do you think it will take them to mop up what's left?'

'We can't leave them here,' Leycock shouted. 'You don't know they're dead . . .'

Gillon swore viciously. 'No, I don't, but in a few minutes they will be and so will we. We came to get the information that Jack Liu had for us and we got it. Unless we take it out, none of this makes any sense and none of *them* were ever worth a damn. It turns out to be one big joke. So you go to hell!' Gillon started off into the trees and after a moment, Leycock followed.

For the rest of that long day, Gillon climbed through the somber forest toward the glacier, hardly aware of Leycock struggling along behind. Restricted now to the northern side of the river, the map indicated that they must climb ridges that reached to twelve and thirteen thousand feet, cross one of the most treacherous glaciers in Asia and the mid-slopes south of Janart Peak at 15,000 feet. In spite of the implacable hatred which obscured everything else, he was well aware that he must manage to elude heavy Red Chinese patrols to cross the border into the Soviet Union. It was an impossible task; but Gillon no longer cared whether or not it was possible. It was something that he would do. His indifference toward the Red Chinese had become a consuming hatred, for all that they had been the butt of the Kalmucks' jokes and rudeness. That he would deliver the packet of information to the Soviets, he no longer doubted. And he would deliver it gladly on the chance that the Soviets would use the information to initiate a pre-emptive strike that would destroy a regime that would order and carry out such wanton killings.

All through the endless afternoon, wherever there was a break in the trees to the east, they could see the thin plume of smoke that marked the valley where the bombs had fallen and set fire to the forest, making of it a grand funeral pyre. Gillon pushed himself to the limit of his endurance and then beyond, not stopping even for the briefest rest, knowing that within hours, the Chinese troops would have found the bodies of Stowe and Dmietriev – and their own tracks leading up the ridge. As the afternoon waned into evening, he began to hear aircraft high above flying endless search patterns over the forest.

Darkness fell and still Gillon pushed on, ignoring Leycock's exhausted urgings to rest. The trees had begun to thin and by the time the shaven moon had risen, they were climbing upward through open terrain, pitched steeply on the southern face of a wide ridge that, according to the map, gave onto a narrow plateau, on the far side of which rested the Subarcho Glacier. Beyond the glacier was a last terrible climb of two thousand feet to a pass that gave onto the border.

The sky had clouded over during the afternoon with high, thin cirrus that covered the sky from horizon to horizon. As the night advanced the mild wind blowing from the peaks above died and the air grew still and cold. A thin mist began to fill the air, a mist composed of tiny ice crystals, and which burned bare flesh wherever it touched. The moon was a pale disk through the ice, which, as the night progressed and the mist thickened, began to disappear.

Leycock stopped and screamed at Gillon, screamed with all of the same frustration and tension that was serving to drive Gillon on. Gillon did not hear him, the profanity and curses that Leycock flung at him did not register. Leycock stumbled after him, panting hoarsely in the thin air, and grabbed at his shoulder. Gillon, shocked into awareness by the abrupt check, whirled. Leycock ducked, parried the straight-arm punch and slammed Gillon in the chest with a flailing elbow strike that smashed him back into the snow. Gillon rolled with the force of the blow and was on his feet in the same motion, but Leycock had fallen back and Gillon found himself staring into the muzzle of his carbine.

'Damn you, damn you!' Leycock screamed, stumbling forward to his knees. 'Stop . . . we've got to stop or we'll freeze to death!'

Gillon started forward, oblivious to the weapon; then, suddenly realizing, fell back a step, his hands hanging loosely at his sides. His knees buckled and he too all but collapsed into the snow.

'All right,' he choked. 'We'll stop . . . but only for a few hours.'

Leycock got to his feet and wearily shrugged out of his pack. Together, they pitched one tent, driving the pegs deep into the hard-packed snow with their carbine butts. Leycock dragged their packs inside and laid out the sleeping bags, then called to Gillon, who had remained kneeling in the snow by the last peg, staring with unseeing eyes at the now almost invisible disk of the moon. Leycock crawled over, grabbed his arm and half dragged him into the tent. Gillon roused long enough to crawl into his sleeping bag. He was asleep before he had zipped it closed.

CHAPTER SIXTEEN

It was two hours short of dawn when Gillon woke abruptly. The silence was almost absolute – interrupted only by Leycock's curiously ragged breathing in the high, thin air of the plateau. For nine days they had never really been free of sound; aircraft engines, the incessant wind, the crunch of snow underfoot and the eerie gunshot-like report of cracking trees in the intense frost, the action and noise of the caravan.

But now there was silence and it was oppressive. Gillon twisted, pulled aside the tent flaps and looked out. The night was utterly black at first and then he saw the pale glimmer of the moon to the west. The ice mist had thickened to a shroudlike consistency and the air was utterly still. Not the faintest breath of wind stirred and as the mist settled it began to burn the exposed skin of his face and hands. He shivered and re-closed the flaps, then dug the Primus stove out of his pack, moving awkwardly in the confined space of the tent and the encumbrance of his sleeping bag.

He stared blankly at the pale blue flame as it cast a

230

dim light in the tent while the pan of snow melted, then roused long enough to add tea leaves, a double portion for each of them, and the water boiled quickly. The boiling water early reminded him that he and Leycock were running for their lives across one of the highest mountain ranges in the world. They had crossed the southern slope of Janart Peak the previous afternoon and were now on the 16,000-foot-high plateau beneath Pobeda Peak, the highest mountain in the Tien Shan at 24,000 feet. He felt the tension of the situation begin to tighten his stomach muscles into a hard cramp and he knew that it would not relax until he was safely across the border – or dead. He swore to himself, more in exasperation with his own recalcitrant body than at the circumstances that had placed him in this situation. The water took on a darker color than the surrounding gloom and he nudged Leycock, then poured two mugs full of the lukewarm liquid and dug out the last of the foil-wrapped ration packs. Leycock had two remaining and they each had part of the hard-baked, unleavened bread left that was a main staple in the Kalmuck diet. After that, he estimated that in their physical condition and at these altitudes and temperatures, they had at best an additional twenty-four to thirty-six hours before they would be too weak to move. He recalled an account he had read of Scott's death in the Antarctic less than fifty miles from an emergency cache of food and his own bewilderment as to why they had not been able to exert that last two or three days' effort to reach it instead of slowly dying of starvation in their tent. Now he felt he understood.

Leycock woke slowly and Gillon had to shake him violently several times to get him into a sitting position. The strong tea helped to revive him enough to eat and Gillon knew that unless they got out soon, they were finished. He had come to depend on Leycock's strength and never failing sense of humor, but the past nine days of violent exercise at high altitudes had taken their toll. Leycock's face was sunken and pinched and pale patches which indicated the beginnings of frostbite were visible on his nose and forehead. His eyes peered out dully between the lowered hood and the ten days of bearded stubble giving him that haunted concentration-camp-inmate look. Gillon knew that his face must look the same.

Silently, they forced the inadequate rations down with gulps of tea, then rolled their sleeping bags, struck the tent and folded the stiffened fabric into Leycock's pack. Gillon had donned his face mask and settled snow goggles over the eye holes. Over his parka, he pulled the rainproof poncho to shield himself as much as possible from the tentacles of ice mist that seemed to search out every gap in the fabric of their cold-weather clothing. Leycock followed his lead and, wordlessly, they shouldered their packs and carbines and, compasses in hand, started forward. The glimmer of moonlight through the clouds cast no appreciable light and Gillon used his flashlight freely, knowing that the mist made its dim, frozen light invisible beyond a few feet.

Within an hour, they were climbing up through the jumble of ice and rock that led to the northern reaches of the Subarcho Glacier. No one in his right mind would have attempted this climb in the darkness, but both men knew only too well that they had no other choice. They traveled as carefully as was possible, testing for hidden crevices and faulty snow bridges, and a small amount of luck remained with them. Temperatures had been low enough in recent weeks that the winter's accumulation of snow had frozen into solid névé that at least provided firm footing. It would have been different, Gillon knew, if temperatures had been even a few degrees higher, as this would have been sufficient to increase the internal movement of the ice to twist and wrap the surface into dangerous configurations, opening up chasms in the ice that the heavy snows of winter could not have bridged.

Slowly, almost imperceptibly, the darkness thinned as they struggled across the rugged surface with its great blocks of ice, twisted and smashed by the passage of the glacier across the stubborn rock of the mountains. It was well toward midmorning before they were finished with the glacier and clambered down onto the wind-packed snow of the high slopes once more. Here the travel was faster – or would have been if their reserves of strength had not been exhausted. The sun was a pale ghost of silver light gliding through the ice cloud. On the one hand, Gillon was grateful for the concealment offered, while at the same time he cursed the bitter, strength-sapping touch of the mist. While it remained, there was no chance that the Chinese would be able to spot them from the air. Within an hour, they had both become shrouded in suits of frost whose coldness penetrated the insulation of their clothing, even without benefit of wind. Gillon stared around at the mountains, half hidden in the frozen mist. They were climbing up through a narrow pass, or col. On either side, the peaks closed in around them the higher they climbed, funneling their route into a pass which the map indicated was less than two miles ahead. The oppressive silence held sway for a moment more: then he heard, faintly in the distance, a booming begin to grow into a steady roar, sounding very much like the roar of jet aircraft engines being run-up prior to takeoff. For a moment he was puzzled by the sound and he and Leycock exchanged half-puzzled, half-apprehensive glances as the booming sped toward them. A barely seen shadow, like the forward wall of a high-explosive bomb concussion, swept down the pass toward them, and seconds later the wind struck in full fury, screaming through the rocks and ice. They half turned and crouched, shielding themselves against the wind.

Only once before had Gillon encountered such a wind and that had been deep into the High Sierras of California, years before. He had heard the same distant booming then, far off among the peaks, and the wind had come sweeping down through the passes at thirty and forty miles an hour. That night it had rained with all the fury of a hurricane and before morning the storm had become one of the worst summer blizzards that he had ever experienced. As they struggled forward, Gillon could only hope that this wind did not presage another such storm for them.

All through the interminable day, Gillon and Leycock struggled upward against the mountains, the temperature and now the wind, taking what advantage the covering mist offered. They stopped briefly for rest every hour and for fifteen minutes at noon to eat. More time than that, they both knew they could not spare.

By midafternoon, the mist was beginning to dissipate somewhat under the repeated onslaught of the wind; but it remained a thick layer of cloud above the twenty-thousand-foot level. A dare-devil pilot, one who did not care the least about his own life, could have flown in to search for them . . . but even so, visibility was so poor that one moment's inattention, and the mountains would destroy the aircraft.

They reached the top of the pass at 18,000 feet three hours before dark. The cloud-wreathed peaks of the central Tien Shan lay before them, clothed in majestic robes of newly fallen snow and highlighted on their higher slopes by the pale sun. Heavy snow clouds clung tenaciously to the peaks, wrapping them in angry rolls of gray and black. The sight of the peaks and their coverings of snow and cloud sloping down into the deep valleys below was breathtaking; a sharply etched lithograph done in grays, whites and steel blues. To the north of where they stood reared the fortress-like Pobeda Peak and beyond was the Tengri Khan. Both peaks were enmeshed in a battle with the snow cloud that surmounted their 24,000-foot masses. Gillon turned away from the twin peaks to examine the valley directly below them when Leycock grabbed his arm and pointed back down the pass. Gillon swung around and peered into the mist.

At first, there was nothing to be seen but the sun-brightened mist and snow. Then the movement of two unsubstantial black specks riveted his attention. Gillon shrugged out of his pack and quickly dug his binoculars out of his pack.

Through the glasses, the dots resolved into the figures of two men struggling toward the top of the pass but the mist was still too thick and the distance too great to discern details. Gillon tapped Leycock on the shoulder and motioned to the rocks along the side of the crest. Leycock nodded and wordlessly the two men picked up their packs and carbines and climbed up into the rocks to a point where they would be invisible from below. Gillon laid his carbine across the top of his pack and settled himself to wait, watching the figures below through his binoculars.

Within thirty minutes, the two men below them had moved close enough for them to be identified as Dmietriev and Stowe. He and Leycock exchanged surprised glances and Gillon continued to watch through narrowed eyes as the two men came on slowly, stopping to rest often on the last, six-hundred-foot climb up the col. The tracks that he and Leycock had left would be plainly visible and Dmietriev and Stowe seemed to be following the same, exact route. Painfully, the two men struggled up the last steep stretch and slumped exhausted into the snow below where they were crouched.

Gillon nudged Leycock and they slid down out of the rocks to confront the surprised pair. Dmietriev saw them first and jumped to his feet, fumbling for his carbine. Stowe, emaciated and barely conscious, glanced up slowly and the relief in his face was clearly visible.

The four men stared at each other for a long moment until Dmietriev said hoarsely, 'They wiped out the entire caravan.' He turned then to stare off down the far side of the pass toward the magnificence of the twin peaks, his expression one of indescribable sadness.

'We watched them from the top of the ridge,' he continued quietly. 'Troops came in by helicopter and they rounded up anybody left alive, then shot all the animals. The helicopters carried the survivors out and left the troops to start after us.'

Stowe nodded absently as if in confirmation.

'Yeah, we saw some of it,' Leycock said. 'We didn't think that you two had gotten out of the valley.'

There was a sense of unreality in the scene, Gillon thought, of four men quietly discussing the massacre of dozens of people while they themselves sat only a few miles from the scene of their own probable deaths at the border.

'It was very close,' Dmietriev admitted. 'We were almost taken once, near the crest. But we shot at two of the soldiers and were able to hide in the trees until dark. We did not think to catch up with you on this side of the border.'

'You knew that we had gotten away?' Gillon asked sharply.

Dmietriev nodded. 'He saw you go' – he hooked a thumb at Stowe – 'but we did not know about Mr. Leycock . . .' Again, that feeling of unreality. For nine days now they had depended every second of their lives on one another, and yet they were not on a first-name basis.

Gillon nodded. So Stowe had seen him going up through the trees. Just where in hell had they all been when the Migs had started their runs? he wondered. He remembered that Stowe had been behind him, which explained why he would have seen him climbing up through the trees. Leycock had pushed on ahead as he often did, as if the pace of the caravan were too slow for him. But he had not been out of his sight . . . he never was. He did not recall where Dmietriev had been at that moment, only that he had been near the end of the caravan, some fifty feet behind him the last time he had checked. Dmietriev, then, had been the one out of sight for a few minutes, just before the Migs struck.

Of a sudden Gillon remembered one final item that had not registered until now – from the crest he had seen a red smoke marker streaming upward from the trees to the rear of the caravan. But the Migs had struck from the northeast at an angle to the caravan's line of march, from behind the ridge, where the sound of their engines would be obscured. He had automatically assumed that the flare had been dropped by one of the aircraft, but now that he thought about it, he remembered that the smoke marker had come from the trees several hundred yards behind the caravan. If the marker had been dropped from an aircraft, it would have to have been during the third pass at the earliest. The first had taken them on the flank. The second pass had been made from directly ahead as the aircraft turned to run back along the length of the column. And by then no marker would have been necessary because of the smoke from the bombs. And Dmietriev carried the remaining explosives in his pack, plus four smoke markers which they had intended to use to mark the landing site for their own pickup aircraft.

Almost stunned by the sudden realization, Gillon

stared at the three men crouched with him in the rocks, sheltering from the wind. Now it all fitted together completely; the smoke marker was the key to the puzzle. Dmietriev had to be the Chinese agent; he *must* have called in the Migs with that marker, figuring that they would either be killed by the Migs or captured by the Chinese troops being helicoptered in. Either way, the Chinese would have had the packet of information. Those damnable markers could be seen for miles, miles which the Migs and copters could cover in minutes. And the aircraft exploding prematurely – Dmietriev had checked the explosive pack one last time before they jumped. And it would have been easy enough to change just one timer, reset it to explode a few minutes sooner than Rodek had planned. That had brought Chinese troops into the exact area hours sooner than they had expected. Jack Liu had been right after all. Those troopers he had killed in the forest on the third night had been moving to an ambush site when they had accidentally stumbled onto them; otherwise they would have all – Jack Liu and his people included – been taken the next day. Not daring to look at Dmietriev for fear his thoughts were written too plainly on his face, he glanced down at the snow-covered ice beneath his boots. Any doubts he had about Liu's analysis were resolved now. There was no doubt in his mind that the big Russian had betrayed them all.

The western side of the pass and the line of peaks were beginning to emerge from the shroud of ice and cloud. What the hell did he do next? he wondered. What did he do about Dmietriev?

His head ached with the effects of exhaustion and altitude and he found it impossible to think clearly. And he needed to do so, needed time to think this out clearly and concisely, to be absolutely sure that he was correct.

'It's clearing off,' he said tightly. 'We can make the border tonight and we'll try and cross in the dark, after the moon rises.'

While the others murmured assent, he went on. 'There's a ledge about a quarter of a mile down into the pass. I saw it earlier. I think we would be better off waiting there than up here.'

Leycock nodded. 'With the sky clearing, they'll be desperate to get search planes in before dark. We heard one an hour ago.'

Stowe seemed to have regained a measure of strength during the brief rest and he flared up immediately.

'For Christ's sake, how the hell can they know where we are? There are a dozen different ways we could have gone. I say, let's get to the border as fast as possible while we have enough light to climb down.'

Gillon's patience snapped. The last thing he needed now was Stowe's continued sniping.

'You bloody bastard. How stupid do you think they are? Of course they know where we are . . . there's only one way to cross the border in this area without hiking twenty miles or more farther and that one place is through this col. They can get up here a hell of a lot faster than we did. They could have parachuted troops down onto the glacier or even into the valley here. They could very well be down there now waiting for us to come bumbling along.'

He snarled at them, 'You do what you want, all of you. If you want to try for the border now, you're welcome to. But I'm damned well going down to that ledge and wait.'

Without another word, he picked up his pack and trudged off, shrugging his shoulders into the straps. He did not look back; Leycock, ignoring the other two, followed immediately. Dmietriev and Stowe exchanged glances and Dmietriev got to his feet and started after them. Stowe watched the three of them go, and if Gillon had turned just then, he would have seen the big man's eyes narrow and his face take on an expression of suspicion, rather than anger, as he studied the departing backs of each in turn. After a moment, realizing that they could not afford to be separated at this point in the game, Stowe stood, hefted his pack over one shoulder and started after them.

It took them an hour to negotiate the steep slope to reach the ledge that Gillon had selected. It was a rocky outcropping some twenty feet wide, jutting from the almost vertical rear wall, which curved slightly outward to form a shelter. The ledge dropped sharply for some twenty feet before it began to decline in a more gradual manner until it reached the valley floor. Gillon and Leycock reached the ledge before Dmietriev, who had stopped to wait for Stowe.

The wind had stiffened to a force-eight gale by the time the four of them were safely down on the ledge. The bulk of the ridge behind them effectively cut off the pale, setting sun and although the valley floor was still light, on the ledge they were in deep shadow – a frigid shade made more intense by the wind. Gillon emptied his pack against the ridge wall and with his knife, sliced along the top seam of the tent fabric. With pegs, he fastened one end to the ledge and the other to the cliff itself, forming a shelter against the wind. While Leycock followed his example, he, Stowe and Dmietriev each went through their packs discarding everything but canteens, ammunition and skis. They would have no further need for the snowshoes that had served them so well during the long days and it was with some regret that Gillon abandoned the lightweight polyester-strung aluminum frames.

The two tents, fastened side by side, formed an effective wind shelter and they heated and ate the last of their rations. Stowe argued that they should conserve some of the food until they were certain that the Soviets were waiting for them on the other side of the border.

Gillon laughed at him over the loud snapping of the tent fabric in the wind. 'If they aren't, we're dead. Unless there is at least half a division of Soviet troops waiting for us, nothing will stop the Chinese from coming across after us . . . and if they do, they'll catch us. This is it, buddy. It's tonight or never . . .'

He took a perverse pleasure in seeing Dmietriev nod in agreement. He had made certain that the explosives Dmietriev had emptied from his pack had been moved to his side of the ledge. And he had not been surprised to notice that one of the smoke flare canisters was missing.

After they had eaten, he picked up his binoculars and

went out onto the ledge. He had decided on his course of action and as he studied the valley floor and the mountain slopes on the other side in the fast-fading light, he went over the plan one last time, looking for any flaws.

They had laid their collective plans for crossing while eating the last of the meager rations. Moonrise was due for midnight. Until then, they would get all the rest they could for the final dash. As soon as the moon was high enough to shed sufficient light to see by, they would ski for the border as fast as possible. There was no other choice but a direct push for the wire and hope to God the Russians were waiting for them, alerted by the Red Chinese activity in the area, and could provide any covering fire required.

Gillon's plan was as simple as he could make it. Following Liu's advice at last, he would leave an hour before moonrise, purposely leaving the others to make their way across as best they could. If the three of them made it, they could deal with Dmietriev afterward. If not, then the problem would have taken care of itself. For a moment, but a moment only, Gillon had supposed himself half-insane even to contemplate abandoning Stowe and Leycock, but savagely he had thrust the thought away. At this point in time, the morality and sanity of the situation were the least of his considerations. That packet of information was going to the Russians and nothing more was standing in his way.

A few minutes later, Stowe crawled out of the shelter, binoculars in hand. Wordlessly, he joned Gillon and in strained silence they both watched the valley below.

The final hour to sunset dragged on and on. Gillon watched the sky fade from gray to blue, a hard, clear blue as the sun made its final bow toward the horizon. Aircraft had appeared in the last remaining minutes of light to cruise back and forth, searching for any trace of their quarry. Gradually their sound faded as the sky turned black, leaving only the incessant wind whining around them to break the utter stillness of the mountain night.

CHAPTER SEVENTEEN

As the evening ran sluggishly into night, the crystal clarity of the sky disappeared behind an overcast that grew steadily darker and more angry-looking by the hour. The wind had increased in velocity as well and it flapped the make-shift wind shelter they had constructed from the tent panels with vicious force. Just as the last remaining light faded from the valley, Stowe nudged Gillon and pointed across the valley to a point centered between the shallow slopes where a very thin line of barbed wire was barely discernible above the snow. A tiny black speck moved along the fence and as they watched, several others came into view.

'Which side are they on?' Gillon asked quietly.

Stowe waited a moment before answering. '. . . On the Russian side, I think . . .'

'Let's hope to hell you're right.'

'If nothing else, all the troop movements in this area would have alerted them . . . and just maybe they are smart enough to put two and two together,' Stowe muttered, half convinced.

Gillon hoped that the Russians did have sense enough to realize what was going on. Coded messages should be swarming back and forth between the border and Moscow . . . the last thing he wanted was to be shot by Russians as he tried to cross.

Far down the valley almost out of sight around a shallow bend in the mountain flank was a watchtower. They estimated its distance at twelve miles, too far away to tell if it was occupied.

In a desultory way, he and Stowe discussed the planned approach to the border. Except for drifted snow, there was no cover of any kind. They speculated that the border was probably mined up to a quarter of a mile deep on both sides and decided that the snow was deep enough to prevent the mines from exploding. As a safety precaution, Stowe suggested cutting up the remaining four pounds of gelignite into quarter-pound cubes. Using ten-second fuses, they could clear a path through the minefield with sympathetic detonations if it became necessary. It was not a plan to inspire confidence, but then, Gillon thought ruefully, nothing about this mission ever had, and in any event, after all they had been through and still expected to face, a few mines hardly seemed worth bothering about. But he agreed anyway and they both returned to the shelter.

Knowing that the mission was drawing to a conclusion, Gillon was aware of a deepening lassitude. He could see it in the faces of the other three as well. They had done their job; the weather had worked both for and against them and now that the final task was almost complete, he dared not allow himself to become careless.

When they had finished with the explosives and were slumped in various attitudes of exhaustion, Gillon put his share of the explosive away into his almost empty pack and shoved it against the wall next to his carbine.

'Okay,' he announced, mustering as much forcefulness as possible. 'Moonrise is at midnight. By oh one hundred or so, it should be high enough to see by, and that's when we go. Until then, we are going to break into two-hour shifts . . . outside. If the Chicoms come over that pass, I want as much time as possible to get down into the valley.'

The other three groaned, but no one argued, and Gillon pointed to Dmietriev. 'You lead off. Stowe, you take the second, Leycock, third and I'll go last.'

Dmietriev nodded and got slowly to his feet. He picked up his carbine and paused at the entrance. He looked back at the three upturned faces, his own expression blank, then stepped out onto the ledge.

He awoke sluggishly, forcing himself out of the drugged depths of exhaustion. Leycock was prodding his arm with the carbine. Gillon sat up to see his haggard face peering at him, almost hidden by the low hood and the ten-day growth of heavy beard.

'It's your turn,' Leycock said softly, then shuffled to his pack and sank down with a groan. His chin dropped forward onto his chest and he was asleep instantly.

Gillon got slowly to his feet, using his own carbine

as a cane, astounded at the variety of ways that his body could ache . . and all simultaneously. He stepped out into the wind and cold that had grown more bitter with each passing hour.

He checked his watch. Twenty minutes to make sure they were all sound asleep and he would go. In spite of his exhaustion, he could feel the tension twisting his abdominal muscles into knots. He glanced up at the sky. It had become sharp and clear as the last of the aborted storm dissipated and the Milky Way was an almost solid river of stars between the valley walls.

He swore under his breath at the cold and forced himself to pace up and down the length of the ledge. The wind whipped his parka against his back and deep into any opening it found. With the wind speed at forty to fifty miles an hour his difficulties in covering that last mile on skis would only be increased.

Gillon reached the far side of the ledge and started back. He paused for a moment to peer upward, searching for any movement along the crest of the pass. There was none and the night was quiet but for the steady whine of the wind. Reaching the center of the ledge again where it pulled away from the wall, he stopped and stared down into the valley, which had become a pale blur barely visible in the starlight. With the binoculars he searched in the direction of the watchtower but could see nothing in the starlit blackness except the dim glimmer of snow. There were no lights of any kind along the border and he knew that the Russians would be foolish to try to maintain a garrison here during the winter. Resupply would be difficult at best in the summer and impossible in the winter. Blizzards that lasted for days and the constant wind that blew for weeks at a time were effective deterrents. But he also thought he knew the Russians well enough to realize that no matter what the weather or terrain, from the Arctic to the Crimea, the Sinkiang border to Western Europe, they would never for an instant leave a single inch of frontier unguarded. There were plenty of Russian troops over there, of that he was certain, and they would be waiting for them.

Gillon paced up and down the length of the ledge

several more times until finally, the moon, much reduced from its round opulence of a few days before, began to gleam behind the eastern peaks where he could see them through the gap in the ridge. Now was the time. To delay longer would rob him of desperately needed time and he turned toward the windbreak to gather his skis and equipment.

Dmietriev was standing directly in front of him, a pistol held comfortably in his right hand; the dark, cylindrical shape of a silencer mounted on the muzzle. His expression was carved from ice and his dark eyes stared at Gillon unwinkingly. The dead, flat expression told him more eloquently than words that if he so much as twitched, a bullet would issue from the end of the silenced pistol.

'Turn around and let the carbine fall,' Dmietriev said quietly. There was no trace of hesitation or deference in his voice and Gillon turned slowly, letting the weapon slide off his shoulder and down his arm into the snow.

'Walk to the edge.'

He did so, then turned back to Dmietriev, who motioned him to start down the slope. The pistol held steadily on the center of his chest.

'Climb down until I tell you to stop. If you do anything else, you will die. Do you understand?'

Gillon nodded. He knew that within a few minutes Dmietriev would shoot him to death anyway, but there was absolutely nothing that he could do about it. His own pistol was inside his parka, inaccessible. His knife he could probably reach, but to use it effectively, he would first have to sidestep the bullet that Dmietriev would fire reflexively and then whip the knife into Dmietriev's eye. He would never avoid the first shot and he knew it. Dmietriev had him; there was no way that he could move fast enough.

They went carefully down the steep slope, feeling for footholds. Gillon thought about throwing himself headlong down the slope, depending on the darkness to shield him until he reached the meager cover of the snowdrifts below, but the reflected light was bright enough that Dmietriev would be able to see him for a good twenty feet – ample time to fire.

'Stop.'

Gillon stopped, his back muscles tensing uncontrollaby. He heard Dmietriev coming closer.

'Give me the packet,' Dmietriev said quietly.

Gillon shook his head. 'It's in my pack . . . we'll have to go back . . .'

'You're lying,' Dmietriev said without inflection. 'I have searched your pack and it is not there. Give it to me or I will shoot you and take it from your body.'

Gillon turned carefully, expecting to be told to stop, but Dmietriev said nothing and when Gillon was facing him, he simply motioned for him to raise his hands. Gillon did so and clasped them on top of his head.

'The packet . . .' he repeated, and Gillon knew that he had no other choice.

'It's inside my parka.'

'Use your left hand and do not touch the pistol that you have in the shoulder holster nor the knife behind your neck.'

'Very observant,' Gillon muttered, and when Dmietriev did not reply, did not even indicate that he had heard, he lowered his left hand slowly and unzipped the parka, pulling it wide. The wind tugged and flared the fabric out of his hand. Awkardly, he struggled with the zipper on the pocket. Dmietriev watched him, never moving, never blinking. He was like a great cat waiting for his prey to make one move, one wrong move and then he would spring, snap once and it would be finished.

Gillon got the pocket open, pulled the packet out and held it at arm's length.

'No. Throw it to me . . . throw it carefully or I will shoot you before I catch it.'

Gillon had no doubt that he would do just that and he tossed the packet carefully against the wind, so that it landed in Dmietriev's outstretched left hand. The Russian tucked it away inside his own parka, then stepped to his left and slipped his skis off his shoulder.

'Now . . . back up five paces and sit down . . . keep your hands on top of your head.'

Gillon did as he was told and Dmietriev knelt down, still holding the pistol rock steady. He undid the lashings that held the skis and poles together. Getting to his feet again, he thrust the ski poles into the snow beside his skis and paused.

Gillon had curled the fingers of his left hand into the material of his hood. A quick push backward and he could reach his knife and throw in one swift movement, but Dmietriev never gave him a chance.

The Russian walked around behind him and Gillon felt the brief touch of the heavy pistol. He took a deep breath, readying for the final blow.

'I am sorry this must be done,' Dmietriev said. 'We have been through much together and I had hoped we would finish together. But one of the four of us is a traitor. I know it is not me, but of no one else can I be sure. I cannot take the chance that you are the one, although I am certain that you are not.' He pushed Gillon's hood back and reached a cold hand into the collar and extracted the throwing knife.

'I was betting it was you,' Gillon said wearily. 'I would have put money on your having brought the Chinese down on the caravan.'

'On the caravan?' Dmietriev shot back, clearly surprised.

'Yeah. Someone set off a red smoke marker behind the caravan and you were the last one in line . . . and you were carrying the explosives.'

Dmietriev was silent for a moment. 'I see.'

Dmietriev paused and Gillon heard him fumbling for something. A moment later, there was a sharp bang and he flinched. He spun around in time to see a flare of light blossom for a brief instant near the border before it plummeted into the snow and disappeared. Gillon realized that anyone not looking at that spot at the exact time would never have seen the flare.

'Turn around,' Dmietriev ordered sharply, and Gillon did so.

'They will now be waiting for me,' Dmietriev said quietly. 'If you can, make for the same spot and we will be waiting for you . . . on the other side of the border. But we cannot wait long . . . the Chinese will not let a mere border stop them from attempting to retrieve the information in this packet.'

'Listen, you bastard,' Gillon snarled, but a crushing blow from the pistol butt knocked him face forward into the snow. As his face touched the icy crystals, consciousness fled.

The ledge jutted just above his head, brightly outlined in the moonlight, and Gillon reached for it, hooked his fingers over the solid rock and struggled to pull himself up. He was almost finished and he knew it. He had no idea how long he had been unconscious but when he had come to, there had been no sign of the big Russian intelligence agent but for two thin ski tracks leading toward the border. In a daze, Gillon had started back up the slope . . . not really aware of what he was doing, but dimly realizing that he must have his skis to stay alive. When Dmietriev crossed the border, all hell could break loose and there would be no chance of anyone else crossing at that point. Beyond that, his mind refused to function. Who then was the double agent? Unless Dmietriev was lying . . . If any of them were to survive now, they would be forced to co-operate. Whichever of the other two it was, he should be quick to realize that the reception waiting for him in Peking without that packet was not going to be a hero's welcome.

The climb had finished what little strength remained to him and he rested for a moment, his fingers still hooked over the ledge. Strong hands grasped and jerked him upward, dragging him painfully over the rock. For a moment he thought it was Stowe or Leycock but as he struggled to his knees, his arms still gripped tightly, he saw clearly in the moonlight the faces that surrounded him and he knew for certain then that they were all finished this time, for good and all.

'Get up, you son-of-a-bitch.' Gillon looked in the direction of the voice, not wanting to believe. Leycock stood with his carbine cradled in his arms and a sneer on his face.

'Get up,' he repeated.

Gillon got painfully to his feet with the assistance of the two Chinese soldiers who continued to hold his arms. He glanced at Leycock, then at the others. Eight

Chinese soldiers, all dressed in white snowsuits, were with him on the ledge. Three held their rifles ready but the rest were standing relaxed, weapons slung over their shoulders. The reason was obvious. Stowe was standing next to a tall Chinese whose captain's insignia gleamed on his fur hat.

'So you two were together all along,' he muttered huskily.

Stowe shook his head, still grinning. 'Yep. But until the cavalry showed up, I figured Leycock was on your side. It seems we were both planted on you all in case something happened to the other . . . sort of a fail-safe arrangement, you might call it.'

'And I thought that Dmietriev was the one . . . the flare was missing from his pack . . .'

Leycock laughed, thoroughly enjoying himself. 'I thought that would tie it for you. I took the flare that morning while the tents were being packed and dropped it as we came over the ridge. I used one of the time-delay fuses.'

'Made up for breaking the radio too early, then, didn't you?'

Leycock snarled at him. 'All right, so I made one mistake. But I did manage to pull it out and that's all that counts.'

'When you went back down the pass that second day, was it just to count Chinese or to talk with them?'

'What do you think?' Leycock smirked. 'They've been right behind us for quite a while.'

Gillon shook his head. 'Both of you . . . I never even thought of that . . .

'Then it was one of you that warned the Chinese that we were coming . . . in fact . . . told them about the Rome meeting and had Phan killed, then led them to protest to the Russians so that we had to go through that little act at Ala Kul.'

Leycock smirked at him. 'Yeah . . . that was me.'

Now that it was over, he did not even feel bitter. He was beyond that now. The packet had gone with Dmietriev . . . the Russians had won and everyone else, himself included, had lost.

Gillon smiled at Stowe. 'It's all for nothing, you

know,' he said softly. 'Dmietriev has the packet. He took it from me and by now he should be almost across the border.'

Stowe and Leycock both laughed. The soldiers grinned at one another; even though they did not understand what Gillon had said, they must have been expecting this reply.

Stowe spoke in Chinese and the soldiers' grins turned to laughter.

'Not very damned likely,' Leycock said finally. 'They've got two squads of troops strung through the valley by now waiting for anyone to try. They moved in after dark and dug in. Dmietriev will never make the border.'

Gillon stared at him, his brain frozen, unable to think coherently. The scene was a surrealistic painting, white-clad soldiers, the dull splash of white from the windbreak against the black rock, the varied attitudes of the participants and all washed in pale moonlight. He looked around, unable to focus on any one detail until his stare was suddenly riveted by the sight of Leycock's pack, half in and half out the windbreak. He looked up to see Stowe watching him carefully. Without thinking, Gillon glanced back at the pack, which he knew contained Leycock's share of the explosives which they had divided earlier.

Stowe stepped forward slightly and the muzzle of his pistol wavered toward the pack. Puzzled, Gillon looked up at Stowe, who nodded imperceptibly.

The Chinese officer snapped out an order, breaking the intense expression on Stowe's face, and one of the soldiers pushed Gillon toward the rock wall. He stumbled toward Leycock, who suddenly swung his carbine at him in a vicious arc. Gillon saw it but was unable to do more than deflect the blow; it hit him in the ribs and he stumbled forward to his knees, almost going off the ledge.

Before anyone else could move, Stowe shoved the officer out of the way and shouted Leycock's name. Leycock, startled, turned toward him as Stowe raised the pistol at arm's length and shot him through the neck. Gillon saw the surprise on Leycock's face through his own haze of pain as Leycock swayed forward under the impact of the bullet. Stowe had not waited to see the effect before he had continued around in the same smooth motion and shot the Chinese officer in the face; three rifles crashed simultaneously and Stowe was slammed back against the rock wall.

'Go!' he gasped. 'Now!' And Gillon saw the pistol wobble up to point at the pack. Without an instant's hesitation, he pitched himself over as the pistol roared and the face of the ledge erupted into incandescent gas. The concussion of the exploding gelignite, even though deflected partially by the ledge, slammed him against the snow and rolled him over and over down the ice-hard slope until he slammed against a snow-covered boulder. He lay on his back for an indeterminate amount of time, staring up into the hard, blue-black sky, his mind refusing to work properly while the blaze of flame and smoke died away above him. No sound, no movement of any kind came from the ledge. Beyond, he could see clearly the side of the ridge leading up to the crest of the pass and it shone balefully in the moonlight.

After a while, Gillon rolled over onto his stomach and got to his hands and knees. He knelt in the snow, breathing in deep gasps and wondering if he could ever manage to gather enough strength to stand. He took it step by step; first, forcing himself upright, but still on his knees, then he brought one leg up, and finally got onto both feet. The sky spun and he stumbled forward onto the boulder and waited for the vertigo to pass. His ribs grated against each other and he gasped in agony as the muscles cramped down, almost doubling him into immobility. The cramp eased after several minutes and by degrees he forced himself erect once more and, without thinking, began to hobble down the remaining slope.

Bits and pieces of conversation, scraps of scenes came and went without pattern. Dmietriev talking to him earlier, pointing out the place to cross the border . . . the red smoke marker . . . the Chinese soldiers on the ledge . . . Stowe telling him . . . warning him? . . . that more soldiers were waiting for anyone to cross the border. All of it mattered no longer. To stay was to die . . . to attempt to cross was only to struggle that much longer against the inevitable, that last bit of effort that kept you alive, because luck was made of anticipation and struggle . . . he laughed out loud and found that it hurt.

He went downslope, shuffling one foot in front of the other as if he were an old man. It seemed that he no longer controlled his body and it tended to go where the terrain pushed it. The valley swept away before him and he did not trust the scenes that his eyes displayed for him. The landscape wavered in the watery moonlight; shadows took on the menacing shapes of trolls, then those of soldiers rising up from the drifts to reach restraining claws and he wondered insanely if the people who lived in these mountains told tales of middle-earth creatures as did the Scandinavians.

The slope flattened and the valley floor became level. The snow was hard-packed under the wind that whistled endlessly through the wind tunnel of the valley. A thin line came into sight, black against the glimmering white. As he stumbled on, the realization grew in him that this was the border fence.

It seemed that he walked for an endless time barely conscious of the snow lighted by a lopsided moon. He was not aware of the long line of figures sweeping down the slope behind and it wasn't until the rifle fire began to kick up spurts of snow around him that he realized he was no longer alone.

He stopped and found that he had to turn his entire body to see the twelve ski troopers bearing down on him.

The shock of surprise brought him fully awake and he broke into a shambling run toward the fence. The rifle fire around him was increasing and he still had nearly a quarter of a mile to go to the fence. Something yanked violently at his right sleeve, throwing him off balance in mid-stride and he crashed into the snow, stunned by the shock of the fall. After a moment, he struggled up and brushed the snow from his face mask and eyes.

A shallow snowdrift was between him and the leading skier, now less than a hundred yards away. Almost with resignation, he fumbled his pistol from beneath his parka and methodically checked the magazine; it was fully loaded and he laid his hand, the pistol resting comfortably in his grip, on the top of the snowdrift and began to watch the lead figure over the blade sights.

The distance narrowed to fifty yards, then forty, then thirty. The soldier saw him crouching behind the drift, flung his rifle up and snapped off a shot. He missed, the bullet striking the snow well to Gillon's left. Gillon kept his eyes on the lead skier, blocking the other soldiers from his mind. His man was approaching him directly and he had a clear dead-on shot to a full target. The soldier raised his rifle, steadied himself and Gillon stared directly into his eyes . . . at twenty yards, they fired simultaneously. The trooper's shot sprayed snow into Gillon's face before he went down in a cartwheel of snow, rifle and skis flying. Gillon saw only that the soldiers were still several hundred feet behind and he was up and running, the will to live suddenly overpowering once more. Gillon ran like he had never run before; he didn't bother trying to dodge bullets by zigzagging; he merely raced for the fence like a cornered animal, all thoughts of the minefield gone.

The darkness along the fence erupted into bright flame and a bangalore torpedo tore the barbed wire strands apart. Through the gap poured Russian soldiers, firing past him at the pursuing Chinese troops. Gillon raced on, ignoring the whistling of his breath and the agony in his chest. He ran for his life a final time.

Fifty yards from the fence he tripped and crashed headlong into the snow but was on his feet in one rolling motion. A gasp of pain brought him up short and he swung around, pistol leading him to the body of a man lying in a crumpled heap . . . Dmietriev.

Russian soldiers lined the fence, some on their knees, other prone, all pouring rifle fire into the Chinese troops, who were still advancing, but off their skis now and scuttling forward from one snowdrift to another. Gillon crawled quickly to Dmietriev and eased him over. As he did so, Dmietriev curled into a tight knot, hands clutched to his chest. His exhalations came in ragged gasps. Each inhalation produced a curious whistle and Gillon gently pulled his hands away. In the moonlight, the blood that covered his white snow-parka was black.

He had been shot through the lungs, yet he was still fighting to talk, his lips moving in spasmodic jerks. Gillon bent closer to hear what he was whispering.

'Packet . . . don't know how . . . no shot . . . no one heard . . .'

'Shut up, shut up . . .' Gillon hissed furiously. His badly shaking hands yanked at the zipper on the parka. The zipper refused to work and he wrenched it apart and peeled back the jacket, then gagged. Dmietriev had been shot from behind with a softnosed bullet which had been cut into a dumdum. It had torn a gaping hole in his chest and Gillon wondered how he had survived this long. There was nothing that could be done and he knew it . . . no way to even carry him back . . . to move him would kill him instantly.

Gillon pounded the snow in anguish, mouthing obscenities unintelligibly. Dmietriev opened his eyes and they brought Gillon up short with their desperate message. His mouth worked but no sound came.

The volume of gunfire increased as a machine gun opened up. Gillon jerked his head and saw the Chinese troopers diving for cover but even as they did, reinforcements in the form of two more groups were coming up from either side . . . a few moments more and they would have him cut off from the border.

Gillon tore the plastic-wrapped envelope from the pocket and turned to see a soldier beside the fence waving frantically in his direction.

A bubbling sound beside him drove him to his feet and he ran.

He knew that he had been hit. A Caucasian face, bent close to his, sobbed with exertion as he dragged him over the snow and through the gap in the fence. A stretcher was waiting and Gillon was lifted gently onto it. A man with a red star on his winter cap bent and spoke to him in Russian. Gillon shook his head. They were all dead except him . . . all of them. He unclenched his fist and dropped the packet into the officer's hand. Then the face disappeared and the stretcher was lifted. The sound of gunfire died behind them and he watched the lopsided moon swaying from side to side as the soldiers hurried along, watched it until the only light in his eyes was that reflecting from the moon.

A Selection of Crime Thrillers from Sphere

ASSASSIN	James Anderson	30p
THE ALPHA LIST	James Anderson	35p
VICTIMS UNKNOWN	Richard Clapperton	30p
THE ABDUCTION	Stanley Cohen	30p
ONLY WHEN I LARF	Len Deighton	35p
THE WHITE LIE ASSIGNMENT	Peter Driscoll	35p
A COLD FRONT	Bridget Everitt	30p
SUPERFLY	Philip Fenty	30p
ACROSS 110TH STREET	Wally Ferris	35p
CZECH POINT	Nichol Fleming	30p
SHROUD FOR A NIGHTINGALE	P. D. James	35p
UNNATURAL CAUSES	P. D. James	35p
KLUTE	William Johnston	30p
LINE OF FIRE	Roger Parkes	30p
TOLL FOR THE BRAVE	Harry Patterson	30p

A Selection of General Fiction from Sphere

THE TAMARIND SEED	Evelyn Anthony	30p
THE ASSASSIN	Evelyn Anthony	35p
CALICO PALACE	Gwen Bristow	65p
SOCCER THUG	Frank Clegg	30p
A VERY LOVING COUPLE	Hunter Davies	30p
THE ONE-EYED KING	Edwin Fadiman	45p
JOSEPH	Mervyn Jones	75p
THE LAST PICTURE SHOW	Larry McMurtry	30p
NORTH CAPE	Joe Poyer	35p
THE BALKAN ASSIGNMENT	Joe Poyer	35p
SUMMER OF '42	Herman Raucher	35p
THE WESTBANK GROUP	Henry Sackerman	35p
WHAT MAKES SAMMY RUN?	Budd Schulberg	30p
THE STEWARDESSES DOWN UNDER	Penny Sutton	30p
GARDEN OF SAND	Earl Thompson	50p
THE SWITCH	Patricia Welles	35p
JOHN ADAM IN EDEN	Christopher Wood	30p
KISS OFF!	Christopher Wood	30p
BACKLASH	Natalia Zabaneh	30p

All Sphere Books are available at your bookshop or
newsagent, or can be ordered from the following address:

Sphere Books, Cash Sales Department,
P.O. Box 11, Falmouth, Cornwall.

Please send cheque or postal order (no currency), and allow
7p per copy to cover the cost of postage and packing
in U.K. or overseas.